W9-AYD-719

m

Crime
on Her Mind

Crime
on Her Mind

A Collection of Short Stories

Carolyn G. Hart

Five Star
Unity, Maine

Additional copyright information may be found on page 268.

All rights reserved.

Five Star Mystery.
Published in conjunction with Tekno-Books.

Cover photograph by Jason Johnson.

February 1999
Standard Print Hardcover Edition.

Five Star Standard Print Mystery Series.

The text of this edition is unabridged.

Set in 11 pt. Plantin by Al Chase.

Printed in the United States on permanent paper.

Library of Congress Cataloging in Publication Data
ISBN: 0-7862-1735-9 (hc : alk. paper)

Contents

Introduction

I love writing about women protagonists. This is not simply because I am a woman. I chose to see the world through the eyes of fictional women because women make terrific sleuths.

Recently, I heard of research that indicates men and women listen differently. Men focus completely on the speaker. Women hear the speaker, but their brains are so organized that they hear everything going on around them. They are, indeed, incapable of tuning out surrounding sounds, so, of course, they receive a good deal more input in any situation than does a male listener. I believe this is simply one difference between women and men that gives women sleuths an edge.

Women are curious, insightful, attuned to their surroundings, sensitive to moods, aware of nuances. In short, women are nosy and there is no better attribute for a sleuth.

The mystery itself, especially the traditional mystery, provides a great forum for women. The reason goes to the heart of the function of the mystery in literature. Mysteries, as Agatha Christie once observed, serve the modern world as the medieval morality play served the Middle Ages. In the mystery, readers see what happens to lives beset by sin. Every mystery has to do with human relationships. When one of my series detectives, young and eager Annie Laurance Darling or old and seasoned Henrie O (Henrietta O'Dwyer Collins), sets out to discover who committed murder, she really wants to discover what fractured the relationships of the characters. She will find out what went wrong in these people's lives.

Who succumbed to evil? What dark passions have bubbled to the surface? And it always comes down to those basic human failings, greed, anger, lust, cruelty, fear, jealousy, and hatred.

Women care passionately about relationships and are always eager to seek out personal truths. This is why I created Annie Darling, a young and eager mystery bookstore owner, and Henrie O (Henrietta O'Dwyer Collins), a retired reporter with a zest for life and a talent for trouble. They differ in age, background, and attitudes, but both Annie and Henrie O always want to know everything about everyone.

This collection contains two Death on Demand mysteries, eight Henrie O adventures, and two non-series stories. Most of the stories have a common theme: Relationships gone awry and women sleuths who want to know why.

I hope you will want to know why, too.

NONE OF MY BUSINESS, BUT . . .

I listened to the heavy thumps on the stairs. They must be taking the body down. I had left the front door ajar. Not because I was curious, but simply because I knew I would have to talk to the police. At that point, I had no intention of getting involved, other than offering what information I had. As far as I was concerned, Mollie Epsley was a budding virago who would have been a full-blown bitch by age thirty. That had been easy enough to figure out in the two weeks she'd lived in the apartment next door. In my judgment, her lissome blonde beauty wasn't a mitigating factor, though it blinded most men to her defective character. Women, of course, see through that kind of female with ease. As for Calvin Bolt, he was a poor excuse for a man, willing to endure any kind of abuse so long as Mollie let him stay around. And he was an M.I.T. graduate with a thriving electronics firm! But, as we all know, business acumen isn't necessarily transferable to the bedroom. And vice versa.

So I had no personal interest in either of these creatures. I was merely prepared to cooperate as a good citizen must when peripherally involved in a case of homicide. Actually, I had only one consuming interest at the moment, and that was to meet my deadline. My fall had been about as fractured as Lavinia's leg, but what can you do when your oldest friend, both in years and events, falls down dew-slick marble library steps and ends up in a body cast and traction and desperately needs someone to complete her semester courses? If you are Henrietta O'Dwyer Collins, you arrive one midnight in a sleepy college town in the depths of Missouri and find yourself the next day explaining the 5Ws and H to several classes full of embryonic journalists who think news is the equivalent of sound bites. It was my pleasure to disabuse them of this concept. When they found out I'd covered wars, revolutions, and earthquakes, they tried to con me into regaling them with my adventures.

I am rarely connable.

I do, however, have an intensity of character which served me well during my reporting years, but which has always been a drawback otherwise. When I take on an assignment, I give it my all. Whether it requires pursuing reluctant principals, staking out a love nest, researching land titles, tracking down eyewitnesses, or — in Lavinia's case — teaching idiot-box refugees basic reporting skills, I will go to any lengths to succeed.

When I took over Lavinia's classes, I thought it would be a simple task. Suffice it to say, it was not only not simple, the challenge of eliciting decent prose from the couch potatoes became a time consuming obsession, with the result that my editor had gone from plaintive pleas to angry rumblings, and I *had* to get the finished draft of Istanbul Transfer in the mail post haste.

That's why I was up and working at a quarter to midnight Monday night and heard yet another episode in the drama of Mollie and Calvin.

I had no idea at the time that it was the final episode.

Nor did they, of course.

It was the usual. Mollie had only lived next door for two weeks, but, believe me, it was the usual. Slamming doors. Shouts. Screams of fury.

There is quite a difference between screams of fear and screams of fury. Mollie Epsley worked herself into a towering state of rage several nights a week. The object of her scorn, of course, was the hapless Calvin. Unfortunately, the walls were thin enough that I could hear only too well the substance of every argument. Monday night she was focusing on his lack of virility, which she described colorfully enough to satisfy an Ambrose Bierce fan.

I was writing at fever pitch, my CIA heroine escaping the clutches of the evildoers via a rope ladder dangling from the parapet of an Adriatic villa, when the entire wall behind me trembled.

I turned and glared at it.

More thumps.

Books, probably. Glass would break and there was no sound of splintering.

Mollie's voice rose, gut ugly, into a vicious screech. "If you can't get it up, then get the fuck out of here. Do you hear me! Get out!"

Instead of telling her to go to hell, he begged, "Mollie, don't. Please, don't." It was more than his usual whine, it was a sob. There was another crash, and he cried out in pain. Blinded either by tears or emotion, he must have stumbled into a chair. Mollie erupted into derisive laughter. "Going to claim a war wound? Better be careful or you'll fall down like an old lady. Maybe you are an old lady!"

My eyes slitted like a cat's. I take strong exception to derogatory comments linked to age.

The stairwell reverberated with Calvin's blind rush down the steps.

Then it was silent, except for an occasional slam or bang in the next apartment and Mollie's continued cursing. The dear child hadn't quite got it all out of her system yet.

I tried to concentrate on the glowing green letters on my monitor.

My eyes felt like over easy eggs that had overed too many

hours before, and my heroine, Eileen Cameron, dangled limply in the purple night, awaiting my inspiration. But I couldn't get past Calvin's sad plea to Eileen's brisk resourcefulness.

"Damn."

I shoved back the chair and stalked out to the kitchen, because the drama had yet to play out. In a little while, Calvin would return and there would be a loud and teary rapprochement, ending up with squeaky bedsprings that played hell with my concentration. So I did some slamming and banging of my own en route to producing a cup of hot chocolate. I have always delighted in life's sensual pleasures, so I added a dollop of whipped cream and a handful of Toll House chocolate bits and determinedly closed my mind to the recent episode and concentrated on Eileen. The scene began to take shape in my mind: Instead of dropping to the ground and thereby falling into the hands of the bearded and turbaned watchman, Eileen enters the second floor bedroom window of the prime minister's mistress and —

That's when he began to scream.

I tipped over the mug of chocolate — thank God I was at the kitchen table and not at the word processor where my precious manuscript pages rested — and hurried out to the landing.

Calvin Bolt clung to the doorframe of Mollie's apartment, his face contorted in an agony of grief. He made a high whistling sound, eerily like the shriek of a tea kettle, as he struggled to draw breath into shock-emptied lungs.

I knew it was going to be bad.

It was.

I looked past him just long enough to take it all in. Mollie's once-voluptuous body arched backward over the red-and-green plaid couch, shiny blonde hair spread like an open fan.

My gaze riveted just long enough on that swollen, bluish face, the eyes protruding, the tongue extended, a classic case of strangulation. I drew my breath in sharply, then turned back to Lavinia's apartment and the phone. As I made my report, Calvin blundered past my open front door and headed blindly down the stairs.

The police, in the form of a fuzz-faced patrolman, arrived within minutes and directed me to remain in Lavinia's apartment until further notice. "And don't worry, ma'am, we've got an alert out for Bolt and a guard downstairs."

"I'm not at all worried."

I didn't work, of course. Although I had no personal liking for either Mollie Epsley or Calvin Bolt, I don't like death. Especially unnecessary, premature, violent death. Nobody my age does. Surviving this long in a world fraught with perils is as much an indication of stubbornness as it is of chance.

I'd seen a lot of death over the years, starting when I was younger than Mollie. It was, in fact, during the war that I had seen victims who had died like Mollie, garroted with a thin, fine wire, the twisted ends poking out from the fleshy trench. I not only saw such victims, in the course of duty I — but that is a closed chapter and one I prefer not to recall.

I continued to consider the method of Mollie's murder. In the 1940s, in Occupied France, it was the method of choice for OSS and SOE agents when a Nazi had to be removed, quickly, quietly, efficiently. It was quite out of the ordinary in this the Year of Our Lord Nineteen Hundred and Ninety.

I drank coffee, fought off the perennial desire for a cigarette, and thought about the night's events. By the time a gentlemanly knock sounded on the apartment door, I'd reached some conclusions.

The man in the doorway wasn't fuzz-faced, but he didn't look old enough to be a police lieutenant. However, I've reluctantly begun to accept the fact that the world is now run by children, doctors who could pass for Eagle Scouts, lawyers who've never heard of Clarence Darrow, copyeditors unaware of the identity of the Former Naval Person. I have not, however, accepted the premise of these youthful upstarts that anyone over sixty is superannuated. So we got off on the wrong foot right from the start.

He gave me a reassuring nod and spoke in a deliberately gentle voice. "Mrs. Collins? Mrs. Henrietta Collins?" He had sandy hair, an unremarkable build, a polite, noncommital face, and weary eyes.

"Yes." I don't like the cellophane-box approach, so I may have snapped it.

"Lt. Don Brown, Homicide. I know it's very late and this has been an upsetting experience, but I would appreciate it if I could talk to you for a few minutes. I'll be as brief as I can. It all seems pretty clear cut."

"Indeed?"

He heard the sharp edge in my voice and that surprised him. Those weary eyes widened, and he really looked at me. I caught a glimpse of my reflection in the hall mirror. I like to be comfortable when I work. I was barefoot and wearing baggy blue sweat pants and a faded, oversized yellow t-shirt emblazoned with the Archie Goodwin quote, "Go to hell. I'm reading." Otherwise, I looked as I had for many years, dark hair silvered at the temples, dark brown eyes that had seen much and remembered much, a Roman coin profile, and an angular body with a lean and hungry appearance of forward motion even when at rest. Lt. Brown glanced at Lavinia's living room, a recreation of Victoriana that should have been aborted, then back at me.

"I'm a guest. Come in." I led the way, gesturing for him to take the oversized easy chair, the only comfortable damn seat in the place, and I dropped gingerly onto a bony horsehair sofa.

He glanced at his notepad. "Sure. This is Mrs. Lavinia Malleson's apartment. She teaches at the college and you've taken her place for the semester. Right?"

"Yes."

"Now, Mrs. Collins, if you could tell me what happened here tonight, ma'am."

I went through it, quickly, precisely, concisely. When I reached the part about Mollie's taunts at Calvin, he wrote furiously and carefully didn't look toward me. But he was frowning as I neared the end.

"You heard Ms. Epsley — the victim — you heard her *after* somebody — you think Calvin Bolt — went downstairs. Are you sure it was her?"

"Certainly. She had a lighter step. Besides she was still swearing. Look, she started raising hell with him about a quarter to twelve. It went on for maybe ten minutes, her yelling, him whining, then he left. And she was still banging around after he went down the stairs. The usual pattern."

Brown's sandy brows knotted. "How much later was it when he found her and yelled — or acted like he found her?"

So that was his perception. My daughter, Emily, has often warned me against what she perceives as unfortunate bluntness on my part.

But facts are facts.

"Not an act, Lieutenant."

He had the gall to give me a patronizing smile. "Now, ma'am, I know this has been a shock and it's hard for —" and I swear he went on to say "— a nice little old lady like you to believe anybody you know could've done such an awful thing. But Ted Bundy was downright charming and —"

"Lieutenant, only a fool could think Calvin Bolt committed that murder."

His face flushed a bright red. Not an indication of a very stable blood pressure.

"Ma'am, murder is my business. Think about it: The neighbors report screams, followed by someone running downstairs, at approximately five minutes before twelve. Your call, reporting the body, came in at twenty past twelve. From your own testimony, the victim had engaged in a violent quarrel with the suspect. Now, it's pretty obvious he staged the discovery of her body for the benefit of witnesses. When you went to call the police, he got scared and beat it. Well, he won't get far. We've got cars out hunting —"

With the artistry of television, the fuzz-faced patrolman burst in. "They picked him up, Lieutenant, down on the bridge over the river. Grabbed him before he could jump."

They left in a flurry of excitement.

Which meant I didn't get a chance to complete my report to Lt. Brown, how tonight had been the repeat of the other soap opera episodes, right up to the final moment. Nor did I have the opportunity to share with him my conclusions, so his later claims that I was deliberately uncooperative are absolutely unwarranted.

I cleaned up the hot chocolate mess and poured a glass of sherry. I do like Lavinia's taste in sherry. Cream, of course. As I sipped, I came to the regretful decision that I had no choice.

It was up to me to find Mollie Epsley's murderer.

I am not a woman to shirk my clear-cut duty.

"Henrie O!" Lavinia's voice rose in dismay Tuesday morning. The familiar nickname is special to only my oldest and dearest of friends. It was coined by my late husband, who always claimed I packed more twists and surprises into a single day than O. Henry ever thought about investing in a short story. Rather gallant of Richard, I always thought. "Oh, Henrie O, are you all right!"

"Of course I am," I replied briskly and perhaps a little irritably. Lavinia does have a tendency to bleat. "It wasn't nice, but the point is, Lavinia, the damn fool police have arrested that pathetic Calvin, and he didn't do it. So, I need some facts."

That settled Lavinia down. Lavinia is quite good with facts. Despite her motherly, meatloaf appearance, she was a top financial reporter in Chicago for many years. I made a sheaf of notes.

That was how I spent the day, gathering data, a good deal of it on the victim.

Mollie Epsley was twenty-seven. Never married. Which didn't surprise me, despite her remarkable blond loveliness. She'd finished high school, attended a secretarial school, and refined her skills at a paralegal institute. She was by all accounts very quick, very competent, and very overbearing. She found it difficult to hold jobs, and I didn't have any trouble finding out why. As the office manager at one law firm snapped, "She wouldn't mind her own business. Always poking and prying, wanting to know too much about people. And the more they tried not to tell her, the more determined she was to know."

This sounded promising. "Did she try to use her knowledge for gain?"

The office manager quickly backed off. "Oh, no, nothing like that. She loved to gossip. She liked to know things about people and tell the world. Especially things that would make them uncomfortable. She was a nasty, spiteful woman."

I would agree to that.

Calvin came off as one of life's losers.

"Just a damn sap," his cousin said sadly. "No guts. No sense. But believe me, Mrs. Collins, he would never hurt anyone. He would have been better off if he had lashed out now and then. But he didn't, and I'll never believe he could strangle anyone. I don't care how awful she was to him."

So Calvin was ineffectual and pathetic, but neither of those qualities translated to violence. However, a cousin's testimony and my opinion wouldn't sway the lieutenant. No. I had to come up with some hard facts if Calvin were to be saved.

Some of my legwork had already been accomplished by Judi Myerson, an enterprising reporter for the local newspaper. She hadn't written the lead story on the murder. That belonged to the police reporter, Sam Frizzell. I scanned it, but it didn't tell me anything I didn't know. After all, I'd been right on the spot. But Judi, probably a young reporter, was assigned to do a sidebar on the Scholar's Inn apartments and the residents' reactions to the murder. I could tell she'd put heart and soul into it and come up with very little. But that's what interested me. Judi'd rung every bell in the apartment house and had found no one who really knew Mollie.

That was important. Not a surprise — she'd only lived there two weeks — but important.

Of course, I didn't spend all my time on the telephone. I sallied forth several times.

My first outing would have appeared desultory to any observer. It was early October, a nice time of year for a walk. Of course, anyone my age (most damn fools think) can walk only a short while and that at a limited pace. So it was easy for me to wander about the grounds of Scholar's Inn. (It was interesting to speculate upon the motives of the businessman who chose that name. Was it prompted by wistfulness or stupidity?) The apartment house was built as a quadrangle. A tiled pool and patio occupied the center area.

Three locations suited my hypothesis, a clump of patio chairs near the back of the pool, the parking area just past the back gate, and the laundry facilities. Each provided a clear view of Mollie's apartment windows, and each was within earshot.

It had rained most of Monday, steadily, persistently.

A little rainwater still glistened on the webbed patio chairs. I studied the patch of earth where the chairs sat. No impressions, no footprints.

The parking area was asphalted. Now, at midday, most of the slots were empty. The residents of Scholar's Inn worked or attended college, for the most part. Many were students and many of those led what I would term irregular lives. Up late. Out early. Arriving and departing on no set schedule. Part of the background noise to the apartment was the muted thud of slammed car doors. At all hours. Not, then, a likely spot for surveillance. Especially not on weekend nights.

That left only the laundry room. As usual, the door to the laundry area was ajar. I stepped inside. A sign in bold red print enjoined: NO SMOKING. Added to it, across the bottom, in thick black printing was the message: AND THIS MEANS YOU, BOZOS. A tiny smile touched my face. I was on the right track.

Bud Morgan, the custodian, was an ex-smoker. He reviled all smokers, and the laundry facilities were within his domain. He exercised his power. Tenants who wished for unruly toilets, etc., to be repaired made it a point to respond to his directives. No resident dared smoke in the laundry room or was unwise enough to drop errant butts at will on the grass or walks. But that angry black scrawl indicated someone was flouting his orders. And the offense must have occurred recently. The addendum had occurred since my last visit to the laundry room three days ago.

Bud was going to be furious. Several mounds of ash spotted the green cement floor. The smoker had stood close to the doorway with its excellent view of Mollie's apartment. But there were no butts on the floor.

I glanced around, then bent to my left to peer into the empty steel drum beside the door that served as a trash receptacle. There was only a little trash. Someone had thrown away an empty box of Tide. A mound of dryer fluff was draped over it. Leaning over, I gently poked at the debris. On the rusting bottom of the drum, I found a single pink baby's sock and four cigarette butts. Unfiltered Camels.

I considered calling Lt. Brown. Truly I did. But I could imagine his reaction. So what if I had found four cigarette butts in a trash can! My leap from the cigarette butts to a stranger on the premises, stealthily staking out Mollie's apartment for several nights in a row — witness Bud's vituperative addition to the NO SMOKING sign — would be a hard one for the sandy haired lieutenant. Of course, it had to be that way. Someone knew that Mollie goaded Calvin night after night. Someone knew the pattern and had taken advantage of it. When a murder is necessary, how delightful to position it after the victim has engaged in a violent quarrel. However, I could see that the weary lieutenant might have difficulty in positing all of this from Calvin's sad sack personna and four cigarette butts. So, after due thought, I followed standard investigative procedures. I used separate envelopes for each item and listed the date and location of the discoveries. I used eyebrow tweezers for retrieval, of course. If fingerprints existed — on the cigarette butts — I certainly was careful to preserve them.

Further, I had satisfied the major requisite of my reconstruction. I had found the area where the killer had waited, listening to the customary quarrel and anticipating Calvin's departure.

It didn't take long to track down Mollie's closest friend. She didn't have many. She corroborated my conclusion that Mollie was unacquainted with her neighbors. A neighbor would have had no need to observe from the laundry room.

I had by this time a shadowy picture of the killer and an inkling of motive.

Don — Lt. Brown — later insisted I could have had no such ideas at this point in the investigation.

Nonsense.

It was all quite simple.

Mollie's murder — despite her blonde beauty and her troubled relationship with Calvin — had nothing to do with sex.

Simple garroting with no physical disfigurement is not customary for sexually motivated killers.

Garroting from behind with a fine wire (as opposed to manual strangulation) is not customary modus operandi in crimes committed under emotional stress.

Rather, the manner of her death indicated premeditation and calculation, the opposite of impulsive violence. This was unmistakably an execution. And the method hinted both at the perpetrator and at the motive.

A quiet, effective means of silencing an enemy.

The murderer was either a former OSS officer, a member of the French Resistance, or someone who knew a great deal about that period. The murderer smoked. The murderer was swift, competent, and dangerous. And the murderer counted Mollie as an enemy.

Three more phone calls and the facts began to pile up. Secreted among them, I felt certain, was both the name of a murderer and the reason for the deed.

Mollie had been temping for two weeks at the law firm of Hornsby, McMichael, and Samuelson.

In Mollie's three previous temp engagements (Jetton and Jetton, Foster, McCloud and Williams, and Borden, Frampton, and Fraley) there was no employee with whom she had contact who was of the appropriate background (served in Intelligence during World War II or possessed a great deal of knowledge about that period). Besides, all of the other law firms had non-smoking offices.

It was a different matter at Hornsby, McMichael and Samuelson.

Horace Hornsby didn't smoke. Now. He'd been dead for twenty-five years. He was, when alive, partial to Cuban cigars. Sinclair Samuelson didn't smoke. He was the yuppieish youngest partner, a tri-athlete who flung himself from pool to bicycle to track before and after work.

Marvin McMichael smoked. McMichael was a distinguished veteran of the European theater in World War II. A colonel at war's end. In the OSS.

My final visit of the day, just before closing time, was to the law offices of Hornsby, McMichael, and Samuelson. I wore a black dress I'd found in a back corner of Lavinia's closet, a dyed black straw hat (God, where *had* she bought it?) adorned with a limp spray of fake violets, and black orthopedic shoes. (Lavinia's closet is full of frightful surprises.) The right shoe pinched my foot abominably so I listed to starboard.

I windowshopped next door, gazing intently at an astonishing assortment of porcelain elephants. Small towns have the enchanting quality of offering a potpourri of offices and shops along a main street. Observation would have been difficult in a huge city building.

My patience was rewarded a few minutes before five. I had no difficulty in recognizing Marvin McMichael. The morgue attendant at the newspaper had been very helpful and McMichael's image from innumerable photographs was firmly fixed in my mind.

He didn't notice me, pressed close to the curio shop window, but I saw him clearly. He was taller than average, with a lean athletic build and a noticeable shock of thick white hair. His muted gray plaid Oxxford suit was a perfect fit. Iron gray brows bunched over cold gray eyes. He had a distinguished, if severe, face with chiseled features, a smooth high forehead, beaked nose, thin-drawn lips. He walked briskly, head high, shoulders back, striding down the street with all the arrogance of a Roman senator.

I looked after him speculatively for a moment, then turned and entered the office. As I approached the secretary, I checked my appearance in the ornately framed mirror over the goldleaf side table. For a moment, I didn't even recognize the apparition in black. What a hoot.

My voice quavered just a little as I addressed a young woman whose hair looked as though she'd been on the receiving end of a hundred volts. "Hello, I'm Matilda Harris and I'm here to get my niece's things. I called to let you know I was coming." I dabbed a scented handkerchief to my eyes. Unfortunately, I'd dabbed on too much of Lavinia's cologne — I never use the stuff — and I almost strangled. It came out to the good, however, as Frizzy Hair, beneath her sleek exterior, was good-hearted and kindly. She rushed to get me a glass of water and by the time I could breathe, we were on excellent terms, sitting side by side on a brocaded bench.

"Oh, you must be Mollie Epsley's aunt. Oh, Mrs. Harris, we are all *so* sorry. It's such an awful thing to happen. No one's safe anymore. And to think it was her lover who killed her! I'd never have believed it, from what she said about him."

Calvin's arrest had been reported, of course.

I sighed heavily. "We never know what will happen in life," I observed darkly. Not, by the way, a tenet I accept. It's quite easy to know what's going to happen, especially when unstable elements combine. "And it's so very sad," I continued lugubriously, "because Mollie was enjoying this job so much. She told me just the other night — such a dear girl — so good to telephone her old aunt — that this was one of the most challenging work experiences of her life."

Frizzy Hair blinked. "But Mr. McMichael almost fired her —" She clapped a red-taloned hand over artistically carmined lips.

"Oh, that." I tsked. I crossed mental fingers and heaved a sigh. "Sometimes Mollie just didn't use good sense."

"I couldn't believe it," the receptionist said, her eyes wide. "I'd *told* her Mr. McMichael always kept that drawer locked and she said every lawyer needed a good secretary to keep things straight and she was going to put the files *she* was in charge of in first class shape."

"A locked drawer always was a challenge to Mollie. Couldn't keep her out of them when she was a little girl. She always had to see inside everything! But I'm sure she smoothed it over."

Frizzy Hair nodded, but her light brown eyes were faintly puzzled. "I guess so, 'cause she was at work Friday just like nothing had ever happened. But Thursday night, I heard them going at it." She shivered. "His voice was like an icicle down your back. I didn't hang around to hear anything after he told her she was fired." She looked nervously over her shoulder. "Mr. McMichael left for the day just a few minutes ago. I don't know that he'd like for me to talk about the cabinet. See," she confided, "he doesn't know I overheard any of it. It was after work last Thursday. I'd forgotten my car keys. I'd taken them out of my purse earlier to poke out that little aluminum thingamabob when the ring came off my Tab can." She led the way into a small office. "Let me tell you, I got out of here in a flash when I heard him talking to her. I couldn't believe it when she was here Friday morning, just like nothing had ever happened."

Mollie's work area was nicely appointed, a golden oak veneer desk and standing beside it a wooden filing cabinet. Through a connecting door, I could see the sumptuously decorated office of Marvin McMichael, senior partner. Mahogany desk. A massive red leather chair. Red and blue Persian rug. A ten by eight foot wall painting, an impressionist's swirl of brown and gold and rose, of a polo player at full gallop.

I'd tucked a grocery sack into the absurdly large crocheted handbag I'd also borrowed from Lavinia. I sat down behind the desk, pulled out the sack, shook it open, and, with little mews of distress, began to empty out the few personal effects Mollie had left behind from her two week's occupancy: a package of Juicy Fruit, a plastic bottle of Tylenol caplets, three emory boards, a plastic rain hood, a comb, a hairbrush, some loose change, several coupons, and an ad for a white sale. I added a Kleenex box from the lower right hand drawer and a pair of low heeled shoes. I sighed again, cradled the shoes in my lap, and looked mournfully at my guide. "If I could just sit here for a few minutes. A silent reverie. I feel so close to Mollie here."

The receptionist looked at me uncertainly, darted a glance at the open door to McMichael's office, and said slowly, "I don't know. I mean, I guess it's all right. He's left for the day."

"Just for a few minutes. For Mollie's sake."

"Oh, well, sure. I mean, yeah, I understand," and she backed out into the hall.

I was on my feet and crouched beside the locked cabinet before the door closed behind her.

Funny how you don't lose some skills. I picked that lock in a flash and eased out the drawer.

Empty.

As I'd expected.

It didn't take more than a minute and a half to determine that there was no locked receptacle of any kind in McMichael's office.

That didn't surprise me either.

But I had some ideas about where the contents of that filing cabinet might be.

At the appropriate time, I would share my conclusions with Lt. Brown.

An envelope of silence surrounded me as I walked through The Sahara. Obviously, the clientele of this dimly lit watering hole rarely shared the ambience with elderly women clothed entirely in black. I would have stopped at the bar for a sherry, but my time wasn't my own.

I found the phone booths near the restrooms. The first booth was occupied. I stepped into the second. I already had the numbers committed to memory.

The first call was short, if not sweet. McMichael, after a long, thoughtful silence, was coldly, cautiously responsive. I was more relaxed as I dialed the second number and my eyes scanned the booth, absorbing some of the au courant graffiti: Safe Sex Saves Lives, Cocaine Kills, and X Exxon. Since my mind, yesterday and today, was going back in time, I remembered some from the war years: Kilroy was Here, Uncle Sam

26

Needs You!, and V for Victory. Autres temps, autres moeurs.

"Brown, Homicide."

"Lt. Brown, Henrie Collins here. I would appreciate it if you could join me. I've made an appointment with Mollie Epsley's murderer."

Don Brown reminded me just a bit of Richard. Very difficult to manage. He didn't want to meet me at the door to the men's room of The Sahara.

But he did.

He didn't want to ride on the backseat floor of my Volvo to the Scholar's Inn.

But he did.

I didn't tell him the name of the murderer until we had successfully crept up the back stairs to the apartment.

He'd glared at me. "That's ridiculous. Why, he's been an elder in his church, worked with youth groups for years."

That didn't surprise me at all. I said so. Lt. Brown glared again.

And he most especially did not want to recline beneath Lavinia's dining room table, well hidden by the lace tablecloth which hung to the floor.

But he did.

The knock came earlier than scheduled.

That didn't surprise me.

McMichael would have scouted the area as soon as it was dark, to be certain he wasn't walking into a trap. But there were no official looking unofficial cars and no brawny young men lurking in this residential neighborhood.

As I opened the door, I backpedaled, I hope gracefully.

"Come in, Mr. McMichael. You are a little early."

He stepped inside. Tonight his noticeable shock of thick white hair was hidden beneath a tan rain hat. A spear of light

27

from Lavinia's Tiffany lamp illuminated his face. Cotton wadded between gum and cheek subtly distorted his face, but nothing could disguise that beaked nose and those thin lips. There was no trace of elegance in his shiny rayon raincoat. I would have wagered the farm that it was a long-forgotten item from a back closet of the firm.

"Your telephone call wasn't clear." His voice was thick. It's hard to move the jaw when impeded by cotton, but the tone was as cold as ice-slick cobbles on a winter street. He stepped inside and unobtrusively nudged the door shut with his elbow. His hands were stuffed in the pockets of the cheap raincoat.

I walked into the living room, putting several feet between us, then turned to face him. "To the contrary," I replied pleasantly. "It was eminently clear. Or you would not have come."

"What do you want?"

I didn't permit my face to reveal my satisfaction. Lt. Brown was sure to be listening with ever increasing attention.

"Oh, to have a little talk with you." I made a vexed noise. "I would offer you a cigarette, but I don't have your brand."

The tightening of his facial muscles emphasized the protrusion of his cheeks.

"Camels, I believe," I continued cheerfully. "But perhaps you don't wish to smoke right now. We do have so much to discuss. I find crime an interesting subject, worthy of study. As I'm sure you do, Mr. McMichael. And to have murder occur so close to you — actually to an employee of yours."

"The police have arrested the murderer," he said harshly. "The case is closed." He took a step toward me.

"Yes, I know. Poor Calvin. I do feel he needs help. So I'm sure you won't mind explaining to the police how you found

28

Mollie last night — and how you left her."

Another step. His shoulders hunched. I could imagine the cool feel of the thin wire against his fingers in the pocket of that coat.

"There's nothing to connect me to her. Nothing."

"I saw you. And I know why you came."

That stopped him for an instant.

"Mollie snooped. Lots of people know that. When the police find out how she opened that locked cabinet at your office —" I paused, looked at him inquiringly. "I suppose you thought that was the safest place to keep it. You certainly didn't want that kind of material at home. For years your mother, old Mrs. McMichael, lived with you. And you've always had a housekeeper. Josie's her name, isn't it? She's a bit of a tartar. You couldn't have unexplained locked drawers in her house! I suppose, too, it was convenient to keep that material there. You often work such late hours."

He came closer, step by step.

"You never expected your safe world to be invaded by someone like Mollie Epsley. A snoop. A sneak. A loud-mouthed virago. And once she'd seen the contents of that cabinet, she had to die, didn't she? But you wanted to be sure you killed her without a breath of suspicion attaching to your firm. So you followed her. I've checked your record, you know. SOE in France. A colonel, by war's end. You know how to follow people — and how to kill. I spotted the wire at once. Do you know, that was your only mistake. That and smoking in the laundry room and positioning the crime so that poor Calvin took the rap. Rather ugly, don't you think? I doubt, however, that you spend much time empathizing with others. You watched Mollie's apartment Friday night and Saturday night, too, I imagine. And the pattern came clear. A quarrel. Calvin running out into the night. And, always, a

29

good twenty minutes before he slunk back. Enough time for murder. More than enough. I doubt it took you more than five minutes at the most."

He was almost to me now.

In the dining room, I saw the lace tablecloth switch.

McMichael lunged for me.

I suppose, despite his own agility, he'd relegated me to the class of a helpless old woman.

When he made his move, I wasn't, of course, still standing where he expected. As I landed on my feet, after vaulting over the horsehair sofa, I watched him whirl to face me.

His face was suffused now, an ugly purple.

"Yes, you old bitch. I killed her — just like I'm going to kill you!"

Youth does have its innings. McMichael was no match for Lt. Brown, who executed an excellent rugby tackle, although he occasionally rubbed his right shoulder the next morning as we drank a fresh pot of coffee. I did glance at my watch at one point. I had to be in class in another twenty minutes.

"Okay," he admitted finally. "I see how you got there. The murder was just like a war-time execution and that let out Calvin. If he'd lost it, he would have slammed her up against a wall, choked her with his hands."

"Correct. Poor Calvin would never have come up behind her and looped a wire over her head."

"Yeah. I should have seen it. But how the hell did you get from there to McMichael?"

It was all so simple, but I did manage to keep that tone out of my voice. After all, the dear boy had been handy in a pinch.

"Once I tied it to the war, that limited the murderer to someone of my own age or someone with a deep knowledge of

30

World War II and Intelligence training. I combed through personal friends of Mollie's. No one fit. I backtracked over her most recent jobs. No one fit. I came to her final employer — and there was McMichael. I expected to find the murderer among people she had dealt with very recently. Whatever she'd learned, she hadn't broadcast it yet. I imagine she was enjoying her power, teasing him, as a cat toys with a mouse. That would have been her style. But she'd come up against a desperate man."

Lt. Brown finished his coffee. He gave me a peculiar look. "Okay. I can see all of it. But how the hell did you know she'd discovered actual physical material that he would kill to keep secret?"

I poured us each another cup. A quarter to nine. Time enough.

"It had to be something that on the face of it was so illegal or so heinous that anyone seeing it would immediately be shocked to the core."

"You were right," he said grimly. "I got a search warrant this morning and in the trunk of his car —"

"You found pornographic pictures that he'd taken over the years of children he'd molested at church camps and in youth groups with whom he worked."

I suppose the witches of Salem must have elicited similar stunned responses in somewhat different circumstances.

"My God," he breathed. "You're right. My God. Sure glad you're a law-abiding citizen."

I smiled pleasantly and reached for my briefcase. As we walked downstairs — I en route to my class, he, I presume, to the station — I will admit I enjoyed his admiring sidelong glances.

And no, I didn't tell him that I'd picked the lock on McMichael's Mercedes in his garage Tuesday evening before

I made my phone calls at The Sahara. Obviously, the hidden material could as easily have been cocaine or a stash of cash.

It is good to encourage reverence for one's elders among the young.

NOTHING VENTURED

I make it a rule never to involve myself in the personal lives of my students.

The Meriwether affair was, of course, an exception. When I pointed this out to Don — Lieutenant Don Brown, Homicide — I must say he was downright rude about it. Young people do so hate to admit not seeing the forest for the trees. Rather an occupational hazard for the young, I'm afraid. Admittedly, I had an advantage over the police — both Darrell Meriwether and Barbara Hamish were my students, and I'd watched the progress of their love affair. Lieutenant Brown went so far as to suggest that my judgment might be deficient in gauging passion. I merely raised one sardonic eyebrow until he looked away. As his face reddened and he tugged at his collar, he muttered something about the heat in the room. I forbore to point out that the steam heat is extinguished by the university in April and sharp nights tinge the rooms with an almost subterranean chill despite the daytime warmth.

Odd to think Darrell Meriwether's life was forever affected by last Thursday's weather. His life and that, of course, of his roommate, Paul Feder.

Thursday, April 18, was the kind of spring day celebrated by poets, billowing flagships of clouds, a robin's-egg-blue sky, a spurt in temperature sufficient, despite April's chilly undertone, to draw gardeners forth from winter's hibernation.

Paul Feder decided to wash his car.

That much was established beyond doubt.

He had time to wash almost half of the jaunty red 1957 four-door Plymouth. A mound of still-damp rags nestled beside a half-full bucket of cold soapy water.

That was the scene in the driveway after Darrell's hoarse and frantic shouts to the 911 operator brought two squad cars, Lieutenant Brown's unmarked Ford, and a siren-wailing ambulance to the quiet residential neighborhood.

I didn't know any of this until late that afternoon. I was in my office at the journalism school, where I'd just finished talking to a reporter on our university newspaper, the *Clarion*, which also serves as the newspaper for our town of Derry Hills. The reporter was worried about libel, a specter that haunts all journalists, and I had assured her it wasn't libelous for *The Clarion* to report that the police were seeking a missing bank employee to inquire about the disappearance of a small fortune in bearer bonds that the employee, one Hazel Dublin, had checked out of the vault that morning. The story sounded intriguing, but the reporter knew little more than those facts. The bank president declined to comment. I suggested a number of inquiries to make, felt the old adrenaline surging through my veins, and had just settled back to my grading of the last of a three-part investigative series required of students in Journalism 3705, when Barbara Hamish stumbled in, her narrow, sensitive face white and stricken, her eyes wide with horror and shock. Barbara is the kind of student that teachers, especially old professionals converted to teaching like myself, dream about — articulate, eager, ambitious, with a scholar's love of language and an adventurer's love of life, enough idealism to believe in truth to keep men free yet savvy enough to see the meretricious so inextricably woven into even the most heroic institutions.

In short, nobody's fool. She was presently an outstanding staff member of *The Clarion* and someday she would be a first-class reporter.

But right now she was confronting emotions she'd never even dreamed about.

"Mrs. Collins." Her usually vibrant voice was reedy. "Mrs. Collins — Darrell's roommate's been murdered — and they've arrested Darrell. Please, the police won't listen to me. Please, you've got to help us."

The police in this small college town are well trained, especially my young friend Lieutenant Don Brown, who has a degree in criminology and is going to night law school. He does not arrest capriciously.

But I knew Barbara and I knew Darrell.

This is not to say I consider my students to be exempt from suspicion of wrongdoing merely because they are my students. In fact, I expect any day now to hear of the arrest of my least favorite graduate student for drug clearing. And there is little I would put past the sophomore who is always late for Editing 1003. She is dishonest, unethical, and probably into the kind of sex that Don — Lieutenant Brown — considers an unfit topic for conversation with me.

Therefore, Barbara's impassioned plea that Darrell couldn't be guilty didn't impress me.

What did impress me was the basis for the arrest. The DA, a dark intense young man much given to quoting Freud — I do think someone should inform him that Freud is now hopelessly out-of-date — decided Darrell and Paul were not merely roommates but homosexual lovers and Darrell beat Paul to death in a raging lovers' quarrel.

"That's crazy — so crazy. Oh my God, Mrs. Collins, Darrell wouldn't — Paul wouldn't — they didn't —" Tears streamed down Barbara's face. "It's so awful for the police to say something like that when they didn't even know Darrell and Paul. Just because two guys room together doesn't mean

— oh my God, Mrs. Collins, what am I going to do?"

She came to me because at one time in my varied reportorial career I covered the police beat for a large metropolitan daily. And lots of murders. I knew, of course, that Barbara could be wrong. Darrell could be in love with her — and with Paul. In fact, that could provide a pretty motive all its own, a dual involvement. It happened. Lots of things happen. The DA could be right. But he could also be wrong — and if he was wrong, two nice young people's lives would be destroyed.

I only hesitated for an instant. I'd seen the attraction between Darrell and Barbara, watched it grow from hesitant wondering glances to the exchange of lovers' lingering looks, and there was never a false note. And now desperate blue eyes beseeched me. I've never imagined myself as a rescuer of dreams — but life throws us some odd tasks and we are the poorer when we turn our backs on challenge.

"I'll see what I can do. May not be much." I delivered it in my usual crisp fashion.

"Oh, Mrs. Collins. Thank you. Thank God."

That put a heavy burden — and so did the wet warmth of her cheek against mine.

Don Brown slumped in the hard-backed chair that fronts my desk. It was amazing how quickly he'd arrived on the campus after I'd called to say I'd be dropping by his office to discuss Darrell Meriwether's arrest. Not, of course, because Don was pining for my sage input. Rather, he would do almost anything to keep me away from the crisply modern Derry Hills Police Department. The chief seems to have an almost pathological dislike of elderly women — or perhaps it is one particular elderly woman, Henrietta O'Dwyer Collins.

I was tempted to don (not a pun, I wouldn't do that) my Gray Power T-shirt and sally forth without a prefatory call, but it is never wise to ruffle the feathers of the bird one intends to devour. So I called, and as I expected, Don quickly arrived.

I made no comment about his execrable posture. My own, if not Prussian, is certainly erect, in keeping with my general appearance, a lean and angular body usually attired in sweats, a Roman-coin profile, and dark hair silvered at the temples. I've no intention of going gently into that dark night, and I have no patience with those who confuse age with decrepitude. I know a ninety-two-year-old marathoner. But this was not an appropriate time to encourage Don to mature gracefully. Instead I poured him a cup of my best Kona coffee and assumed a most benign expression, one I'd used successfully any number of times, notably when I shared a cell with an accused murderess and suckered a word-for-word description of a murder-for-hire scheme. She was most indignant when I testified against her. Really, it was one of the high points of my career, a ten-part series entitled "Cellmate with Murder."

"Come off it, Henrie O."

Was it fair for Don to use my late husband's nickname for me? Richard always said it with laughter, claiming I packed more twists and surprises into a single day than O. Henry ever thought about investing in a short story.

I narrowed my eyes, letting the smile lapse.

"That's better," Don drawled. "More than a hint of a barracuda at large." He rubbed the back of his neck. Even sprawled in an uncomfortable chair, Don Brown was, on second glance, an impressive young man. At first glance, one was tempted to see only his carefully blank and unresponsive face, his nondescript sandy hair, his somewhat slight build. It took a second glance or a perceptive viewer to notice his firm chin, his supple, sensitive hands, the litheness of a long-distance runner, the glitter of intelligence in his weary blue eyes.

"So what's your angle on the Feder kill?" He massaged the back of his neck again.

A sure sign of tension.

Why?

With an arrest that quick, it should be open and shut. No problem. No sweat.

I felt a quiver of the old magic, the second sense that a story was out there, just beyond my grasp. Don wasn't certain.

But this wasn't the time for a frontal assault.

I didn't, however, try my benign look again. If it wasn't working, it wasn't working. Indeed, I leaned forward, propped a chin on my hand, and, exuding quiet interest, said merely, "Darrell Meriwether's a student of mine."

Don didn't ante.

"He didn't do it."

"Oh, for Christ's sake." A swallow. "Pardon me, Mrs. Collins."

I raised an eyebrow.

"Oh hell, Henrie O, what do you expect? Don't you think we know our job?"

"You don't know Darrell," I said authoritatively.

It was his turn to look sardonic. "Knowing Darrell doesn't make a difference." He held up his hand to forestall me. "Listen, I know more about Darrell Meriwether now than his mother does, and I'll grant that there's nothing — I mean zero — to indicate he was likely to go off the rails and kill somebody. But it sure as hell looks that way." He sat up straight to snap facts faster than linotype keys used to clatter. "Darrell Meriwether and Paul Feder shared a one-bedroom — two twin beds — garage apartment on Calhoun Street in the old part of town. Victorian houses. Two-story frames, mostly. In good repair. One of those revitalized neighborhoods. An especially desirable street because it dead-ends into a ravine, so not much traffic. The ravine curves around, runs behind the houses on the south side of the block, which includes the Murray property with the garage apartment Meriwether and Feder rented. Thursday morning, April eighteenth, the city sewer department was busy digging up half the street just past the Murray house — four guys, including a foreman. Not a single car went past their excavations between nine and ten A.M. Paul Feder was alive at nine A.M. He called in to the math department to say he would be in later that morning, he had a toothache."

Don gulped his coffee. "That's the kind of fact that drives a detective crazy. Because, you know what Feder did then? Did he go to a dentist? Or to the drugstore to buy some of that red junk that numbs your gum? Nope. He proceeded to wash his car. According to friends, he was nutty about that car. He loved stuff about the fifties. So, was this just one of those little lies people do? Or did he have something special planned? Was he maybe expecting someone to come over? All we *know* is that he started to wash the damn car. Okay, about this time Meriwether decides to cut his morning class and go for a jog. Why? Such a great day. That's what he says, anyway. So neither guy is keeping to his regular schedule. Usually, at nine o'clock on Thursdays Feder would be at the math building and Meriwether in class at the journalism school. So anyway, according to Meriwether, he trots off. There's a bridge that crosses the ravine right behind that property. It connects with a nature path that goes into Primrose Park. Meriwether comes back an hour later. Feder's car is about half washed. The bucket's next to the right rear wheel. Meriwether lopes up the steps to the garage apartment. The door's open — according to him. He opens the screen door and, again according to him, he finds Feder's body sprawled in the middle of the living-room floor, face down, his head battered to a pulp. Meriwether says he went into shock and he tried to pick up his roommate, carry him to a bed. He says maybe it was crazy, he never thought about it, he was just trying to help, then he realized Feder was dead — very dead — and there's blood everywhere and then Meriwether picks up this golf club — funny thing is, it turns out to be *his* golf club — because he stumbled over it on the way to the phone and he sees it's got blood and hair all over the head, so he starts to throw up — then he calls us and we come. The call logged in at ten-oh-three."

"Why not?" I asked equably.

Don downed the rest of the coffee. "Meriwether was there. We can prove it. His fingerprints are on the golf club. We can prove it. Meriwether's covered with blood. We've got pictures. And there's absolutely no suggestion that anyone else — anyone at all — had any reason for killing Feder. Talk about a well-liked guy — he was voted the most popular instructor in the math department last fall. He was social chairman for the young bachelors' club in town. When he was an undergrad, he was social chairman of his fraternity. One of those 'he-never-knew-a-stranger guys.' Bonhomie to the max. Loud, full of jokes."

"So why did Darrell bash his head in?"

"So who knows? Maybe Feder cracked one joke too many, and it drove Meriwether nuts."

"I understand the DA says Darrell and Paul were lovers."

Don shrugged. "That's the way the DA reads it. He saw the shambles of that living room and said it had to be a crime of passion and that's all he could figure. But nobody may ever know what triggered Meriwether. Maybe Feder made some kind of crack about Meriwether's girlfriend. Who knows? And it doesn't really matter. Cops don't have to prove motive." He sounded belligerent, but it didn't quite hide the defensive note. "We have to place the accused at the scene of the crime and prove opportunity. We can do that. And besides that, it doesn't look like anybody else *could* have done it."

Don pulled his notepad out of his pocket, flipped it open, and handed it to me. As I studied the sketch, he explained.

"Look at it this way, there're two houses on the south side of the street with a driveway between them, the drive to the Murray house. At the foot of the drive stands the garage apartment. Out in the street, maybe twenty yards past the Murray house — not close enough to see Feder's car in the driveway but damn sure there — is the sewer crew. Nobody drove past that crew from nine in the morning *until* two cop cars, an ambulance, and me came squealing in there about half past ten. Besides that, they got an A-one loafer on that crew and he told us there was just one old man walking a poodle who went along the sidewalk during that hour. Not including, of course" — heavy sarcasm here — "two little girls about four on tricycles."

Before I could interrupt, point out that this contingent of beady-eyed sewer repairmen certainly couldn't speak for approaches through backyards on the south side of the street or from the footbridge used by Darrell, Don concluded briskly. "Moreover, we've checked every house on the block and nobody had more than a nodding acquaintance with Feder. We've checked Feder's friends — and believe me, that guy knew a hell of a lot of people — and we haven't picked up any quarrels, any disputes that might lead to murder."

I suppose I must have looked skeptical.

"Nope. This is on the level." He glanced longingly toward the thermos, and I refilled his mug. "This guy was Mr. Popularity."

But Paul might have had secret images and passions no one knew about it. Don was a good cop. He would have asked the right questions. But people lie.

I stuck to the point. "If Darrell could cross that footbridge, so could someone else." I continued to study Don's map.

"Sure." Don sipped at his coffee, relaxed now. "But who? We don't have any candidates among Feder's friends. I mean, for Christ's sake, we're talking major motive when a killer strikes that savagely. There would have to be some kind of indicator, as many people as we've interviewed. Are you postulating a vagrant killer? Somebody who came across that bridge and thought, 'Hey, why don't I break into that garage apartment? Never mind there's a car in the drive and somebody's obviously washing it, but I'll break in and kill whoever's there.' No way, Henrie O."

The session with a red-eyed, haggard Darrell Meriwether almost broke my heart. He was unshaven, in too-large orange dungarees, and his voice sounded hollow through the mesh in the plate glass that separated us. He tried manfully to keep his mouth from trembling, but couldn't quite. He kept shaking his head. "Nobody would've killed Paul. I tell you, Mrs. Collins, he was a great guy. Everybody liked him. And he didn't have anything worth stealing. I mean, we didn't have any money, either of us. Grad students. That's why we roomed together. As for what the police" — his pale face flushed — "that's crap. Pure crap." Then his face crumpled. "Barbara — oh God, Barbara doesn't —"

"No, she doesn't. That's why she asked me to see what I could do."

For an instant hope flared in his eyes, then died. He buried his face in his hands. "I didn't do it. Oh God, I didn't do it."

42

I didn't get much sleep that night. Much of the ground I covered was old. I fed the last of my information into my computer about half past two. I slept until six, then struggled up, lusting for coffee.

I read the morning papers during breakfast, of course. My day can't start any other way. Feder's murder and Meriwether's arrest were the lead story. I read it carefully, but didn't learn anything new. The latest Middle East Crisis was the second lead and the bottom of the page was filled with the fourth in a series on the origins of animals used in research, including kidnapped pets. A small story at the bottom of the page caught my eye:

POLICE SEEKING BANK EMPLOYEE

Police are seeking Hazel Dublin, an employee in the customer service department of the First National Bank, for questioning in the disappearance Thursday morning of an unspecified number of bearer bonds from the bank.

I didn't see a sidebar interview with an acquaintance or coworker of Hazel Dublin. If it were my story . . . But those were other days. After breakfast, a dull ache in my temples, I reviewed all of my notes on Darrell Meriwether and Paul Feder.

If the seeds of murder were buried in the past of either young man, they were too well hidden for me to find. And if I couldn't find them, no one could.

I don't intend to sound arrogant. Merely factual. I know of no investigative reporter better than I.

So, it didn't look to me as though it was a personal murder.

What was left?

Happenstance.

Paul Feder was in the wrong place at the wrong time, like the customer who walks into the gas station when a robbery's in progress.

I could imagine Don Brown's shrug and offhanded response. "In the wrong place at the wrong time? Henrie O, he was in his own damn driveway!"

April is fickle. Friday morning was gray, and a sharp wind rustled the leaves of the big magnolia. I studied Paul Feder's half-washed car. No one would have chosen to wash a car this morning. I shivered. Not simply from the raw day. If yesterday had been like this, Paul Feder might have gone to the mathematics building and he might be alive today.

If my premise was correct.

And I felt it had to be.

Something happened within Paul Feder's view after he started washing his car at 9:00 A.M. that made his murder imperative.

What?

A *Saturday Evening Post* cover during Norman Rockwell's heyday couldn't have exuded more small-town charm: two Victorian frame houses on large lots, a chat driveway, several oaks, the glorious magnolia, two blooming red buds, a screened-in porch on the house next door, a hedge-lined path to the footbridge over the gully, daffodils budding.

Here's where Paul Feder stood. I glanced at my watch. Half past nine.

I surveyed it all once again, noting this time the fenced backyards. This wasn't to say that those fences couldn't have been scaled. Certainly they could have. And certainly someone climbing those fences would have attracted Feder's attention.

But so would someone coming from the path to the footbridge.

In fact, any such person would pass within only a few feet of Feder.

If someone crossed that footbridge on Thursday morning between 9:00 and 10:00 A.M., the destination had to be either the Murray house or the house next door. That observant, effort-allergic worker among the sewer repair crew would have mentioned anyone coming out of the drive by the Murray house.

So no one had.

The wind rustled a stand of cane near the footbridge. It sounded almost like light, swift footsteps. I shivered.

No one answered my knock at either the Murray house, 1205 N. Calhoun, or at the house next door, 1207 N. Calhoun. I walked slowly up the drive to the street, the chat crackling beneath my Rockports. A boom box next to the excavated hole in the street twanged country music. Two workmen knee-deep in a pit shoveled dirt. A third leaned against his shovel.

Such would have been the scene Thursday morning. I didn't bother to approach the sewer repairmen. Don Brown was a good cop. No point in re-traveling that ground. Instead, I glanced up and down the street. Most of the houses had that shuttered, somnolent air of houses whose occupants are elsewhere.

But across the street and two houses down, an elderly woman sat on the wooden front porch with one shawl around her shoulders, another over her lap.

As I came briskly up her walk she smiled, but her eyes were sharp and curious. "Good morning."

"Hello. I'm considering buying a house here." I pointed down the street at a For Sale sign. "I believe in finding out what I can about a neighborhood before I move into it."

"Oh, this is a wonderful neighborhood." Then her smile fled and her eyes darkened and she looked toward the Murray house. "Even though — I saw you down there. I suppose you know —"

"Yes. And I'll have to admit that's made me nervous."

She gestured for me to join her. "Forgive me for not getting up." It was brisk, not self-pitying. I saw then that the bottom shawl didn't quite obscure the tires of her wheelchair.

I dropped into the wicker chair beside her. "Yesterday —"

"I wasn't here. A doctor's appointment. I left just before nine." She looked across the street again. "I didn't know those boys, but I've watched them come and go. They're nice boys. I find it hard to believe —" She shook her head.

Reporters have to ask a lot of questions. Sometimes they get half answers, fake answers, stupid answers. Sometimes they ask and ask and ask and never find the facts that they need. And sometimes they get lucky. It was my day for luck. The kind of luck, however, that springs directly from effort. If I had not come to the site, if I had not looked for a witness, etc. As I am fond of telling students, "Nothing ventured, nothing gained" is perhaps the most profound adjuration refined through time by our species. I am enormously dismayed by the passivity that rules — and ruins — so many lives.

Olivia Briley had lived all of her life on this block, and the past five years, since a car wreck injured her spine, much of her days had been spent on her front porch.

"I don't feel so trapped, you see, when I'm outside."

"What do you think happened over there yesterday?" I gazed across the street, but I have excellent peripheral vision and I caught the uneasy look on her face.

"I don't know," she said slowly. "The paper said they'd arrested the other boy. I — it seems so unlikely."

"Who else could have done it? A tramp from the park?" I

46

tried to appear candid, not, I know, an expression that sits easily on my rather world-weary countenance.

"Oh, maybe that's what happened. Oh, maybe so."

A child could have detected the false note of eagerness in her voice.

"And they'll catch him and then our neighborhood will be safe, just as it's always been."

Oh, sure. And our preppy president's Points of Light will burst into a radiance that will succor the thousands of mentally ill expelled from institutions to enjoy their freedom to roam America's seediest streets. And if you can buy that, I have some excellent oceanfront property in Arizona. . . .

I made encouraging noises and drew her out about this wonderful neighborhood. It took a while to gently maneuver her back to the houses that interested me, 1205 N. Calhoun and 1207 N. Calhoun.

Suddenly that false note was back in her voice. "Zenia Murray's a perfect neighbor. Just look at her tulips. Have you ever seen anything so glorious? Now, that's the kind of neighbor who helps property appreciate." Faded brown eyes stared at me earnestly.

"And Mr. Murray?" I asked.

"Oh, he's been dead for years."

"So Mrs. Murray lives alone and refits out her garage apartment?"

She was a definite beat too long in answering, but I merely stared blandly across the street as if this were the most inconsequential chatter, just a curious woman wanting to know about prospective neighbors.

"No. Her nephew lives with her." Her lips firmed in disapproval. "But she has to do everything herself, that good-for-nothing nephew of hers never lifts a hand. He never holds a job for more than a few months, then he goes on unemploy-

47

ment. Shiftless, that's what Rex Timmons is. And slamming out of the house when something doesn't suit him, going over to the park to work out. Shows off his muscles and picks up girls, that's what he does. I've told Zenia she's a fool to put up with it, but she says Rex is her dead sister's son and she just can't turn him out. I've seen those young men hanging around the park. Up to no good. Buying, selling drugs. Thursday morning? I'm sure he wasn't out of bed yet. Not Rex. As for Zenia, she's a teacher and I saw her leave for school just a few minutes before the cab picked me up to go to the doctor's office."

"And the house next door . . ."

"Oh, he's such a *nice* young man. He went up in my maple and rescued Sweetie Pie, my new kitten. She was just a little thing and last winter she got out and the first thing you know I heard this terrible mewing and Sweetie Pie was way up in the tree and too scared to come down. Burt Samson's his name. Friends? Why, you know, I never thought about it, but I don't think I've ever seen anyone visit him. Now, isn't that funny? Because he's such a nice young man. But perhaps he's shy. He's tall and gangling, you know, with brown hair and he wears horn-rims. So civilized in his appearance. Now, as for friends — those two young men — the ones in the garage apartment, they had people over all the time. Sometimes they'd play basketball for hours with that hoop on the garage. And to think —" She pressed a suddenly trembling hand to her cheek. She stared across the street. "Oh, I should have said something. I should have *done* something!"

I scarcely dared to breathe.

Then she did look at me, her faded brown eyes stubborn and sad. "I knew something was wrong — over there." She gestured with a wrinkled, ringless hand. "But people won't believe me when I tell them — I saw blood against the moon the other night and I *felt* evil, felt it. But who would have believed me?"

The first call I made when I reached the campus was to my favorite police lieutenant. After a long, thoughtful pause, Don responded affirmatively to my request for information in re criminal activities in Derry Hills within the past forty-eight hours. Then I settled down to my modem-equipped computer. I have some very interesting access codes, quite illegal to use, to credit bureaus, college records, hospitals, banks, and other entities, which make the gathering of information simplicity itself. Most software safeguards wouldn't give pause to a computer-literate ten-year-old. I supplemented the data retrieval with a number of old-fashioned phone calls. It's amazing what people will reveal to strangers over the telephone to a voice of authority.

In less than an hour, I'd gathered and printed out a good deal of information on Rex Timmons and Burt Samson.

REX TIMMONS — B. April 26, 1966, Jefferson City, Missouri, son of Byron Timmons and Cecily Murray Timmons. Only child. Father a fireman, died when struck by falling masonry in a house blaze in 1970. Mother a clerk at a local department store, died of breast cancer in 1980. Rex came to live with his Aunt Zenia. A "C" student in high school, he took a business course from the local junior college but dropped out during his second year. Employed sporadically. Heavy into physical fitness and war games. Hangs around the Tenkiller Gym, dates girls he meets there. No lasting relationships. Most recently worked at a rental car agency, cleaning up cars. Fired last week for telling a supervisor to fuck off when he was told to redo a car. No credit record, no bank account.

BURT SAMSON — Born in Little Rock, Arkansas,

November 3, 1963. Father Harold T. Samson, independent insurance agent, mother Aline, high school counselor. Youngest of four sons. Football, track athlete in high school. BBA in accounting from the University of Arkansas, 1984. Employed as auditor by small accounting firm in Little Rock until moving to Derry Hills last winter. Financial officer at local software plant. Plays outfield in a softball league. An accomplished rock climber. Excellent credit. Combined credit-card debt presently $6,984.82, monthly payments to GMAC for car loan, balance in checking account at First National Bank in Derry Hills, $398.36; savings account, $4,678.21.

Then I studied a copy of two black-and-white photos from college yearbooks at a local library (fax machines are so helpful).

Rex Timmons crouched like Rambo assaulting a hill, an AK-47 replica (I hoped) cradled in his arms. He looked comfortable in the jungle-issue camouflage uniform — and reckless. His hair was cropped short. He had muscular arms, a rugged face, and a wild look in his eyes.

Burt Samson gripped a slim coil of rope and looked up at a granite overhang. (No glasses; contact lenses for climbing?) His face had the finely honed look of a man on a quest, total absorption, rapt concentration. Of course, it focused the mind wonderfully when an incorrect choice might bounce you against cliff walls to your death.

Two agile, strong, physically attractive young men.

Don Brown slumped into the chair opposite my desk and eyed me quizzically. "I thought you were working on the Feder kill."

"I am."

He waggled a file folder. "So why the inquiries in re unsolved crimes in the twenty-four hours preceding Feder's murder and missing person reports filed after his murder?"

"I have a wide-ranging interest in my community."

He didn't say bullshit. He merely looked it.

But he had the information for me. I eagerly reached for the sheet of paper he held out. I didn't, as he later told a mutual friend, "snatch" it from him.

CRIMES

Nick's Pizza, 312 N. Broadway, robbed after closing Wednesday night by an armed man (white, skimpy blond beard, mid-twenties, six feet tall, thin), $436 in cash taken.

Clint's Texaco, 584 S. Porter, robbed shortly after 9:00 A.M. Thursday by knife-armed teenagers (one white, short, fat; one black, tall, muscular), $215 taken.

First National Bank, 105 Main Street, twenty ten-thousand-dollar bearer bonds reported missing at 10:00 A.M. Thursday. The bonds were checked out of the vault at 8:30 Thursday morning by Hazel Dublin, who delivered the folder to the desk of Margot Wood, vice-president, soon after. Wood opened the folder shortly before ten; it was filled with obviously fake bonds. Dublin was called for, but had left the bank sometime earlier. She was last seen going into the women's rest room about nine o'clock. Her apartment has been under a stakeout since the alarm, but she has not returned there. Coworkers expressed shock at the suggestion Dublin might have absconded with the bonds.

MISSING PERSONS

Hazel Dublin, 27, reported missing by E. P. Dunlap, a vice-president of First National Bank. Apprx. five feet seven inches tall, 130 pounds, medium-length blond hair (perhaps dyed), brown eyes. Oval face. No distinguishing scars, so far as known.

Lily Raymond, 45, reported missing by her husband, Jack Raymond. Didn't come home from work (Waitress, afternoon shift, Stars and Bars Grill, 2834 W. Council). Raymond admitted they'd quarreled that morning, says she may have gone to Kansas to her mother's.

Don Brown folded his arms across his chest. "Missing Persons isn't my bailiwick but I talked to the detective in charge. The bank employee's fade is one for the books, Henrie O. You'll never guess what's turned up." He waited with the air of a magician about to perform a dazzling trick.

Richard always told me showing off was bad form. But sometimes I can't resist.

"Oh, I might have an idea or two," I said casually. "Such as, she's only worked there for six months or so, and she never had much to do with anyone. Polite, pleasant, competent, boring. And I'll bet Hazel Dublin isn't her name, but the name of a bona fide bank employee who left employment in a Midwestern bank about the time this 'Hazel Dublin' came to Derry Hills. I've no doubt the real Hazel Dublin was astonished at the suggestion she had moved to Derry Hills and gone to work for the First National Bank."

Don Brown's blue eyes widened. He sat up very straight. "Hey, wait a minute, Henrie O, how did you know?"

"I'm right, then."

And one step closer to the murderer of Paul Feder.

Of course, Don pressed me for details, but I wasn't ready yet. I promised to share the results of my investigation by the next morning.

"Why not now?" It was his tough cop voice.

I told him I had yet to hear from some sources and I

couldn't quite prove my case.

"Your case?" he sputtered. "Now, wait a minute, if you know anything at all about this woman it's your duty to share it with the authorities immediately. As in, right now."

"I don't *know* anything," I retorted crisply. "I am merely making deductions that any reasonable person might make from information we've shared." I should have left well enough alone, but I was, I admit, irritated by his attitude. "It's obvious that the Derry Hills Hazel Dublin was a temporary creature created for the sole purpose of obtaining a job at the First National Bank, a simple matter when the persona offered was that of a trusted employee with several years' experience at a bank in a Midwestern city. Am I not correct?"

"Peoria," he said finally, in a strained tone.

"Further, upon examination, I am sure that the Derry Hills police, under a duly authorized search warrant, have discovered that 'Hazel Dublin's' apartment is empty and contains nothing which might indicate her true identity."

"Plenty of prints," Don snapped.

My smile was not quite pitying. "So few young women have ever had occasion to be fingerprinted, and, of course, the lack of fingerprints on record was quite important in her selection."

"Selection? Wait a minute. You're talking criminal conspiracy." He leaned forward, his intelligent blue eyes intent and demanding. "Selection — who selected her?"

"I have some thoughts on that, but I can't share them yet. And the sooner you depart, the sooner I will be able to pursue my investigations."

Reluctantly, he stood. "Taxpayers pay us to investigate crimes, Henrie O."

I smiled cheerily. "I always sleep well at night, knowing that the stalwart enforcers of the law in Derry Hills are shielding its citizens from the forces of evil."

My office door has an automatic stopper on it, so he was foiled in his effort to slam the door behind him.

Dear Don.

I spent a half hour or so at my computer, but I wasn't surprised when I pulled up nothing of interest about Hazel Dublin. No credit record, no local involvement, no circle of friends.

I was just hooding my computer when the phone rang.

Don didn't bother with a salutation. "So I'm not stupid, Henrie O. You've got some kind of wild idea our disappearing bank employee is hooked up with either the Murray house or the house next door, and Feder saw her — or saw something — that could tip us off about the bonds. I mean, I won't go into the psychology of the deal — what kind of woman — even a thief — is going to batter some guy's brains out? And Feder was a good-sized man. But, cops have to investigate all kinds of wild tips."

My hand tightened on the receiver. "Have you talked to Timmons or Samson?"

"Sure. But don't sweat. Just in case you're on the right track, I didn't mention Dublin. Pressed 'em both on where they were when Feder was killed. Timmons still claims he was asleep. Samson got edgy, said he'd told us he was at his office — but nobody can prove he didn't slip out the back way."

I sighed in quick relief. I didn't want either of the chickens to know a fox was sniffing about.

"Although Timmons is no angel. Slouchy guy. I can see why you might suspect him of some kind of crooked deal. Be nice to know where he gets some of his spending money. But he and the guy next door" — a rustle of papers — "Burt Samson — are clean as a whistle on this Dublin character.

54

Neither one of them has any connection to Dublin at all."

"Of course not."

He breathed deeply.

"The first requisite, of course, was that Dublin avoid contact with whichever one is involved."

"Henrie O, I'm telling you you're on the wrong track. There isn't any link."

"Oh, my dear, of course there is. But don't worry, in the morning I'll be able to tell you which one it is. I'll give you a call and you can get the search warrant."

"I'd have to have probable cause." His voice was tight.

"Dear Don, I know you can persuade the judge. You see, you're going to get an anonymous tip over the phone. 'Bye now." I hung up on what sounded very much like a roar. Perhaps the abrupt cessation of our call was a bit rude on my part, but I didn't want to tell Don I had one further investigative foray yet to make, one that was absolutely essential.

He wouldn't have approved. He has such strong feelings about legality.

I ignored the shrill of the telephone as I locked my office door and departed.

I was careful, of course.

I dressed in dark gray sweats and wore a cap. I rode my bike to the park and left it well hidden among the fronds of a densely grown weeping willow. Willows are among the earliest trees to green. So convenient. I carried a useful implement in one pocket that makes it quite easy to open almost any door unless it has a very sophisticated lock. My other pocket bulged a bit from the container of mace. The mace was just in case, but I expected no trouble. I'd done some checking. Zenia Murray wasn't due home from school until

5:30, which gave me thirty-five minutes clear. Much more than I needed. Rex Timmons was at the Tenkiller Gym pumping iron. Burt Samson was on his way from the software plant to the Derry Hills softball fields. His team had a game scheduled at 5:15.

It took me eight minutes to check out both cellars.

I'd never doubted what I would find.

I did have one other useful tool with me, a squeeze bottle filled with water.

The patch of earth that had been disturbed in one of the basements showed up clearly, six feet long, two feet wide. Recently disturbed earth absorbs water quickly. Hardpacked earth is almost impervious.

Now I knew.

I didn't wait until morning, of course. I'd told Don Brown morning because I didn't want a policeman sticking to me like glue. I punched in the numbers to his office (the dear young man works such long hours, but I knew I could catch him before he left for his night law class). "This is an anonymous phone call."

"Very funny, Henrie O."

"Is something wrong? You sound quite grim."

"I am not amused, as Queen Victoria once remarked."

"I do so admire literate policemen. But there is work to be done. You can get Judge Crowe on the phone." I told him the address for which he needed a search warrant.

"Look, there has to be probable cause —"

"As I said, this is an anonymous phone call from an informant. On Thursday morning, the missing bank employee, aka Hazel Dublin, came across the bridge over the ravine and was seen by Paul Feder, who was washing his car. She entered . . ."

56

Of course, Don Brown got the search warrant and found the grave, just where the anonymous informant reported it would be, and the body of a young woman, who was identified as the missing bank employee. The bearer bonds were found secreted in the lining of a backpack in a second-floor closet.

The Clarion ran a superb story, written by one joyous young woman reporter, Barbara Hamish:

> Reconstructing what is now seen as a double crime, police theorize that Rex Timmons, who has been arrested for murder, conspired with an unknown young woman to steal bearer bonds from the First National Bank, Timmons intending all along to murder the missing bank employee and enjoy the fruits of the crime by himself. Unfortunately for Timmons's scheme, police believe 'Hazel Dublin' was seen entering the back door of Timmons's home by Paul Feder. Police believe that sighting sealed Feder's fate. After killing 'Dublin,' police theorize that Timmons went outside and told Feder he had arranged earlier to borrow Feder's roommate's golf clubs. Going upstairs with Feder, Timmons took a club and battered Feder to death.

I accepted, of course, when Don asked me out for a celebratory steak. One of the many pleasures of living in the Midwest after so many years of food on the run is the availability of the best beef in the world. As for the cholesterol mania, mankind has thrived on beef for millennia, and that's good enough for me.

Don was excited. Knowing where to look, the police had discovered much. Timmons had met "Dublin" at a war-games competition in Chicago. "Dublin" was identified as

Miriam Ventriss, who had lived in the same apartment complex in Peoria with the real Hazel Dublin. Don described the swift compilation of detail as soon as the basic form of the crime became apparent. But finally, he ran down and looked at me quizzically. "Okay, Henrie O, just between the two of us, how the hell did you know which guy did it? It could have been either one of them. God, I had cold chills — I could just see the wrongful search suit if you'd been wrong! How the hell did you know it was Timmons?"

I hadn't known, of course. In fact, I'd expected to find the grave in Samson's cellar — after all, he'd been an auditor. So, of course, it was a very good thing indeed that I'd made my illegal entries. But I had no intention of revealing my prefatory survey to Don.

"I wish," I said sincerely, "that I could reveal my sources. But you know how it is —"

He gave me a startled look. "There really is an anonymous tipster? Who the hell?"

But he knew better than to pursue it. An old reporter never confides.

HENRIE O's HOLIDAY

The pieces clicked into place just before the rose red sun made its swift plunge into the darkening tropical water. One moment I was sitting on the terrace — not quite wishing a prompt end to my suddenly less-interesting vacation — and the next I was tingling with excitement, an old hound responding to scent, quite convinced that I was present at murder in the making.

Obviously, during the past few days — despite my absorption in Jimmy — I'd been cataloging facts, making assumptions, assaying character, drawing conclusions.

It was as clear to me now as the crimson splash of the Caribbean sunset that Frank Hamilton — boyish, diffident, appealing Frank — intended to murder his wife, Winona. His much older wife, Winona.

"Mrs. Collins?"

I realized, from the tone, that Alice Korman had spoken several times.

"Yes, Alice." I turned a little in my chair and smiled at the dainty blonde from Montana.

"They said your husband had to go back to the States. An emergency. I'm so sorry." She peered at me with sympathetic blue eyes. "Is there anything we can do?"

Such a nice young woman. Earnest. Full of goodwill. And, at the moment, I wished she were back in Montana. I wanted to move closer to the Hamiltons. Much closer.

I suppose I dealt a bit summarily with Alice. "Jimmy isn't my husband."

"Oh." A bright flush flared in Alice's cheeks. Not the

last wash of the sunset.

I grinned. Alice apparently was one of the benighted millions who believes sex ends at fifty. And assuredly by sixty. No way, José. Neither Jimmy (Jameson Porter Lennox Jr. to the readers of his rapier-sharp investigative books) nor I would ever see sixty again. But, over the last decade, both of us widowed, we'd met several times a year in various resorts for R&R (rest and relaxation in military parlance, and we all know the most zestful and relaxing of human pursuits). As in most endeavors, from bicycle riding to bedroom romps, the more you do it . . .

"Oh, I'm sorry. I didn't mean —" She lifted a hand to her mouth, overcome with embarrassment.

"Quite all right. And kind of you to offer. But there's nothing anyone can do. A family matter. He'll be fine." My smile had slipped away. I'd driven Jimmy to the airport that morning so he could fly back to Maryland in response to a despairing call from his daughter, Rachel. I doubted his arrival would help. But I understood why he went. Call it loyalty. Call it love. Call it foolish. But call it decent.

So there was nothing I could do at this moment — a hostage to my carved-in-cement airline ticket for three more days — to help Jimmy and his daughter. But perhaps I could help Winona Hamilton.

As I'd expected, Alice, her face still beet red, fled the terrace as soon as possible, murmuring something about dinner and clothes and her husband, Burt.

Under cover of the fairly boisterous cocktail-hour bonhomie among the tourists whose lives would briefly touch for a week at the Crystal Lagoon resort, I was able to focus on the Hamiltons, the spring/autumn honeymoon couple from Peoria, Illinois.

I'd noted them at once upon my arrival. Honeymoon couples are certainly the norm on St. Thomas, but this was a couple with a difference, unashamedly fiftyish Winona whose warmth made every stranger a friend and whose merry brown eyes sparkled with eagerness, and young (late twenties?), slim, tousle-haired, shy Frank, who glanced often and eagerly at his wife, seeking approval.

Tonight was no different. They sat close together on a wicker sofa, holding hands, murmuring occasionally.

Then Charlene Sandler, her chestnut pageboy shining in the flare of light from the hurricane lamps, strode briskly across the terrace, confidence in every line of her lithe, youthful figure. Her slightly husky voice — I had the sense it evoked quite different responses in her listeners depending upon sex — could be heard by all present. "Frank, I missed you at the scuba diving this afternoon."

Frank shot her a look of such irritation that I noticed it immediately, then he darted a sideways glance at his wife. Winona's cheerful face was still for a moment; then, ignoring Charlene, Winona stared determinedly out to sea.

Charlene could scarcely have announced a fact more interesting to me. I decided to deal myself in.

Leaning forward, I addressed Frank. "I suppose Mrs. Hamilton's close call yesterday took the fun out of scuba diving?" Actually, since I'd been present, Winona had never been in any real danger. The facts were simple. Five Crystal Lagoon guests were diving in some fifty feet of water from a raft moored near an upthrust of rocks out in the crescent-shaped bay. Lillian Brewster, co-owner of the resort and a certified dive instructor, was supervising. Jimmy and I rented resort equipment. Winona and Frank brought their own. Charlene Sandler rented. The Hamiltons went over the side first, followed by Jimmy and me. When we were about forty feet down, Jimmy, true to his nature, headed for an enticing

61

grotto. I swam after him, but slowly, fascinated as always by the swirl of aquatic life around me, a curious barracuda, a sea turtle that must have been young when Darwin explored the Galapagos, a fist-size fish that glowed green and rose and yellow.

The water around me suddenly rippled.

I turned and realized at once that Winona's air supply was gone. She was flailing wildly, beginning a too-fast, panicked rise. I gave a massive kick with my flippers and reached her in time. Grabbing her arm, I yanked once hard. Terrified eyes bulged behind her mask. Calmly I offered her my octopus, the spare regulator available on every tank. She grabbed it, and finally sense prevailed. After all, she must have practiced this maneuver fifty times when she'd learned to scuba. I was concentrating on Winona. As long as she remained calm, she was safe. Jimmy swam close. He gave me the circled thumb-forefinger, good-going sign. As for Frank, he was swimming away, unaware of the drama behind him. Winona and I, both breathing from my tank, ascended slowly. We hadn't been down long enough that a decompression stop was needed. We broke the surface and swam to the raft. Winona clung to the ladder. Charlene and Lillian hurried toward us. As Winona gulped in air, still frightened, Frank came up. When he heard his wife's choking report, he embraced her. "Winnie, God, how awful . . ." His voice shook. I felt relieved from duty and went back down, glad to resume my dive. So I didn't know what had ensued when the Hamiltons regained the raft. I could make up for that missed opportunity now. I looked directly at Winona. "What caused the malfunction of your equipment?" I'd asked questions for one newspaper or another for more than a half century. I am difficult to ignore.

"The pressure gauge was broken. I checked before I started down and it registered three thousand psi, but all of a sudden I ran out of air." Remembered panic flickered in her eyes.

It is terrifying, even when you know what to do, to run out of air.

Charlene frowned. "Was the gauge broken?"

Winona glanced at Charlene, then looked away as if the sight hurt. Charlene was slim, but definitely curvaceous. The pink halter didn't cover much of her firm, rounded breasts. Her shorts were short. She'd dropped into the chair next to Frank's, and her lightly tanned body was a young man's dream.

Hmm.

"It must be." Frank's voice was just a little high. "Before we left the States, I took everything to our dive shop and had them go over it. They must have missed it."

I gave him an unwavering stare. It had demoralized much stronger men than he.

"I'm going to give them hell when we get home." It would have been more impressive if his voice hadn't quavered.

I didn't shift my gaze. The gauge could have been rigged. "Accidents happen, don't they?"

"God, if it hadn't been for you!" He gave me such an emotionally charged look, I was startled. "It's horrible to think what could have happened. If it hadn't been for you . . ."

"It turned out okay," I said briskly. Then I arched an eyebrow. "But that's Winona's second close call. Isn't it?"

Did I imagine that the silence at our end of the terrace was suddenly strained? A raucous peal of laughter sounded from the group around the bar.

"I don't know what you're —"

Charlene interrupted Frank. "That's right!" she exclaimed, giving me a sharp, swift look. "On Monday Mrs. Hamilton stumbled over that skateboard on the steps

63

coming down the hill."

Resort cottages in St. Thomas cling to steep, rocky, sharply shelving terrain. At some points, the steps connecting the various levels of the resort skirted steep drop-offs. The island of St. Thomas is the cliff-gashed top of a sea mountain. Roads are narrow and twisty, gouged into the mountainside. Gradients range from steep to steeper. It takes a good heart and strong legs to climb the steps, and in fact, the resort keeps a minivan going up and down the hairpin roads during the day to spare the guests undue exertion. But almost everyone chooses to walk — carefully — down the steep steps from the upper cabins to the resort center and the dining area.

I'd heard about Winona's early morning fall at lunch on Monday. The hero of the hour was Bob Humphrey, a huge young man. Fortunately for Winona — and a disappointment to Frank? — Humphrey was jogging up the steps, getting in shape for ski season, when Winona stepped on the misplaced — or quite carefully placed? — skateboard. The skateboard was traced to a sandy-haired little boy who loudly denied having left it on the steps. He kept saying, "I left it down by the pool, Mom. I know I did." I, for one, was ready to believe him.

Winona said good-humoredly, "Children aren't perfect. That's what I tell my son now about his little boy."

Charlene leaned forward. The halter gaped wider. Frank stared briefly at the cornucopia offered, then averted his eyes.

"So you have a son, Mrs. Hamilton." Charlene's lips parted in a silky smile. "How old is he?"

Winona's face reddened. She looked at Frank, then jumped up. "I'm going upstairs." Her eyes blinked rapidly, hiding a spurt of tears.

Frank scrambled to his feet. "Wait, wait, I'm coming, too."

Such a devoted young husband.

I was damned hungry by the time the Hamiltons approached the dining room that night, but my patience was rewarded. I was standing half-hidden behind a palm. When they passed, I waited an instant, then sped after them. When I caught up, just before they reached the doorway, I called out cheerily. "I'm in luck tonight. I was held up by a call from the States and thought I might end up eating alone. How nice that you've just come down. Let's ask for that lovely table out on the end of the terrace, the one where you feel you can see halfway to Miami."

I beamed at them.

As I'd expected, they were no match for untrammeled effrontery. Besides, Winona's good nature precluded rudeness. Soon we were sipping cocktails and studying the menu. I noticed — and so, of course, did Winona — that Charlene, gorgeous in an apricot sarong, sat nearby at a table for one. Frank didn't glance her way once. Which was a dead giveaway. There wasn't a man in the room unaware of Charlene, and that included the waiters. Despite her surface patina of tanned healthiness, there was an underlying edge of sensuality that couldn't be missed.

I was my most charming, lightly regaling them with episodes from my past — with an emphasis on crime coverage. I chatted about Dolly Foster, who'd killed three husbands and four children with arsenic before anyone became suspicious, and discussed the puzzling case of Joseph Timmons, the high school football coach in Dallas who walked out of his last class one May afternoon and was never seen again, and my theories as to what happened, and recalled sultry Astrid Bruno, who was convicted of murdering her husband though she claimed a witch had done it, and why I thought she was telling the truth.

If I do say so, I had their attention. One can't talk about the most elemental human passions without eliciting interest, because even the most staid and boring humans harbor violent emotions. Think about it.

"Dear me, Mrs. Collins, you've led a very exciting life." Winona finished her last bite of swordfish, grilled with lemon, and winked at Frank. She was in high good humor this evening, even willing to put up with war stories from an old newshound. "But don't you find it upsetting — to deal with people like that?"

I raised an eyebrow. "People like what?"

"Why, all these criminals you've told us about. Isn't it depressing?" She reached out a plump hand to pat my arm sympathetically.

Frank watched her adoringly. Then he turned to me. "Winona's the most understanding person in the world."

I glanced at Winona. Surely he'd overdone it now —

But she simply smiled back at him, and you would have thought this table was the honeymoon center of the world, it exuded such tenderness.

But I was determined to break through that cocoon of ignorance. "All these people I've told you about were solid, middle-class churchgoers, who paid their bills and helped their neighbors out when they could. Interesting thing is, most murderers are very ordinary people. That's why we always get quotes from their friends about how shocking it is, how unbelievable, that so-and-so was a really nice person." I speared a pimiento and said briskly, "Most murders are committed by people we know, people you'd never suspect of murder. What's even more certain, lots of murders are never detected."

I had Frank's attention. He had started to raise his cocktail glass, but he slowly replaced it and stared at me. "Never detected? What do you mean?"

"Accidents. Funny thing, how so many accidents aren't accidents at all." I met his gaze directly. Was that a flicker of panic in his eyes?

Winona fingered her wineglass. "That's dreadful. It would be so awful," her voice dropped, "to think someone you trusted, someone close to you . . ."

I studied her with interest and irritation. Had it not yet occurred to her to question her own "accidents"? Obviously not. Well, the week wasn't over. I still had time to get her attention. But for the moment, I had one more task to accomplish. I managed it as I spooned into my dessert. Peach melba, my favorite. "Is there anything special on tap tomorrow?"

Winona clapped her hands together happily. "Oh, yes, I can't wait. I'm driving up to a bird preserve. Did you realize . . ."

I learned a great deal about tropical birds, their habitats, interests, adventures, and predilections, and found her a fascinating, vibrant conversationalist. I also learned that she was going alone in their rental car — "Frank? Oh, Frank's a sleepyhead. I can't think of any reason he'd ever get up at four-thirty."

"Not for birds." His glance at her and his meaning was so clear that she blushed.

I complimented her on her willingness to negotiate the hairpin roads since, as an American, she wasn't used to driving on the left as is the custom on St. Thomas.

She gave me a dazzling smile. "Why shouldn't I? I've never been afraid to try anything."

I would have been a good cat burglar. There's something

in me that loves the midnight dark and the feeling of a world at rest — and vulnerable. After the cabaret closed, I slipped down the steep steps to the narrow, dark path alongside the sea. The Hamiltons had long since said good night. I wondered idly if they'd had sex. It should surely have followed his unmistakable declaration. But I had much more to concern me, and I was eager for the silence of late night to fall.

It was close to 2:00 A.M. when I climbed back up the cliffside. The parking area near the main lodge was quiet and dark, as I'd expected. I always carry a pencil flash, so I had no difficulty finding the Hamiltons' rental car, a blue Ford Fairlane. I also have a useful key chain medallion which has the innocent appearance of an oblong photo frame. (My late husband Richard's picture, bareheaded and smiling, in the bow of a PT boat.) Recessed in the frame are several small but exceedingly effective tools: a knife, a screwdriver, and a lock probe.

It took less than five minutes to puncture all four tires beyond repair.

The next morning I drifted casually through the parking lot as the young man from the local garage fastened the tow chain to the front of the Ford. I was pleased to see it was being towed. I'd thought that would be likely. (Four new tires demand wheel alignment.)

"William?" I inquired.

He shook his dark head. "Edward."

"Sorry. Did they remember to tell you to be sure and check the brake fluid?"

Of course, no one had.

But it never occurred to Edward to question instructions from an old lady who spoke with authority.

That afternoon it came as no surprise to me when I called

the Allenson garage and learned that the Ford had no brake fluid. If Winona Hamilton had driven down the corkscrew road that morning . . .

The office was small, poorly lighted, and smelled like cheap cigarettes. A small crucifix on the back wall was the only adornment. The man behind the desk — Police Lieutenant Cyril Nelson — had listened without expression as I introduced myself and related the attempts on Winona Hamilton's life and her boyish husband's obvious awareness of another, much younger, woman.

Nelson was a big man, barrel-chested, blunt-faced. His blue suit was crumpled and shabby, his white shirt too tight, his necktie loosened and skewed to the left of his chin. The smoke from his limp cigarette wreathed an impassive dark face.

I concluded and he said nothing. My chin probably jutted out a trifle. "You can check with the garage."

Wearily Nelson stubbed out the remnant of cigarette. He dipped open a slim telephone directory. A blunt finger ran down the column. He dialed and asked for information about the rental car. He listened, his face inscrutable, said thanks, hung up. Then his brown eyes surveyed me.

I knew what he saw, a late-sixtyish woman with dark hair silvered at the temples, a Roman coin profile, and a lean and angular body poised to move, always poised to move.

That, of course, was the basics of what he saw. But I knew without asking the lens through which he viewed me. An American tourist, an old woman. Alone. Probably starved for attention, sexual and otherwise. Beginning to suffer the delusions of old age. A lost thimble had to be stolen. Conversations between strangers across a room indicated collusion and danger. Imagining plots at every turn, directed, if not at myself, then at another older woman.

I realized that I should have to call upon a young police friend in the States to vouch for me. I didn't like it, but this was no time for me to stand on pride. Winona Hamilton's life was at stake. "Lieutenant Nelson, please call Lieutenant Don Brown of the Derry Hills, Missouri, Police Department. He will tell you I can be trusted."

A tiny smile pulled at the corners of his wide mouth. At another time and place, I thought I might like Cyril Nelson very much.

"I am certain, Mrs. Collins, that you are indeed a woman of good reputation in your city. And I applaud your concern for your fellow American, Mrs. —" he glanced down at his notes "— Mrs. Hamilton. Unfortunately — or perhaps very fortunately — I see no evidence here of crime. The skateboard?" He shrugged heavy shoulders. "I have three sons. I watch every step I take in my drive. It, too, you understand, is steep and dangerous. And the scuba equipment? Sports equipment often —"

"Malfunctions." I interrupted impatiently. "Of course. But surely the loss of brake fluid another matter."

He tapped the notebook with his pen. "Ah, yes. The loss of the brake fluid. Because of damage to the power brake proportion valve block." He closed the notebook. "You have driven much on our beautiful island?"

My eyes narrowed. "Some."

"Then you know, Mrs. Collins, our roads are rough. There are many rocks." He pushed back his chair, heaved six feet two of muscle to his feet.

Our interview was over.

The resort sparkled in the late afternoon sunlight. Not a cloud marred the azure sky. The water was as smooth and clear as green glass. I found Winona Hamilton reading — a travel guide to the Andes — on the middle terrace.

She looked up and smiled happily.

I looked about.

She answered the unspoken question. "Frank's gone for a dive. I know all about getting back on the horse, but I'm in no hurry."

And, I thought dispassionately, she'd rather die than appear again in her swimsuit in the presence of Charlene.

"How was your trip to the bird sanctuary?" I dropped into the chair beside hers.

She shook her head in disappointment. "I didn't get to go. Perhaps tomorrow. But it was the most surprising thing — the tires on our car were slashed! I wonder if it's because we're Americans?"

"I doubt it. Probably just some boys up to mischief. So you've had a quiet day. No more accidents?"

"Hmm? Oh no, very quiet." Accidents, real or engineered, were far from her thoughts. She was busy planning a trek to the Andes and oblivious to the currents of desire swirling around her.

I went down to the beach after I left Winona. I found an empty hammock among the palm trees, one with a good view of the raft. I watched Frank and Charlene engage in what was obviously a sharp, short, violent argument. It was not, I felt certain, a confrontation between strangers. Clearly they knew each other well. Had Charlene's presence at the honeymoon resort been prearranged? Maybe he'd asked her to come — a side dish, so to speak — and maybe she found seeing Winona as his wife too galling. Maybe she was telling him she was through.

Whatever it was, when Frank flung himself from the raft and swam furiously toward shore, I decided to retreat. I knew the situation was explosive. The rest of the day, I managed to be near Winona Hamilton. Just in case.

At dinner, I stopped by their table. I couldn't quite manage a gush. Too out of character. But I beamed and chattered. "Do you know, I've been thinking about Peoria. I have an old friend who lives there. Used to work on the paper. I'll have to tell her all about you two. She never misses a copy of the paper, so I know she'll keep me up-to-date on my holiday friends." Would Frank take it as intended? WARNING — Don't think I will miss an "accidental" death after you get home.

I was nearing the end of my holiday stay. Should I warn Winona outright?

She would never believe me.

What really irritated me was her total lack of perspicuity. At one point, Charlene came over and asked Frank to dance, and when he started to stammer a refusal, Winona smiled and told him to go ahead.

As I walked up the steep steps to my cabin, I was oblivious to the beauty of the tropical night, the sweet scent of the flowering shrubs, the rustle of coconut palms in the offshore breeze. Time was running out.

Each cabin at Crystal Lagoon is quite separate and private, clinging to the rocky mountainside, secluded in thick brush, but with a lanai looking out to sea.

Quite idyllic.

I unlocked my door and turned on the light. The furnishings in the combination bed-sitting room were spartan but comfortable, a coffee table and straight chairs, a sofa, two easy chairs, a queen-size bed. I showered and stepped out in time to hear the ring of the telephone.

Wrapped in a towel, I grabbed up the receiver.

Jimmy's voice — so far away, yet so clear — made me smile. "Henrie O, I miss you." (Henrie O is the nickname

given to me by my late husband, Richard. He always said that
I packed more surprises into a single day than O. Henry ever
did into a short story. Rather gallant of Richard, I always
thought.)

"Jimmy, I'm having a hell of a time!"

"Oh?" That single syllable packed a lot of questions.

"No, Jimmy. Not another man. Murder."

"Christ, Henrie O, what's up?"

I told him.

"I'll catch the next —"

"No. I can handle it."

A pause, then a swift "I know. I just hate to miss the excitement."

He reported on Rachel's problems, the kind that don't
have easy answers. I didn't try to give him any. But I said I'd
be in touch.

He didn't waste time warning me to be careful. His last
words were "Give 'em hell, Henrie O."

I was still smiling when I propped up the pillows and sat
on the bed. Movement at the periphery of my vision attracted
my attention. I looked toward the wall above the small, adjoining kitchenette. A slim green lizard skimmed toward the
ceiling. Nature's best insect removers. I put on my reading
glasses and picked up the carafe of water from the bedside
table.

I've faced danger many times.

Small-arms fire.

Bombs.

Mobs.

Storms — at sea, in the air.

I stared at the milky swirl in the water. The hair on the
back of my neck prickled.

A moment later, I poured some of the water into a shallow

dish and placed it on the lanai. I closed the door, then watched and waited. Soon the stone lanai swarmed with life, lizards, tiny crabs, a black snake. A brown toad's tongue flickered into the liquid.

It wasn't fun watching the toad jerk backward, writhe, and die, but it was as clear an answer as I've ever had.

I was the quarry.

Five minutes later, I slipped away from the lanai, my destination an unoccupied cabin two levels above. The locked door was no barrier with the help of my key chain. I didn't turn on a light here, of course. I did take the precaution of placing a chair beneath the knob of the door and balancing a broom against the sliding doors to the lanai.

There were plenty of empty cabins. I could safely spend the remaining nights undetected. I never underestimate an enemy.

Fully dressed, I slept lightly because my mind was engaged, considering alternatives. By dawn, I had a plan. (Later, my young police friend in Missouri would demand to know why I hadn't taken the carafe to Lieutenant Nelson. That was simple. Why wouldn't Nelson believe I'd poisoned the carafe myself? It was not, as Don Brown claimed rather bitterly and, I felt, altogether unfairly, that I was proving I had the soul of a buccaneer and the instincts of a barracuda.)

In the safety of daylight, I returned to my cabin. The freshly washed, empty carafe sat on the table next to the bed.

How disappointing it must have been for my visitor. An unmade bed without an occupant. The assumption, of course, would be that I'd not drunk water at bedtime and had departed for an early morning walk. There would be no reason to suspect that I knew I was hunted. Fine. That gave me an edge.

I ate an especially large breakfast and enjoyed every bite,

greeting everyone on the terrace cheerily. I went into Charlotte Amalie soon after. I wasn't concerned about Winona's safety. She was safe as long as I was alive. So it was a relaxed outing on my part, though it took several hours to round up all the items I needed, including a nylon rope and pitons. One of the essentials, a hand-size tape recorder, I had with me, of course. I never travel without it.

That afternoon I utilized the siesta hour, but I didn't assume Frank was resting. I took no chances. Once dressed in my new hiking boots, long-sleeve shirt, and slacks, I took a circuitous approach to the top of the cliff and Point Cagle, the highest elevation within the resort boundaries. Just short of my goal, I wormed through foliage to settle on a low limb of a banyan tree. I waited a full thirty minutes to be certain I was unobserved.

When I was sure no one was about — except a cold-eyed turkey vulture that circled and circled above — I scouted out the rim of the cliff. The view was spectacular, a sheer drop of some three hundred feet to sharp-edged rocks bashed by the surf.

Richard enjoyed mountain climbing, and we did a lot of it, so it wasn't difficult to drive the pitons in place and work my way six feet down the cliff wall. I threaded a short line through the last piton, then climbed back up, removing the other pitons as I went. I hid the loop of rope at the top beneath a clump of rock plant. Then I looked down one more time at the boulders so far below and the waves crashing over them.

As the sun began its plunge into the west, I joined the convivial group around the bar. Two new honeymoon couples. Some businessmen from Miami with women who clearly were not their wives. My own particular honeymooners beamed with happiness. I watched cynically. Frank obviously had spent the afternoon delighting Winona. She radiated contentment, satiety. I tried to understand a man who could juggle sex and murder and still have the face of a choirboy. It was only when he looked toward Charlene that his eyes turned wary and still.

I ordered a margarita — it's the salt I love — and proceeded to wax lyrical about the beauties of St. Thomas.

"My vacation's almost over. And there's only one thing I haven't done."

Ramona, the bouncy brunette who doubled as entertainment director and tended bar during the cocktail hour, gave me a bright, encouraging smile. I suppose Ramona's job description included a passage on dealing with the elderly.

I spoke to her, but clearly enough for all to hear. "I haven't watched the sunrise from Point Cagle. So that's what I'm going to do in the morning. At sunrise. To see the world come alive — oh, I can't wait."

"That's a hard climb," Ramona said doubtfully. "And the edge of the cliff's all crumbly. Uh — Mrs. Collins, maybe I'd better go with —"

"Certainly not," I retorted briskly. "When, my dear, was the last time you were up at dawn?"

"Dawn," one of the Miami bimbos declared, "was meant for birds."

This initiated a round of ribald commentary. Winona Hamilton pretended she hadn't heard. Charlene gave her a disdainful glance.

I took a deep drink of my margarita. I'd earned it. Everyone knew the old lady was going to be on top of Point Cagle at dawn.

And the edges of the cliff were crumbly.

I stayed in a different unoccupied cabin that night. I was

determined that I, not my opponent, should pick the playing field. I doubted the carafe was poisoned again, however, or any other assault planned there. How much easier to shove a helpless old lady off the top of a cliff with crumbly edges. Of course, if Frank were truly smart, he'd drop his plan to murder Winona — at least in the foreseeable future. But the determination to remove me argued an implacable resolve to murder Winona — soon.

I reached the top of the mountainside shortly before dawn. The dancing spot of my flashlight announced my arrival. I wore a loose cotton dress, stout shoes, and (one of yesterday's purchases) a fluffy, cream-colored cotton shawl. Shawls are not a part of my wardrobe, but a shawl was essential. It hid the belt and pouch around my waist

Without doubt, my foe was already in place. Perhaps in the thick cover of that clump of firs, perhaps among the low-lying limbs of the banyan. I was alert for the scrape of a shoe, for the rustle of foliage. Although I gave the appearance of leisure, I went directly to my spot.

Here was my moment of greatest danger. But I counted on my adversary's caution. There would be time given to be certain I was alone, that no one else was about. That gave me time to stand at the edge of the cliff, to give a sharp little cry of vexation as I dropped my flash, to bend down to retrieve it.

That done, I was ready.

I knew as the pink streaks of dawn turned bright and the sky was transformed from pearl to rose that I was silhouetted against the horizon.

A rattle of stones announced the arrival of my pursuer.

I half turned and looked toward the trail.

And felt a flash of anger. Dammit, what on earth had possessed *her* to come — and how was I going to get rid of her?

Charlene Sandler walked toward me.

I tried desperately to think of a way to deflect her, send her back down —

As I've said, I've faced danger many times.

But this time death was walking toward me.

"Nosy old bitch, aren't you?" A tiny giggle hung in the air. Obscenely. "Older even than Winona." Her face sharpened with hatred, making her ugly. Ugly, obsessed, and dangerous.

Charlene stopped a few feet from me. "How could he marry *her?* It makes me sick! I couldn't believe it when he left me." She stared at me, her eyes uncomprehending. "He left me for her. And she's old, old and ugly."

"Not too old," I said sharply, "and not ugly."

I felt a surge of irritation with myself. Not only had I misread the evidence there for all to see — Frank's adoration, real and deep, for his wife — I had been guilty of rank sexism and the kind of prejudice against age that I spend a good deal of my time combating.

Yes, a young man could love an older woman.

Yes, a young woman could be driven to pursue a past lover, in a frenzy to destroy the woman who had supplanted her.

And yes; I was facing a far more dangerous adversary than I'd expected. But all I had to do was lead her on to talk, record her plans to kill, and I would save not only Winona, but Frank.

"It's obvious Frank adores Winona. If anything happens to her —"

A vicious smile twisted Charlene's face into an almost unrecognizable mask of hatred. "Oh, it's going to happen to her, you old bitch. I'm going to kill Winona. She's not going to have Frank. Frank belongs to me. In fact —" she placed arrogant hands on her hips "— I'm going to kill her tonight. An overdose of Valium — because she's so upset by your accident!" Her chuckle was warm and satisfied.

It was the laughter that fooled me.

I didn't expect death to strike with laughter in the air.

So, despite all my preparations, I was caught by surprise.

Charlene lunged at me.

Her hands, palm out, slammed into my right shoulder.

And over I went.

I had intended to fake the strike, the way a movie hero fakes taking a punch.

Instead, a numbing pain seared my right side, but my gloved right hand, hidden in the folds of the shawl, tightened on the nylon rope I'd looped around my wrist as I picked up the dropped flashlight. So I banged over, yes, but my lifeline held, though I slammed hard into the side of the cliff.

I braced myself against the cliff wall and checked the belt looped around my waist. The pouch held the tape recorder — all was well there — and the pitons and hammer I'd need to climb back up the cliff.

"Goddamn you." Charlene peered over the cliff edge. "Why didn't you die?" she screamed.

"Not my time yet," I called up cheerfully, though my shoulder ached like hell. Still, I was flush with adrenaline. "Checkmate, Charlene."

But acceptance of defeat requires rationality.

Charlene leaned over the cliff edge, reaching down, down, trying to grab at me.

And the crumbly edge gave way.

I barely had time to flatten myself against the cliff face as she hurtled by. She plummeted past me, her angry scream turning to a shriek of horror.

I pounded the pitons into the cliff automatically, then removed them once past, a task done so many times over the years that I could do it without thinking. My breathing was ragged, I admit, as I pulled myself back over the lip of the cliff. I dropped the pitons and hammer into the pouch, looped the rope around my waist, then used the shawl to cover it. No one questions how an old lady wears a shawl.

Of course, I had the recording. I could well have made the whole affair public. But why tarnish two lives? Charlene's acts were hers; Winona and Frank didn't deserve the misery and unnecessary guilt that would result from public disclosure. Let them remember their honeymoon with joy.

So I made my decision. I adopted a suitably shaken and shocked expression when I heard the sound of running feet nearing the top of the trail. Although understandably distraught, I would manage to give a clear account of the dreadful accident. So unfortunate — the treacherous, crumbly edge of the cliff.

AN ALMOST PERFECT MURDER

A young friend of mine — Homicide Lieutenant Don Brown, Derry Hills (Missouri) Police Department — insists I can smell murder.

That's extravagant, of course.

But I do like for facts to add up.

When they don't, I ask questions.

On the surface, the facts of Sylvia Fulton's unexpected death appeared reasonable, even if sad and ironic.

Sad because the death of an old friend brings memories, and memories are always, ultimately, sad. Faded lives, faded days forever gone, the ghosts of laughter and vigor.

Ironic because I had not thought of Sylvia in years, and we had only a few seconds to talk before she met her last deadline.

It began with her phone call. I always reach for a ringing phone with a flicker of anticipation, the legacy of almost fifty years as a reporter. Those days were over, yet the swift flutter of eagerness remains. The new, the unknown, the unexpected, delight me.

"Hello?" I can no more quench the questioning lift to my voice than I can suppress a curiosity stronger than any cat's.

"Henrietta O'Dwyer Collins? Henrie O?"

I didn't recognize the voice. "Yes."

"Oh God, that's great. This is Sylvia Montague. Sylvia Fulton now."

I knew the name, of course. She'd done a couple of very successful books on famous criminal trials. And there was one trial in particular . . .

"The Hammonds case," I said immediately.

"You remember."

"How could anyone ever forget?" Sylvia Montague and I both covered that trial. I remembered her well. Tall. Blond. Deep, brisk voice. Oh yes, I remembered. South Carolina summer heat. A sweltering courtroom. And the strangest corkscrew of a mystery I ever encountered. Sylvia and I'd struck up a quick, cheerful friendship and exchanged Christmas cards for a while, but our paths didn't cross again and we'd lost track of each other years ago.

"Sylvia." I suppose my response was pleasure mixed with surprise.

"Actually, I live around here. Saw in the paper where you were in town to speak to the Women's Caucus. I know the program chair so she gave me your number. Understand you gave 'em hell."

I'm not big on buzz words. But empowerment is no joke. I consider myself a foot soldier in a battle that isn't over. Not so long as women still earn seventy cents to a man's dollar. Not so long as glass ceilings keep females and minorities in second-tier roles. Not so long as the power in the U.S. Senate resides in the plump hands of privileged white men who haven't the imagination to understand why sexually harassed women keep their mouths shut. That, or the Honorables don't give a damn.

"You rattled some cages." A hearty laugh.

The laughter brought her so clearly to mind. A big bony face like an intelligent horse, light blue eyes with a sardonic gleam, a wide mouth that smiled easily.

"Good," I said. "One of my specialties." That and never, never, never taking no for an answer. I haven't changed much over the years, in attitude or appearance. I could see my reflection in the motel room mirror, dark hair, a Roman coin profile, dark brown eyes that have seen much and remembered much, and an angular body with a lean and hungry appearance of forward motion even when at rest. No one's ever called me restful. And I still take pride and delight in the nickname given me by my late husband Richard. He called me Henrie O, saying I packed more surprises into a single day than O. Henry ever put in a short story. Dear Richard.

"Henrie O." Sylvia's tone changed. It marked the end of social pleasantries; time for business. "When I saw your name — God, it seemed like an answer to a prayer. It would be god-awful if I were wrong! Listen, if you've got a few minutes this morning, I . . ." Her voice broke off. I heard, faintly, a scraping, rattly sound. "Oh . . . there's Gordon's car." Surprise lifted her voice. "I'll call you right back."

I was left holding a disconnected phone, listening to the flat, mindless buzz. I slapped down the receiver irritably. When the phone rang, I'd been walking toward the door, suitcase in hand, ready to check out of the pistachio-colored cottage and drive down the spectacular coast road to Sausalito. Actually, it was sheer fortuity Sylvia had caught me at all. I'd been unable to resist the temptation of one last slow jog along the road with the gorgeous view of waves crashing against the jagged cliffs. Otherwise, I would have checked out two hours sooner.

I've never waited patiently. I gave it fifteen minutes, then flipped through the phone book and found the Gordon Fulton residence on the winding coastal road just north of Sequoia Cliffs. I dialed the home number. Four rings and the ubiquitous answering machine: "You have reached . . ." I hung up, waited ten minutes, tried again. The same result.

I shrugged it away. I had no reason to hang about, snarling my plans, to see a woman I'd once known for a brief period.

I checked out, left word — for Sylvia should she call again — that I was en route to Sausalito and the hotel where I could be reached.

But on the outskirts of town, I swung the rental car into a gas station. I used the outside phone and once again heard the recorded voice. I called the inn I'd just left. No messages for me.

Maybe wealth and age had made Sylvia inconsiderate.

I didn't remember her that way.

That's why, twenty minutes later, following the directions of the station attendant, I pulled up at a barred gate. There was just room to park. I tried the intercom attached to the gate, above the electronic number pad.

No one answered the intercom. I looked at the gate.

That was another topic I could have discussed at the Women's Caucus — the withdrawal of rich Americans into barred and walled enclaves. Us. And Them. The Rich and the Fearful; the Poor and the Dangerous.

Beyond the gate, the graveled road curved out of sight amid eucalyptus and gnarled cypress.

I looked at the keypad. Members of the household would have devices in their cars to activate the gate. Still, they all would need to remember the number. I glanced up at the bronze numbers adorning the gate, 69.

People are mentally lazy.

I punched in 96. Nothing happened.

I keyed 96 twice in succession. No luck.

I tried 15, then 15 twice. No luck. Okay, how about 30? Nope. Then 45. The gate on its well-oiled hinges swung inward.

That's the trick to managing numbers in our increasingly arithmetically defined society (SS #, PIN #, FAX #, Voice Mail #), pick a number you can't forget. To make it easy, use a familiar number like the address, add the digits, then multiply. To outfox burglars, do times three.

Only problem is, the forces of evil can think, too. I wasn't including myself, of course, in that category as the car bucketed past the open gate and sped up the winding road. When the car swept into the circular bricked drive, I caught my breath. Not even the French Riviera is as gorgeous and compelling as the rocky, wild northern California coast. Sunlight glinted on the red-tiled roof of the Mission-style mansion.

I grinned. Was Sylvia going to be surprised to see me.

But there was no answer when I rang the bell. I even walked around the house, tried the back door, and took a moment to gaze out at the vivid blue water. Sunlight danced on the white caps. The surf crashing below boomed like holiday cannons. I almost followed the path out onto the headland, but I was beginning to feel like a trespasser. Definitely, no one was at home. I retraced my steps and climbed into the car. Obviously, I'd imagined the stress I'd thought I'd heard in Sylvia's voice. In any event, the matter hadn't been important enough for her to call me back.

That's as much consideration as I gave it until I was drinking Kona coffee and eating a brioche on the hotel balcony in Sausalito the next morning and, of course, reading the local newspaper. The story rated a two-col. head in the lower left of the first page:

FORMER NEWS REPORTER, SYLVIA FULTON, DIES IN CLIFF ACCIDENT

Longtime AP reporter Sylvia Montague Fulton died Thursday when her wheelchair plunged over the side of the cliff behind the mansion where she lived with her husband,

Gordon Fulton, a prominent Sequoia Cliffs attorney.

Fulton suffered massive head and trunk injuries in the fall. Police today theorized that Fulton lost control of the motorized wheelchair. There are no guardrails on the path where the accident occurred and a sheer hundred-foot drop to a boulder-strewn bay. Fulton had been confined to a wheelchair since a car accident two years ago in which she suffered injuries resulting in partial paralysis.

No one was at the home when the accident occurred but police report that the victim's watch apparently shattered during the fall down the rugged cliffside and had stopped at 11:22. The battered body, half-submerged in the surf, was found upon her husband's return from his office at shortly after 5 P.M.

There was a good deal more, of course. A summary of Sylvia's career, titles of her two books on famous trials, and personal information. She was Gordon Fulton's second wife. He was a widower when they met. Sylvia's stepchildren were Mark and Delores Fulton. Mark and his wife, Emma, lived in Thousand Oaks. Delores lived with her father and stepmother.

The time of Sylvia's death was the most important fact I gleaned from the news report. I'd talked to her at a quarter past eleven. She ended our call — because her husband had come home. Very shortly thereafter, she fell to her death. She was already dead when I arrived at the house and found no one there.

The question jumped out, of course.

What happened between the time Gordon Fulton arrived and shortly after noon when I reached the house?

Was Sylvia's husband there for a few moments only? Had the accident occurred after he left?

That had to be the explanation if, indeed, Fulton didn't

find Sylvia's body until "his return from his office" late in the afternoon.

The answer was perhaps so obvious that the question didn't need to be asked.

But I've learned over time never to trust the obvious.

Police officers come in all the sizes and varieties common to the rest of humankind — bright or stupid, diligent or lazy, honest or venal, dispassionate or prejudiced. . . . And the combinations are as endless. What kind of havoc can result when the detective is bright, diligent — and corrupt? Imagine the failures of the stupid but honest cop.

But there is a common veneer, a stolid, dogged watchfulness, a cultivated, protective stolidity. Only the eyes seem to be alive in those faces, eyes tainted with despair, dulled by weariness, imprinted with harsh memories, resistant to emotion.

Lieutenant Laura MacKay of the Sequoia Cliffs Police Department was no exception. Her smooth face might have been cast in Plexiglas. But her icy gray eyes probed mine.

"Her husband's car?"

"To be precise, Sylvia said, 'Oh, there's Gordon's car. I'll call you right back.' Did Fulton tell you he'd been home at almost the moment his wife is presumed to have died?"

MacKay tapped a closed folder with her pen. "No." She stared at me without warmth. "What's in it for you?"

"I don't like murder."

"There's no indication it was murder."

"Funny she's got a problem so pressing she calls on a woman she hasn't seen in years, gets off the phone to see her husband, and next thing we know she's dead on the rocks."

MacKay flipped open the folder. "Accident. That's the official conclusion. Could be suicide." Those cold eyes studied me. "Could be murder. Nothing wrong with the chair mechanically. No evidence she blacked out before she fell. We'll never know."

I was ready to plunge into speech, but the lieutenant held up her hand. "We'll check with Mr. Fulton."

My memory of Sylvia's funeral will always be of dark and twisted cypress and a lowering sky and a chill wind that rattled the green canopy over the open gravesite.

There were almost a hundred mourners present. Sylvia would have liked that.

A memory popped into my mind: the two of us seeking a patch of shade beneath a magnolia on the South Carolina courthouse lawn, the sweet sharp burn of cold Coke down a dry throat. Sylvia had thrown back that mane of blond hair and exploded, "Jesus, it's too frigging hot to live! These goddam people must be salamanders."

She would never be hot again.

Her family, looking stiff and forlorn as families always do, sat on the metal folding chairs, eye level with the bronze casket.

The priest spoke too softly to be heard where I stood.

Leaves crackled behind me.

"Fulton says somebody's mistaken." MacKay's voice was as matter-of-fact as a clerk making change. "Says he never left his office that day." The homicide detective hunched her shoulders, jammed her hands deep into the pockets of her gray all-weather coat. She faced the gravesite, her face as devoid of expression as her mirrored sunglasses. "Fulton drives a red '92 Mercedes sedan. Vanity plates: Cheerio." She nudged a clump of springy grass with the toe of her shoe. "Understand she was a sharp woman. Don't suppose she imagined that car." The shiny sunglasses turned toward me.

"Of course, I don't have anybody's word for that conversation but yours."

Cars were parked at odd angles all the way up the road to the Fulton mansion. The turnaround was jammed. Two young men in navy blue suits handled the parking, giving tickets to the visitors.

The house was jammed, too. I was behind a group of leggy middle-aged women. One of them said, "Sylvia always did say to hold her over till a rainy Monday."

"That's what she hated the most. About the car wreck," a breathy blonde murmured. "Not being able to play anymore."

It wasn't hard to guess golf was the game from their weathered faces and rangy stride.

But I wasn't interested in meeting Sylvia's friends. I made a beeline for the family, clustered in the center of a living room large enough to house an Olympic team.

Such a nice-looking family. A voice echoed in my mind. "Such nice people." That was one of my aunt Martha's favorite phrases. It reflected, of course, how nonjudgmental Aunt Martha was. She always saw everyone as good. It certainly would have been her call about the Fultons.

Nice people in deep pain. Gordon Fulton's face looked desolate, like bombed-out ruins. His son, Mark, kept shaking his head mournfully. Sylvia's stepdaughter, Delores, had red and puffy eyes. As the line of comforters edged closer, I heard her say, "Oh, it's so awful. I still can't believe it. Sylvia was the most alive person I ever knew — even after the accident." She rubbed her eyes with a sodden handkerchief.

I was armed, when I reached them, not only with chutzpah but with enough information to do full-length stories on each of them. It's amazing how much you can find out about people if you have the electronic savvy: credit records, property transfers, moving vehicle violations (and any other criminal charges), media coverage, educational backgrounds, hospital records, insurance policies, class attendance records, sales transactions, hotel reservations.

I knew that Mark Fulton, a computer science professor, was teaching his regular eleven o'clock class the day Sylvia died, which spotted him four hundred miles south of the cliffs. His wife was playing doubles at a Thousand Oaks tennis club. Delores was at work at a gift shop in Sequoia Cliffs. Her clerk's number was on a Visa charge logged in at eleven-twelve. Inez and Ernesto, the Filipino couple who worked for the Fultons, were in the waiting room of an oculist at eleven-fifteen.

So I focused on Gordon Fulton. The attorney was, according to his secretary, in his office all morning and had lunch delivered to his desk at twelve-fifteen. I had a plan of the building. There was a private exit from his office that he could have used. The time would have been close, but it was possible. The parking garage was unattended. Building residents used electronic cards to enter and leave.

So, yes, he could have shoved Sylvia's wheelchair over the side of the cliff. But why? I'd dug deep. If Fulton had been carrying on an affair, he was a master of discretion. I hadn't, despite heroic efforts, uncovered any evidence to indicate he was anything other than a model husband, totally devoted to his second wife, both before and after her confinement to a wheelchair. As for money, the second greatest incitement to murder after lust, the bulk of it belonged to him. Sylvia's books had earned tidy sums, but nothing to tempt a man with assets of more than three million.

I would continue to dig.

I came face to face with Gordon Fulton. He was tall and

lean, sharp-featured, his nose a beak, his deep-set eyes hooded beneath thick gray eyebrows. But today he looked shrunken in his gray pinstripe, deep hollows beneath his reddened eyes, his hands hanging limply at his sides.

He tried to focus on me. "Good of you to . . ."

Delores was talking to the woman behind me. ". . . been home just a week. God, we had such a great time. I'm so glad now that . . ."

I held out my hand, gripped Gordon's firmly. "I'm Henrietta O'Dwyer Collins, an old friend of Sylvia's. I was on the phone with her that morning."

"That morning?" Suddenly he really looked at me, his green eyes — remarkably vivid eyes — coming alive.

"I'm doing a book on top women reporters. Sylvia'd agreed to let me poke through her papers."

He still held my hand, clung to my hand. "She was a wonderful reporter. She's worth a book all by herself." A faint flush stained his pale cheeks. "Maybe . . . maybe that's what you might consider."

I've seen a lot of anguish. I've known anguish. And I had no doubt that I was seeing a man who was heartsick, a man suffering a grievous, almost unbearable loss.

But, dammit, Sylvia saw his car! And he'd denied leaving his office.

Fulton was still talking, introducing me to Mark and Emma and Delores, then sweeping me out of the room and into a short hall. He flung open the door to a study at the corner of the house with three walls of windows, encompassing the front drive, the headland, and the open Pacific.

How the hell Sylvia'd ever concentrated in here I couldn't imagine. As we stood there, the morning's heavy mist rolled away. Brilliant shafts of sunlight spilled through the windows. The view was breathtaking and, even through the

91

closed windows, there was the constant, dull boom of the surf crashing into the rocky cliff.

The rapid eager voice stopped. He awkwardly brushed his arm against his eyes. "Everything's here. You're welcome to come any time. I . . ." His shoulders slumped. "I've got to get back — but we'll do everything we can to help." He stared at the untenanted desk for a long moment, then turned abruptly and headed back toward the houseful of mourners.

The one non-window wall, the one with the door through which we'd entered, was covered with framed clips, the big stories she'd covered. A faded news photo of Sylvia with Maggie Higgins near Inchon. The bombing of the Casbah in Algiers. The presidential inauguration of De Gaulle. The Bay of Pigs. The Freedom Walk from Selma to Montgomery. The famous — and infamous — trials. The kidnapping and murder of little Bobby Greenlease. The Manson horror. And more, so much more.

I swung around, moved toward the desk, and stopped dead still. I was looking out onto the drive, packed now with the cars of mourners. This must have been Sylvia's view as we talked on Thursday morning. It was almost the same time, just after eleven. And the brilliant sunlight, diamond-bright, glittered off the hoods and windshields and chrome of the cars.

Eyes squeezed almost shut against the harsh reflections, I could see the automobiles, yes, but I couldn't see through the windshields.

Sweet Jesus.

That changed everything.

"Dammit, Henrie O, think!" I'll admit to occasional vocal self-exhortations. Maybe it's just what I needed because suddenly I understood. I'd gone at it all wrong.

The key fact wasn't what Sylvia said during that brief call

— it was that she'd called at all.

Why call me?

There could be only one reason.

I swung around. I spent fifteen minutes making a careful, thorough survey of Sylvia's trophy wall and felt a sudden cold certainty at what I *didn't* find, the Hammonds trial. When I looked very close, I could see how some frames had been shifted to cover an empty patch. In her bookcase, I spotted copies of both her books. I picked up the second, *Killing Days*, and checked the Index. Yes, there was the chapter on the Hammonds trial, "Murder Down in Dixie." I could imagine how urgently the murderer wanted to take this book, how painful it was to leave it behind. I slipped it into my purse. My purse, always a leather shoulder bag, is large enough to carry a book or two, a gun, a folded umbrella. Whatever the day demands.

I found the butler in the kitchen.

"Pardon me, Ernesto. Mr. Fulton's asked me to look in his car pocket for a list he needs." I nodded toward a door. "Does that lead to the garage?"

"Yes, ma'am." He held the door for me.

One's actions are rarely questioned if sufficient authority is exuded.

I stepped down into the garage.

I saw the Mercedes immediately. Yes, a crimson 1992 Mercedes sedan with vanity plates. But that wasn't what I sought.

Instead, I stared at the pegboard with its neatly labeled row of hooks. Car keys dangled from each hook. I nodded in satisfaction. Then I opened the driver's door to the Mercedes and looked at the visor and the little leather folder clipped there. I unclipped it and pulled out the entrance card to the Lincoln's Inn Parking garage that served the building where

93

Gordon Fulton officed.

Back in the kitchen, I waited until Ernesto returned, bearing a tray of used glasses.

"Ernesto, if you have a moment, please."

He looked at me patiently. "Mr. Fulton's car keys, the extra set. How long were they missing?"

"I'm not certain, madam."

I had the same feeling — pure pleasure — that you get when the horseshoe drops neatly around the stake on the very first throw. Because, if my theory was right, the car keys had to have been missing just before Sylvia died.

"When were they found?"

He was at the drainboard now, transferring the soiled glasses from the tray. "I don't know, madam. They weren't on the board Thursday morning when I needed to move a car. Then, with Mrs. Fulton's accident, I didn't notice. But they were there this morning." He began to fill the tray with fresh cups and glasses.

"So you first missed them Thursday morning?"

He frowned, trying to remember. "Yes, madam, I think so."

I persisted. This was important. Ernesto finally tied the disappearance to Thursday because "I know the keys were there Wednesday night. I moved the car to get ready for the party."

Have you ever drawn a royal flush? That's how I felt. Because the party was the final necessary component to my equation.

"What was the occasion for the party, Ernesto?"

For the first time, the manservant's composure wavered. His eyes filled. "It was a welcome-home party for Mrs. Fulton and Miss Delores. They'd been gone for six months on a trip around the world. They got home on Saturday and

94

the party was Wednesday night and on Thursday —" He busied himself with the glasses.

So, Sylvia and her stepdaughter were out of town for six months. They returned home on a Saturday. The following Thursday Sylvia's wheelchair went over the side of the cliff. The keys to the red Mercedes were not in their usual place on Thursday morning.

Someone at the party . . .

"The party," Ernesto said mournfully. "Oh, madam, it was such a wonderful party. Everyone was so happy to welcome them home. The house was full of laughter and cheer — and to think Mrs. Fulton only came home to die."

Because, and I knew it had to be true, at that party Sylvia saw a face she thought she recognized, but, more than that, Sylvia must have learned some fact at the party that moved her to call me the next morning.

I was remembering Sylvia more and more clearly now, her good humor, her intensity, her capacity for hard work — and her lack of subtlety. There was no guile in her nature.

Had she been less open, less frank, less easily read, she might be alive now.

I surprised myself by going back to the cemetery. But why not? That's where the dead reside and I had a lot of thinking to do about death, present and past.

A particular death, that of Elbert Hammonds of the famous Hammonds case, the case with no clips on Sylvia's wall, the case that was the only link between me and Sylvia.

I settled on a fairly comfortable bench near Sylvia's fresh grave. I opened my purse, pulled out Sylvia's second book, the one containing the chapter on the murder of Elbert Hammonds, and flipped to page forty-six.

As I started to read, I could smell that courtroom, the

sourness of spittoons and the sweaty, talcumed scent of too many bodies pressed too close together in cloying heat.

THE HAMMONDS CASE

Tobacco money made the Hammondses rich. Some said tobacco money stained their souls. Certainly tragedy and scandal were forever linked to the name. Tobacco wealth made it easy for earlier generations to indulge whims, including the construction of Hammonds Castle, a huge, grotesque limestone castle with battlements, corner towers, and a drawbridge over a moat filled with sluggish, algae-scummed water from a nearby swamp. The castle stood on a ridge five miles from the nearest tiny town and through time many stories were whispered about the Hammonds, about the bloody cockfights and worse, about the ghost of a slave girl who screamed for help when the moon was high, about the drunken revelry when Elbert was young, about his wife who ran away (he said) when their daughter was a little girl (but some believed his wife's bones rotted in a nearby swamp), about Elbert's daughter, Lily Belle, who made a loveless marriage, then came home to bear a twin son and daughter before dying.

Oddly, the beautiful grandchildren appeared to work a change in Elbert's soul. He married a local schoolteacher and decorum settled over Hammonds Castle. Elbert doted on Billy and Chloe. Their every wish was his command. And he would never hear a word of criticism about his beloved grandchildren, both slim and graceful creatures with golden hair and sapphire eyes in elegantly boned faces. When the twins were home from college, parties and balls again were held and sometimes there were whispers of drugs and wild nights, especially when their grandfather, now widowed again, was gone on one of his yearly journeys abroad.

The little town was surprised when Elbert returned home in the early spring of 1973 with a new bride, Louise, a young American woman he met in Cannes. Not much to look at, they said in the town. Short straight black hair and red lips bright as a Jezebel's. And unfriendly, keeping to herself and to the castle. Women snickered over morning coffee at the airs the new Mrs. Hammonds put on, with her tulle-swathed picture hats, and, worse than that, always wearing gloves, at home or away, day and night, some said even at meals. Who did she think she was? Everyone wondered how Billy and Chloe would react, but no one expected the stories that began to seep into town, about hot quarrels and slammed doors and threats from Elbert to turn the twins out.

It was on the clear, still morning of April 22 that Elbert was found dead at the foot of the stone stairs leading from the second-floor gallery to the flagstoned central hall.

A dreadful accident.

But a dowdily dressed maid, who had come to Hammonds Castle with the new wife, walked into the police station the next morning with her damning accusation: she saw Billy Hammonds and his grandfather on the gallery just after midnight and they were quarreling bitterly. She hurried past them and was starting up to the third floor and her room when she heard the old man scream, "Don't! No, no, don't!" and she'd run faster to get away from the ugly scene.

Billy denied it utterly. He swore he didn't come in until after 2 A.M. He said he was with a woman. But he refused to reveal her name.

A married woman, of course, that was what they whispered in town.

Chloe insisted her brother was innocent. And she claimed not to have heard a sound that night, though she'd slept restlessly.

It was the young widow who found the new will, the new unsigned will disinheriting Billy and Chloe.

The police arrested Billy. The trial began in late summer.

Sob sisters had a heyday writing about the trial with snide comments about the widow's refusal to attend, about Chloe's desperate face and tear-filled eyes, about Billy, his exquisite handsomeness, his grace and elegance, his charm. There were several grainy photographs in the book, showing a young man with, admittedly, a handsome face but it was almost too delicate, too fawnlike for a man.

I tried to imagine him twenty years later.

The face would still be narrow, fine-boned, aristocratic. That much he couldn't change.

There were several photographs, too, of Chloe. The delicacy better became her. With maturity, she might be today a strikingly beautiful woman.

Chloe needn't, of course, still be blond. That was also true of Billy.

Surely I would recognize them if I saw them.

I put the book down on my lap and stared out over the cypress-and-gravestone-studded hill.

I didn't need to read further. I'd been at the trial the remarkable, unforgettable day the defense brought Billy Hammonds to the stand. He told his story persuasively, his face appealing, his distress evident.

The maid was called. She told her story with relish, her

98

identification of Billy decisive.

The defense attorney rose for cross-examination. I glanced down at the book, skimmed some pages. Oh yes, Mary Trent.

The defense attorney — a big redhead from Columbia, Stewart Warner — led her through the events of the fateful evening.

I found the passage in Sylvia's book:

"So there is no doubt in your mind, Miss Trent, that it was Billy Hammonds you saw that day?"

"I'm sure." She peered through thick-lensed glasses at Billy.

"How close were you to the defendant?"

"I walked right by him. I saw him, all right." She hunched forward in the witness box, her long frizzy blond hair lying lank on her shoulders.

"Despite your evident weak eyes, Miss Trent? Those glasses appear to be very strong. But you say you saw him clearly. Will you please describe the man — Oh, you're sure it was a man?"

"Yes. Yes." A vindictive glare at Billy.

"Will you describe that man?"

The maid lifted her hand — I remembered so well that accusing gesture and the maid's hand, her outstretched forefinger in such sharp contrast to her stubby, foreshortened, deformed middle finger — and pointed at the defense table and the elegantly handsome Billy Hammonds.

"There he is. He's sitting right there."

But her words were almost lost in a growing swell of sound. Exclamations broke out. Some people stood.

The defense attorney, as if surprised, swung around to

look toward the spectators.

A young man walked down the aisle.

Gasps now. And cries of, "Look at him. Look!"

The judge rattled the bench with his gavel. "Silence. Silence in —" His voice broke off.

It was the shock of the doppelganger.

Warner shouted at the witness. "Or is this the young man you saw? Quickly now, Miss Trent. Who did you see that night? The defendant? Or this young man?"

Before the witness could answer, Billy's double whirled and ran from the courtroom.

Oh yes, I'd been there.

As gorgeous a Perry Mason twist as I'd ever seen in a courtroom.

It gave it away, of course, when Chloe ran. She could cut her hair like Billy's and wear his clothes — both were slim and their height and coloring the same — but no woman runs like a man.

However, for the prosecution's case, the damage was done.

It went to the jury. The prosecution denounced the "play-acting," but the jurors took their oath seriously. Certainly no one could ever be certain of the truth. Did Billy kill his grandfather and Chloe's clever ruse save him? Or had the maid perhaps seen Chloe in the darkness of the gallery and mistaken her for her brother Billy? Was Billy lying about his where- abouts that night — to protect Chloe? Were they co-murderers?

The verdict came back Not Guilty. The Scots' Not Proven would have been much closer to the mark.

I put the book back in my purse and pushed up from the bench. I still had much to do.

Want to know a small-town's secrets? Find the old, retired soc (journalese for society, now they dub it women's news) editor.

I tracked down Elvira Murchison the next morning. Her voice over the telephone was reedy but strong. "I always said there was a world we never knew about that murder. I don't know what was strangest, the way Billy and Chloe left town the day after the trial was over or the way we all woke up one morning to find the castle empty with the windows boarded over. Of course, there was talk. Turned out Elbert'd made a new will after he got back to town with his new wife. She got half the estate, Billy and Chloe the other half. The property was sold to a developer a few years later. He turned it into a country club and a subdivision. The castle's the clubhouse, wouldn't you know. But nobody who was there the night of old Elbert's murder's ever set foot in this town again and nobody knows where they went or what they're doing now."

I hung up the phone and looked at the doodles on the pad, Billy's and Chloe's names, intertwined. They would be in their early forties now.

I felt sure I knew where one of them was, sitting pretty in northern California.

It didn't take long in the local newspaper morgue to find the story I was looking for.

PROMINENT ARCHITECT SUFFERS FATAL FALL

Arthur Robbins was found dead this morning by his wife, Elsa, at the foot of the stairs in the hallway of their home, one of the coast's most famous mansions.

A retired member of the architectural firm of Robbins,

Poston, and Berryhill, Robbins was one of California's most celebrated architects . . .

It was the final paragraph that convinced me I'd found my missing Hammonds:

> Robbins's first wife, Marian Whaley, died of cancer in 1990. He is survived by three children from his first marriage, Diane Olcutt of Northridge, Matthew of Sequoia Cliffs, and Anthony of Paterson, New Jersey, and his second wife, the former Elsa Froman, whom he married three months ago in St. Thomas.

There was a good deal in the story about Arthur's tennis prowess. He'd won the Men's Senior Division just the week before.

Damn clumsy of such a talented athlete to fall down his own stairs.

Elbert fell down and died. Arthur fell down and died. Sylvia fell down and died.

Not a lot of originality there, but who can quarrel with success? Ah, Elsa. You must be feeling quite safe and satisfied. But not, I hoped, for much longer.

"Art Robbins? Oh, sure, we were great friends." Gordon's voice held a smile and sadness. "I called Sylvia in Rome when it happened but I told her not to come home. It was too far and would have been too hard on her. Hell of a thing. He'd married this young woman and was really full of bounce."

"A young woman?"

Now the laughter was wry. "Oh, I suppose only in my eyes. Early forties. Seemed nice enough. Never had much to say. But Art had been damned lonely after he lost Marian."

★ ★ ★ ★ ★

To say I was discouraged was to put it mildly. Still I kept the binoculars trained on Elsa Robbins as she clipped flowers from her garden.

For a lovely fresh bouquet, no doubt. Such an appropriate task for a lady of the manor.

Dammit, she wasn't tall enough to be Chloe Hammonds. Much could be accounted for. The dark hair could be dyed. And even a slim woman can add pounds with years. But age doesn't lop three to four inches of height. And the face wasn't right. The fine elegant bone structure wasn't there. This wasn't exactly a coarse face, but those full lips and rounded cheeks could never belong to Chloe Hammonds.

While I watched the new widow, my mind buzzed with questions. Had I missed another accident among the people in the Fultons' circle?

I didn't think so.

Was I off the mark in every respect? Had a car similar to Gordon Fulton's arrived? No.

I held tight to the binoculars.

No.

The only way into the Fulton compound was through that electronic gate. Sylvia's murderer wanted Gordon's car just in case someone saw it arrive just before Sylvia's fatal plunge. Any questions would be asked of Gordon.

And I knew Sylvia had seen her husband's car. She told me so. But there was indirect proof Gordon's car was used. The missing keys. The party the night before when the keys could have been taken. The return of the keys. No doubt the murderer had an extra set made and, once Sylvia was over the cliff, the original set was silently hung on the pegboard, the duplicates used to drive the car back to Fulton's office garage.

103

It all fitted together beautifully — except the woman I was watching could not be Chloe Hammonds so my hypothesis broke down at its most critical juncture. I'd been so certain that Sylvia called me because of our connection with the Hammonds case.

The plump woman put the last flower in her basket. She stood and stripped off her gloves.

And the whole picture came clear.

Once again, I could see that long-ago courtroom and the "maid" pointing at Billy Hammonds, pointing with a forefinger that made her oddly foreshortened middle finger quite noticeable. Sylvia Montague was sitting beside me that day. It was a scene neither of us ever forgot.

Everything I'd ever read or known about the Hammonds case came together and I knew now, though it might be hell to prove, that there had never been a "maid," that she was the creation of Elbert Hammonds's new wife, Louise, that she was the way that bored young wife slipped out of the shadowed castle for freedom, that Billy and Chloe in their youth and beauty and arrogance didn't pay enough attention to realize the maid was never present at the same time as Louise, that the maid's long frizzy blond hair was a wig and her thick wire-framed glasses a disguise, that Louise wore gloves to hide her deformity, not in a twisted attempt to be a Southern belle. Had Billy perhaps noticed the maid's shortened finger and made a callous remark? Was that as much a reason for the "maid's" accusation as the hope of getting more of the estate if Billy were convicted? How Louise must have laughed and enjoyed using her clever creation as a witness to try and convict her stepson of a crime he hadn't committed.

Now, all I had to do was prove it.

The rest of the day I waged a full-scale assault by telephone. There were setbacks: the courthouse in South Carolina had burned to ashes eight years ago. "Files? Why, honey, we didn't save nothin'. I think the devil himself stoked that fire, it burned so hot and so fast." And nothing came of my efforts to trace Elsa Froman before St. Thomas.

When the phone rang, I grabbed it. Maybe this would be the call that would make a difference.

Her voice still had little inflection, but Lieutenant MacKay spoke with unusual urgency. "A gardener working on an oleander hedge saw Fulton's Mercedes Thursday morning. He knew the time. He was hungry and his lunch break would start in fifteen minutes. We're sure of the ID because he saw the plates, Cheerio."

"The driver?"

"Didn't notice."

"Damn."

"Ms. Collins, time we had a talk."

Obviously, Lieutenant MacKay was ready to pursue an investigation now that the substance of my conversation with Sylvia had been confirmed. The presence of Gordon Fulton's red car had to be accounted for before she was going to mark this case closed.

A police investigation . . . Oh yes. That I would like — as soon as I attended to a few matters. "Great. I'll be at your office at nine in the morning, Lieutenant." I hung up.

I was walking out the door when the phone rang. This time, I ignored it.

Strange cars stick out in rich folks' neighborhoods, but it wasn't hard to find a household on holiday. I picked a house two blocks from Elsa's, one with walls screening the parking area from the street.

I settled myself comfortably to wait for total darkness.

Elsa/Louise was a great girl for planning ahead. Probably it wouldn't have helped even if the gardener had glimpsed the driver. No doubt she'd bunched her dark hair beneath a cap and worn sunglasses. Planning ahead all the way.

That's what I was counting on, Elsa/Louise's penchant for planning and her desire always to have a scapegoat handy. She'd taken Gordon's car, which could implicate him if questions ever arose about Sylvia's death. But what else might she have done to make Gordon an even likelier suspect? I had an idea. If I was guessing right, Elsa/Louise was going to be very surprised indeed at the final turn of events — assuming I succeeded in my quest tonight.

I reconnoitered around the house three times. She was sitting in a downstairs den, watching television. No servants were there.

The house, I was certain, was well locked, a sophisticated alarm system in place.

But I'd spotted a balcony on the back of the house and open french doors and the flutter of bedroom curtains.

I climbed up the trellis with no problem. Jogging doesn't do much for arm muscles, but weight training's very effective. I don't consider myself an exercise fiend, but keeping in shape has lots of nice rewards. In addition to climbing trellises.

Bingo. The lady's room, silken sheets already turned down for night.

It took me two minutes to speed across the room to the adjoining bath. Her hairbrush was nicely clogged with black hairs silver at the roots. In her closet, I thumbed through the sporting apparel and snagged threads from the right sleeve of a navy-blue warm-up.

My other stop that night took a few more minutes. I ran lightfooted up the Fulton's dark drive, cautiously working

106

with the lock on a side door to the garage until it clicked open. I grabbed the Mercedes' keys from the pegboard and opened the trunk.

When I swept the trunk with my pencil flash, I knew I'd guessed right. The tire tool was shoved roughly beneath the carpet. I eased up the carpet. In the cone of light, the discoloration along the end of the tire tool was evident. And a wisp of blond hair. I dropped the carpet down and hoped Sylvia hadn't seen that blow coming.

I pulled an envelope out of my pocket and used tweezers to shake strands of hair — dark hair — onto the carpet.

I took more pains with the threads, making certain a clump wedged into the locking mechanism of the Mercedes.

When I shut the trunk, I paused for an instant, then I moved swiftly to the driver's door. The car was unlocked. More dark hair, a few threads, and I was done.

Lieutenant MacKay sent me a clipping several months later.

POLICE OFFICE COMMENDED
FOR BRILLIANT DETECTION

The Sequoia Cliffs City Council unanimously passed a proclamation today praising Homicide Detective Lieutenant Laura MacKay for her brilliance in using the most modern methods of detection to apprehend a cold-blooded and clever murderer.

Through sophisticated chemical analysis, cloth fibers and hair follicles successfully linked Mrs. Elsa Robbins to the bloodstained tire tool accounted responsible for the death of Sequoia Cliffs resident Sylvia Fulton last summer, resulting in Mrs. Robbins's conviction yesterday for Mrs. Fulton's murder. Furthermore, through diligent and far-ranging investigation, Lieutenant MacKay proved the second Mrs. Robbins to be the widow of a South Carolina murder victim twenty years ago, Elbert Hammonds, and suggests that she, not Hammonds's grandson, who was accused of the crime at the time and subsequently acquitted, was guilty of the murder. Police theorize now that the death of Mrs. Robbins's second husband, Arthur, was not an accident as was believed at the time. Instead, police suggest . . .

I nodded in satisfaction when I finished the article. As the reporter made clear, Elsa/Louise was quite a dandy little planner.

But then, so am I.

AN ALMOST PERFECT HEIST

I won't claim I was immediately suspicious.

My involvement began very simply. I was uneasy.

You see, I believe in character.

I'm not saying people are predictable — not quite. I am saying that character tells. When a student — even a serious, responsible student — fails to show up for a critically important class, well, in the university world, that student has blown it. End of chapter because faculty isn't responsible for student attendance.

I could have left it at that.

Sure.

And I could leave a lost puppy on the shoulder of a super-highway, too.

The latter situation is pretty clear-cut. You see the dog, you see the cars, you take action.

This situation involved a leap. But when uneasiness crystallized into foreboding, I knew I couldn't ignore it. Nor is foreboding, given the circumstances, too strong a word.

My young friend at Homicide, Lt. Don Brown, insists that I have an instinct for malfeasance bordering on the uncanny and that only I would have taken action.

I shrug modestly when Don waxes hyperbolic. This simply reinforces Don's conviction that I, Henrietta O'Dwyer Collins, am a human divining rod for evil. That suits my purposes. I like having a buddy in Homicide. Occasionally he'll drop by and pose questions, always hypothetically, and I know I'm having a chance to use my wits to aid justice, a pursuit I enjoy.

But there was no second sight involved in the affair last week. Rather it was simply responding to the accumulated experience of almost a half century as a reporter. If I've learned one truth, it is this: Character tells.

That day, Wednesday, was going as expected. Since I've retired from newspapering, I've enjoyed a second career as a professor in a journalism department quite unlike most others. The journalism faculty at Derry Hills College is made up of former professionals — real admen and women, real reporters and editors, real TV newscasters and writers and producers, real publicists, people who worked in the world and worked well.

In common with the celebrated school in Columbia, the Derry Hills journalism department edits the town newspaper, *The Clarion*, with students serving as reporters. The unlikelihood of two professionally staffed college journalism departments occurring in the same state is proof that the "Show Me" reputation of Missouri is well deserved.

I wear a number of hats in this community of old pros, teaching at one time or another basic and advanced reporting, feature writing, investigative reporting, and magazine writing. This semester I was handling the op-ed page and teaching two three-hour courses. I also had two independent study students.

One of the great pleasures in teaching is getting to know people who are eager and curious and involved in life, the basic motivations of those drawn to journalism.

This semester I was especially enjoying one of my independent study students, Eleanor Vickery. In the parlance of academia, Eleanor was a nontraditional student. In her late thirties, she was back in school working on the undergraduate degree she'd not completed when she dropped out of school to marry.

In the course of our twice-weekly, hour-long conferences (Journalism 4732, Advanced Magazine Articles), I'd learned a good deal about Eleanor and her husband Ray, president of the Derry Hills National Bank. They were the parents of three boys, Sean, Richard and Riley. They loved to camp, ski, and sail. Ray was a Scoutmaster. Sean had just achieved the rank of Eagle Scout. Eleanor taught the junior high Sunday school class at St. Mark's.

Eleanor radiated good humor, and her infectious smile lightened whatever room she entered. With her unpretentious manner and willingness to work, she fit right into the school milieu even though she drove a Lexus and wore designer clothes. I'd met her husband at the faculty's fall open house for students. Ray Vickery was a chunky, ex-football star with bright, thoughtful eyes and a pleasant manner.

As a student, Eleanor displayed a quick, lively mind and a fine concern for doing everything right. She frequently peppered me with questions:

Shouldn't a direct quote be absolutely accurate?

Although government publications aren't copyrighted, wouldn't an honorable journalist attribute any material quoted?

How could anyone defend using an anonymous source?

Why don't newspapers mount a campaign against the government for the price support of tobacco?

What did I think of a famous magazine's practice of presenting information obtained from several interviews as if the material had been produced in a single interview scene?

And Eleanor was always on time for our conferences. Always.

Wednesday morning was our last session for the semester. It was also the deadline for Eleanor to turn in her three-part series on local nursing homes. If there is one absolute in my classroom as in my life, it is meeting deadlines.

I am not an unreasonable woman. An emergency appendectomy, a blizzard, a train wreck, these are acceptable excuses. But don't knock on my door a day late and say you overslept. Or the dog ate it. Or your computer crashed.

So at six minutes after nine A.M. on Wednesday, I looked up at my clock, puzzled and concerned. I knew, without question, that Eleanor Vickery would have called if there were a serious domestic problem, and only something serious would have kept her away. After all, the series was fifty percent of her grade and this morning was the deadline.

At nine-fifteen, I stared at my telephone, willing it to ring. It didn't.

At nine-twenty-five, I placed my hand on the telephone. In my head, the debate raged:

Coming to class is Eleanor's responsibility.

Something's wrong, something's terribly wrong.

There's a name for people who poke their noses uninvited into other peoples' lives: busybody.

I'd bet my life on Eleanor.

At nine-thirty, I called the Vickery house. Four rings, the recorded message, "We can't come to the phone . . ."

I didn't leave a message.

Why should I? It wasn't part of my job description to discover why an excellent and heretofore absolutely responsible student was apparently self-destructing. Failure to turn in the series would result in an F for the course.

That weighed on the one hand.

On the other, I have confidence in my own judgment, and in my judgment, Eleanor Vickery was rock-solid dependable.

112

I went down the hall to *The Clarion* newsroom and I checked the emergency call scanner. No car accidents. No ambulance runs. No reports from the northside police patrol car.

On the one hand . . .

Back in my office, I jabbed the buttons on the phone.

The recorded message . . .

Slowly, I replaced the receiver.

I walked to my window and looked out at the brilliant redbuds and the daffodils swaying in the light breeze.

A gorgeous spring day.

Car trouble?

Eleanor could have walked to the campus by now.

A sick child?

But, once again, whip quick, I knew Eleanor would call if that were the case. Unless it was life threatening and nothing mattered — nothing — but the life of her child.

There are so many advantages to living in a small town.

I'd met Mae Reno last fall when I gave a talk on famous women foreign correspondents to a local women's group. Mae was the program chair; she was also chief nurse at the Derry Hills Hospital emergency ward.

It took me less than five minutes to track Mae down. She rang me back within three minutes. No Vickery patient at the Derry Hills Hospital.

I walked back to the window, watched two laughing coeds slip off their shoes and dangle their feet in a cold pool. Spring madness.

This was Eleanor's senior spring. She was, damn it, graduating in three weeks. I could see her sitting in the chair in front of my desk — her eyes shining, smiling that shy, eager smile — and telling me about the grand celebration Ray had planned. "He just won't listen. He's invited everyone we've

113

ever known and all of my family to a picnic and I'm so embarrassed." And so thrilled. So happy and proud and thrilled.

She wouldn't graduate with three hours of F.

I walked down the hall, stuck a Post-It note to my classroom door, giving my ten o'clock class a free cut, and headed for the parking lot.

I left a trail of dust as my MG bolted out of the lot.

The Vickerys live on Derry Hill's well-to-do north side in a rambling two-story frame house. Very nice indeed but not flashy. They aren't that kind of family.

I drove slowly past.

Eleanor's Lexus was parked in the drive. The front drapes were drawn. Lights glowed in the living room. Mail poked up from the letter box on the porch.

And the morning paper rested midway up the curving drive.

That was the real tipoff — the morning paper in the drive.

People in the news business, including students, get the paper even before they pour their coffee.

I drove around the block, cruised slowly past one more time.

And the newspaper, still sheathed in its shiny pale green plastic wrap — there'd been a forty percent chance of showers today — lay there so innocently.

It wouldn't mean a thing to anyone else that the newspaper had not been brought in yet. Lazy morning, perhaps.

I was almost to the end of the block.

My paper had been propped up on my breakfast table at shortly after six A.M. I'd especially enjoyed seeing a feature by Eleanor in the Life section.

No matter how many years you write and whether a writer admits it or not, a reporter always gets a thrill out of a byline and quickly scans any article the day it comes out.

I turned at the end of the block, braked beneath an oak midway down the block. This was an older part of town, the homes built in the early nineteen hundreds. This neighborhood had sidewalks and alleys. I hesitated, then switched off the motor. It might be better to go on foot.

I like alleys. They remind me of a childhood in Cairo where my father was a correspondent for INS and later, when I was a young teenager and Dad was transferred, of dark and dank alleys in Paris. I always remember those gray stones glistening with rain. This was a distinctly small-town Missouri alley, narrow, yes, but dusty, with metal trash cans lined next to framed garages.

A deep bark exploded next to a chain-link fence. A schnauzer quivered with hostility.

A marmalade cat stared at me unblinkingly from a perch in a sycamore.

I reached the Vickery backyard.

A dark blue coupe was parked next to the Vickery garages. The small car faced out into the alley.

Not too remarkable, after all. The kind of car a housemaid might drive.

I walked along the car, stepped behind it. There was a rental-car insignia on the rear window. Dried mud obscured the license plate.

But there were no traces of mud on the rest of the car.

I looked toward the back of the house. It was so still, so quiet.

Ominously quiet.

But that welling up of unease came from within me, of course. I knew that. The house itself exuded charm and loving care, the paint fresh and white, the window glasses sparkling in the spring sunlight, the comfortable tan wicker furniture on the wide verandas as inviting as the offer of lemonade garnished with a sprig of backyard mint.

I was looking at a perfect example of small-town America at its best. But I wasn't reassured.

This house was too quiet, too drawn in, too lifeless on a gorgeous spring morning. This was a morning made for open doors and bustling activity.

And the morning newspaper lay in its plastic wrap on the front drive.

I glanced again at the rental car with its muddied plate.

My best advice to young reporters: Don't just stand there. *Find out.*

I moved quietly alongside the drive, stepping soundlessly on the thick spring grass, slipping behind spirea bushes until I reached the steps to the back veranda.

I paused on the top step.

Midway between the steps and the back door, a high school letter jacket — maroon trimmed with silver — lay in a crumpled heap next to a shiny green backpack.

Dropped there?

Thrown there?

Whatever, they shouldn't have been there.

I reached the back door, hesitated, then quietly pulled open the screen.

I turned the knob, again so quietly, so delicately.

The door was locked.

And that was odd, too.

This wasn't a city. This was Derry Hills, a little Missouri town. I know the mores. I'd have bet my MG that nine out of ten back doors on this block were unlocked at this very minute.

I slipped along the back porch, went around the corner of the house.

The curtains were drawn at every window I passed. Yet

the windows were open, up an inch or two from the sills. That's what I would expect on a spring morning. But I would also have expected the curtains to be open.

I paused at each window, bent my head, listened.

A bus rumbled past in the street. Somewhere in the distance a dove cooed. Across the street a lawnmower clattered. But the open windows yielded no sound.

I reached the front porch and a bay window.

These drapes were also drawn, yet all three windows were open.

It made no sense.

Why open windows for the light, silky spring breeze, then pull the drapes?

Again, I bent down to listen.

". . . taking him so long? He should be there. I don't like this." The man's voice was uncommonly high — and ragged with tension.

"Traffic backs up on Springstead. The construction." Eleanor spoke rapidly, her tone an odd mixture of reassurance — and fear. "Please, he'll be there — oh, listen, listen there's the car door now."

Car door? I glanced toward the driveway. Sun glinted on the gray Lexus.

Car door?

"You see, it's going to be all right. Just like Ray said. He promised. You'll see," Eleanor chattered. "Please, just be patient."

"That better be him. If he wants to see you and the kid again, by God, it better be him."

I stared at the drawn curtains in frustration, then eased open my purse. My fingers scrabbled against the soft leather bottom. Dammit, where — finally, I found the nail file.

I knelt by the middle window and wedged the slender metal file into the screen, jimmied it to make room, until the tip reached the edge of the curtain.

Carefully, I eased the curtain back just a hairbreadth.

I had a narrow field of vision, a central portion of the living room including an old-fashioned fireplace framed by black marble and a comfortable-looking couch with bright chintz cushions.

But the teenage boy sitting stiffly on the sofa looked far from comfortable, his body rigid, his eyes enormous, his face carefully devoid of expression. He was an attractive kid, dark haired and green eyed. His broad forehead and generous mouth were a masculine replica of his mother's face. He wore a red-and-white striped rugby shirt, neatly ironed blue jeans, white socks, and penny loafers. And he stared unwaveringly across the room.

I couldn't see what he was looking toward.

Here's where I had to make some choices.

Something odd was occurring in Eleanor Vickery's living room. Eleanor had pled for patience. Why?

I didn't know.

Should I slip back alongside the house, try to edge open the curtain in another window? The best I could manage from any window was a narrow slice of the room.

Would I find out more?

Or would I attract the attention of the man with the high voice?

Sometimes you have to go on instinct.

My instinct told me to go for help.

I didn't have a lot to tell Don Brown.

Maybe to a cop who didn't know me, a cop in a big city, Eleanor missing a deadline, the newspaper lying untouched in the front drive, the odd exchange I'd overhead, maybe that wouldn't be enough to act.

But Don is my friend.

And instinct clamored now.

Fortunately, I wear rubber-soled flats. I consider high heels to be exactly on a par with the old, barbaric Chinese custom of binding women's feet — and approved by male society for much the same reasons.

So I was able to slip quietly, so quietly around the corner of the house and down the side porch.

I had to get away without being seen.

I took only one chance.

I assumed since no alarm had yet been raised about my presence that the man in the room with Eleanor was operating on his own, that there was no lookout.

I forgot to allow for one thing. I wasn't in a big city. I was in a small town.

The rattle of magnolia leaves alerted me.

I looked to my left, directly into bulging, shocked eyes. I had only a swift glimpse of a pink-cheeked face and dyed blond hair before the low branches of the magnolia snapped behind her.

Oh, Christ!

I didn't have time — but I had to take time.

I ran to a side gate, opened it, and plunged into a glorious garden bright with jonquils and flowering dogwood and magnificent royal purple iris. I almost took a header into a stone-rimmed pond.

I veered away at the last moment and stumbled over a garden trowel.

She glanced back over her shoulder, her eyes huge, her cheeks flaming from her unexpected flight.

"Wait. Please!" I called out softly.

She hesitated for just an instant, then clattered up the

back steps, slamming the door behind her.

Oh God, nosy neighbors can be wonderful. But not this time.

If the police arrived, sirens wailing — I whirled around and thudded to the alley gate behind this house, running as fast as I could down the alley, hoping the man in Eleanor's house wouldn't be spooked by the sudden eruption of barks.

I'm an old jogger, yes, but an old and slow one. Now my chest ached and my right knee threatened to buckle.

The schnauzer lunged against his fence. A German shepherd leaped like a ballerina. I kept on running. I had to contact the police before Eleanor's neighbor brought them with sirens screaming.

I'd left the MG unlocked, perhaps the greatest distinction between a little town and a city. So I had my mobile phone in hand without a pause, though I was trying to draw breath into my lungs even when the dispatcher answered.

"Lieutenant Brown. This is an emergency. Henrietta Collins calling."

In less than a second, Don was on the line.

"Henrie O?" His voice was tight with concern.

It was my late husband Richard who gave me that nickname, saying I put more surprises into a single day than O. Henry ever put in a short story. At one point early in our acquaintance (when I'd decoyed a killer to my apartment), Don said fervently that Richard sure as hell got it right the first time.

Gasping for breath, the words came out in spurts. "Don, thank God you're there. A call has just been made from 317 Ninth Street, reporting a trespasser at the Hickory residence at 319 Ninth Street. Make sure no patrol car comes to the front of the house. Do that first. Tell them to come to the alley between Ninth and Tenth on Crawford."

"Right."

The line clicked.

I waited.

"Done. Now, what's wrong?"

I like having Don's respect. I like even more that I can respect him. He listens. Even when it's a tough tale to take in. Quickly, I told him why I'd come to the Vickery house and what I'd seen and heard.

"You saw only a teenager? One of the sons? Nobody else?"

"Right. He looked about seventeen. But he was looking at someone. Or something. And he was — I won't overstate it — but something was terribly wrong. The way he was sitting. The look on his face."

"You didn't see the man?"

"No. I heard him. And I didn't like it, Don. He sounded . . . jumpy. He was threatening Eleanor Vickery."

"Is he armed?"

"I don't know. I didn't see him. I didn't see a weapon," I said carefully. "But he must have one. Or he has an accomplice with one. Don, Eleanor and her son are prisoners. I'm positive."

Don took a deep breath.

I could imagine him seated at his desk, his wiry shoulders hunched, his blue eyes intent. Don Brown looks like such an average thirtyish guy, nondescript sandy hair, an almost slight build, a studiedly vacuous face. It takes a perceptive viewer to note the lively intelligence in his eyes, the stubborn jut of his chin, the compact muscles of a long-distance runner.

"No weapon?" That troubled him. If he rousted out the special weapons and tactical team and it turned out Eleanor and her son were quarreling with good old uncle Frank,

Don would be in big trouble.

Big trouble.

"Don, I'm sure she's a hostage — and she's the wife of Ray Vickery."

I didn't have to tell him who Ray Vickery was.

"Eleanor told this man that Ray would do — something."

"Okay." Don didn't say a word about his job, how he'd lose it in a flash if this turned into a fiasco.

One reason I never visit him at the station is because Don's chief appears pathologically hostile to older women who don't sit with their hands folded and their faces molded in halo-sweet submissiveness. Not my style.

"I'll —"

I interrupted. I already had a plan.

He said nothing for two seconds after I'd finished. Another deep breath. "Yeah."

Because once he thought about it, Don knew I was right. He didn't complain. He didn't object. He didn't tell me it was dangerous. He just said, "Yeah."

Much as he didn't like it.

At fifteen minutes after ten, I walked up on the front veranda of the Vickery house.

If all had gone on schedule, Don was even now slipping onto the back porch of the Vickery house.

Next door a crew of painters pulled up and began to unload scaffolding, paint cans, brushes — they were more backup. I couldn't see the alley from here but I was sure it was well populated with Derry Hills's finest.

I wondered if the pudgy blond woman was watching through the slats of her Venetian blinds.

Now to find out what made Eleanor's teenage son stare fixedly across his own living room.

122

This wasn't the first time I'd worn a body transmitter. The unit rode on a belt hidden beneath my bulky cotton sweater. The antenna ran vertically up my right side, again, of course, beneath the sweater. The microphone was clever, slickly embedded in an old-fashioned-looking brooch snugly pinned on my right lapel.

In my right hand, I carried a slender tool that makes opening a door, especially an old-fashioned lock, easier than punching time on a microwave. I also carried a keyring with assorted keys.

With every step, the heavy stun gun in my left sweater pocket thumped gently against my hip.

I piped a shrill greeting as I pattered across the porch. "Ellie, it's Aunt Henrietta! So sorry I'm late. Such a mess!" I was at the door, opening the screen, and shoving the slender length of ridged metal in the keyhole. As I twisted and turned it, I increased the volume. "The jam boiled over and the stove is just stickier than flypaper in August." The lock clicked, the door swung open. I banged inside. "Ellie, Ellie, where are you? I can't believe you aren't ready to go. I'm a good hour late and then you didn't even answer my call."

I'd already tucked my door opener into a pocket. Keys dangled innocently from my hand. "Ellie?"

I reached the archway that opened into the living room.

"Oh my goodness," I said loudly — to be sure Don heard every word — "Young man, why do you have a shotgun? And why are you wearing that rubber mask? Oh my goodness, Ellie, who tied you to that chair?"

Eleanor Vickery was tied to a straight chair with cord wound round and round her. Her hair was straight, her face wore no makeup. A damp dark stain — coffee? — marked the front of her pale peach silk robe. After the first hopeful jerk of her head toward me, the light in her eyes died, replaced by

123

stark fear as she looked up at the huge man standing beside her. His face was hidden by a Halloween mask of Ronald Reagan.

I felt the flicker of fear myself.

Because the shotgun he held in trembling hands was pointed straight at me. And I couldn't make contact with that rubberized, inhuman face. It was like staring into a cold sea or a dark pit.

For an instant, we were a frozen tableau, I poised in the archway, Eleanor imprisoned in the chair, her son perched tensely on the edge of the sofa, their huge captor — God, six-foot-four, 250 pounds — aiming the shotgun at my head.

And weaving through the stillness among us was an odd crumpling sound, like someone crushing tissue.

"Who the hell are you?" The high voice came out almost in a squeal. But the lips of the Halloween mask didn't move.

I felt a prickle move down my spine. I understood now why Eleanor had tried so hard to reassure him. He was teetering on the edge of panic — with a vicious, dangerous weapon in shaking hands.

"Why, I'm Ellie's aunt. Who are you? What's going on here, Ellie tied up and you with that shotgun!" Out of the corner of my eye, I could see Eleanor's son tensing.

Oh God, no!

I clasped a hand to my chest. "Oh, dear. I think I'd better sit down. I feel all faint," and I tottered toward the couch.

The shotgun followed me.

The teenager's shoulders slumped. Just a little.

I dropped onto the sofa. "Oh, this is dreadful, just dreadful!"

"Shut up." The shotgun wavered between me and the boy.

Eleanor drew her breath in sharply. She strained against the ropes. "Don't point it at Sean, don't!"

124

All the while that peculiar sound continued, a shuffling with an occasional crackle or pop.

There was the squeak of an opening door.

The rubberized mask turned a little to the left.

Eleanor, too, looked toward the rosewood table near the window.

Beside me, Sean tensed again.

Unobtrusively, I gripped his arm, gave it a tiny yank.

His eyes jerked toward me.

"No." I mouthed it, tilted my head briefly, so briefly, toward the hall behind me.

Sean frowned.

Then, I, too, looked toward the rosewood table and saw a radio transmitter sitting there.

Footsteps sounded.

Electronic surveillance is no secret to criminals. Now I knew where the sounds were coming from.

A woman spoke.

We all looked at the transmitter, leaned forward to listen. Static interrupted her words. ". . . Mr. Vick . . . boxes look heavy . . . all right?"

Strain thinned Ray Vickery's voice to a husky whisper. "Fine, just . . . Special proj—" The shuffling sounds resumed amid the crackle of static.

I knew what I'd heard, Ray Vickery speaking in a bugged room. I had no doubt the bug was in Ray's office at the First National Bank.

The shuffling, crackling sound that filled the room suddenly stopped. Footsteps sounded again amid the crackle of static. A door slammed. Now the only sound from the bugged office of the bank president was a flat, lifeless buzz.

The big man abruptly began to pace. His masked face moved from the couch to Eleanor and back again, and the shotgun swung from us to her, from her to us.

"Okay, okay. Twenty-five seconds. That's what he's got. Twenty-five seconds to get to his car." He turned heavily and lumbered toward us. "Or we'll take a little trip, kid. You and me." And the shotgun was inches from Sean's head.

A car door opened, shut. Ray Vickery's frightened desperate voice sounded so clearly in the room where his family was held hostage. "I'm in the car. I'm coming. Don't hurt them, please, don't. I've got the money, just like you want." The ignition turned, the motor roared, tires squealed. "As much as I could carry. At least five hundred thousand. Please . . ."

The robber's huge chest heaved. I could see beads of sweat sliding down his neck.

The shotgun went back and forth, from us to Eleanor, from Eleanor to us.

The roar of the car motor filled the room. Ray Vickery talked in a harsh monotone, "I'm coming . . . for Christ's sake, I'm coming . . ."

And I had to make my move.

Soon.

Because Don should be in the house now. And my job was to decoy the robber's attention away from the archway that opened into the hall.

But first I looked toward Eleanor. "Where are Richard and Riley?" I spoke quite clearly. Don needed to know how many of us were in the house.

"They'd already left for school," she said dully. "They catch their bus at seven-thirty."

"Yeah, yeah." The cheery, pink-cheeked Reagan mask nodded. "I knew that." Pride sounded in the high voice. "I planned it down to the last second."

Sean's hands tightened into fists. "He was waiting for me,

outside the back door."

The dropped letter jacket and backpack.

Ray's voice blared from the transmitter. "I'm at Crawford and Pike. Two more blocks. I'm coming . . ."

"Okay, kid. Now, when your dad gets here, we'll let him come inside and I'll tie him up, then you'll move the cash to my car. Then we leave. Together. I'll be safe as long as you're with me." The mask turned toward Eleanor. "Don't try and get loose and call the cops. Don't do it — not if you ever want to see the kid again."

Eleanor shuddered. "No. Oh, no, no, no."

An old cop once told me never to get in an abductor's car. "You're dead if you go. Make him shoot you there." If the robber walked out with Sean, we'd never see him alive again. I could feel death in that lovely room.

I figured I had maybe two more minutes before Ray Vickery arrived. I had to make my move before then.

I had to be quick and I had to be good.

"Stand up, kid."

But even as Sean leaned forward, I gave a wrenching cry and gripped his arm.

"My heart. Oh, my heart." I clung to Sean. With my face turned away from the robber, I whispered. "Police in the hall. Help me across the room, close to him." And I began to struggle to my feet.

Sean took just a second, then he moved, too, putting an arm protectively around me.

"Air. Sean, I've got to have air. The window . . ."

We veered toward the front windows.

Five feet from the robber.

Four.

I put my left hand into the deep cardigan pocket, gripped the stun gun.

127

"Oh, dear," I moaned. "Pain. Oh, Ellie. My angina. Oh dear, so sick. Air. I need air." I wavered unsteadily, Sean supported me.

Three feet.

The robber backed away. "Hey, stay where you are, auntie."

Two feet.

One foot.

I was even with him.

The robber turned to face me.

And now his back was to the archway.

My hand came out of the pocket, gripping the TV remote-sized oblong plastic case. I pressed the button and lunged toward him, jamming the gun into his chest.

"Help!" I yelled.

Sean, God, yes, he was quick and smart.

Sean grabbed the robber's arm, struggled for the shotgun.

Behind me I heard the thudding footsteps, but I kept on pressing, pressing and now it was five seconds and the huge man, screaming, began to topple.

The stun gun hissed and spluttered.

Glass crashed as the nearest windows were breached.

The front door crashed open.

A firm voice yelled, "Hands up. You're under arrest."

And Don was pulling me away. "He's out, Henrie O. That's enough. We've got him."

I do enjoy awards ceremonies.

Chief Holzer handed the commendation medal to my favorite homicide detective. "The entire Derry Hills police department is proud of your extraordinary role in saving the Vickery family last month." He reached out and pumped Don's hand. "Congratulations, Lieutenant."

He didn't even look my way.

Not that I minded.

Later, as I sipped tea at the reception immediately following, cosponsored by the First National Bank of Derry Hills, I gave Eleanor Vickery a hug.

She stood, holding tightly to her husband's arm.

"I'm looking forward to the picnic, Eleanor."

"I don't know . . ." Her face was somber.

"Of course, we're going to have it, Ellie." Ray Vickery looked down at her, a worried frown tight between his eyes.

She was still having trouble.

I knew that. Understood it.

It's hard to recapture the joy of innocence — and Eleanor's world had been an innocent one. She'd never known fear.

I touched her arm gently. "I'm counting on that picnic. Don't disappoint me."

"If it weren't for you —"

"And Don. And a great police force. And Sean."

Her eyes lightened. She looked across the room where Sean stood, deep in conversation with Don.

"And you, Eleanor."

"Me? I didn't do anything."

"You," I said firmly. "You've always done your best, Eleanor. That's why I came to your house. I knew you would never let me down or yourself — or your family."

She stared deep into my eyes.

I knew what she saw, a lean and angular woman with dark hair silvered at the temples, a Roman coin profile, and dark eyes that have seen much and remembered much — and, at this moment, were both stern and admiring.

"Really?" she asked faintly.

"Really."

She looked at me, then back across the room at Don and her son, the center of an admiring crowd.

Some of the old spark touched her eyes. "But you're the one who really saved us." Her voice rose with a journalist's outrage at a half-told story.

I welcome a teaching point wherever I find it. "It's all right. Especially this time. But take it from me, Eleanor. Never trust official sources."

She stood very straight. "No, it's not all right. I want everyone to know what really happened. I'll do the true story for *The Clarion*."

That put me in a pickle. I don't like to compromise facts, but I didn't want to embarrass my only buddy in the Derry Hills police department.

So, I had to share another journalistic truth with Eleanor. "Sometimes, my dear, it's very important to maintain confidentiality because you need access to those sources in the future."

I should have known better, of course. Character always tells.

Eleanor wrote her story. It won first in the intercollegiate press association contest for investigative reporting.

Don was pleased even though he couldn't admit that publicly. He'd wanted me to have co-billing all along.

Chief Holzer wasn't pleased.

But so what else is new?

OUT OF THE ASHES

Don Brown, my favorite homicide detective, lounged against the kitchen counter, watching me with an odd expression.

"I never think of you as a cookie maker, Henrie O."

I squeezed out pink icing to make the final curve of the *e* on a heart-shaped sugar cookie. I tilted my head. The inscription — *Love* — was a bit uneven but readable. "Don't be a chauvinist, Don."

His face squeezed in thought. "Yeah. You're right. Sorry."

I let it drop, though I could have ragged on him a bit more. No, after almost fifty years of newspapering and a second career in teaching, I don't fit the stereotype of a dear little grandma whipping up goodies. But I am a grandmother and I do enjoy cooking, although it's definitely not one of my talents — I paused to swipe up some icing that had overshot its mark — but I resent pigeonholing. I like making cookies, hammering nails, outwitting malefactors — don't try to put me in a mold. Anybody's mold.

I studied the last two cookies on the sheet of waxed paper, nodded, and squeezed out a capital *E* on the first. This would be Emily's cookie. Dear Emily. My daughter. God's greatest gift to me. Then I traced a *D* on the last cookie. I folded a napkin, put the cookie on it, and handed it to Don.

"Valentine's Day." Don's tone was morose. He stared at the cookie, the skin of his face stretched tight over the bones.

Don isn't the kind of guy who attracts attention. He's average height and slender, with a carefully blank, unresponsive face, nondescript sandy hair, and an even, uninflected voice. It's easy to miss the sharp intelligence in his weary blue eyes, the dry, wry curve of his mouth, the athletic wiriness of his build.

And something was terribly wrong with my young friend this gray February afternoon.

I got down two mugs, poured coffee, and gestured to the kitchen table.

Don joined me. But he didn't pick up the mug, and he put the heart-shaped cookie down on the table, untasted.

"Henrie O . . ." He looked at me with misery in his eyes.

Now it was my turn to make judgments, but I had no chauvinist intent. The sexes do differ. Markedly. And it's damn hard for men to admit to emotion.

"Tell me what's wrong, Don." My voice was much gentler than usual. I am customarily cool and acerbic.

But not always.

I reached out and touched his arm.

It was such a young arm. Strong. Lean. With — God willing — so many years yet to live. I silently wished him the best of life — and that includes both passion and pain.

"Everything. Nothing." He gripped the coffee mug. "Hell, a cop shouldn't get married anyway."

"Yes, a cop should. Especially this particular cop." I gave his arm a final squeeze, picked up my own cup. "Any woman with taste would know that."

He didn't manage a smile. If anything, his face was even bleaker. "The hell of it is, she loves me. I know she does. But, damn it . . ." He hunched over the table; his anguished blue eyes clung to my face. "Henrie O, you're a natural when it comes to crime. I swear to God, sometimes I think you can smell it, pick it up like a cat sniffing a mouse."

I lifted an eyebrow. "What does crime have to do with love?"

He told me.

You don't see many happy faces at the courthouse. You're on reality time here, much as at a hospital. Pain, suffering, and despair mark these faces. I don't know whether it's worse in summer or winter. Now the marble floors were mud scuffed and the smell of wet wool mingled with the occasional whiff of forbidden cigarettes.

The DA's offices were on the third floor. I found the cubbyhole assigned to Assistant DA Kerry O'Keefe at the end of the hall.

I knocked.

"Come in."

She was on the telephone, a slender, quite lovely young woman with blond hair and an expressive, intelligent face. She gestured for me to take a seat.

". . . arraignment is scheduled at ten A.M. tomorrow. We'd be willing to reduce the charge to . . ." Her clear voice was clipped and businesslike.

I sat in the hard wooden chair that faced Assistant DA Kerry O'Keefe's gray metal desk and looked at the young woman who was breaking Don's heart.

Kerry O'Keefe wasn't knockdown gorgeous, but hers was a face with a haunting, unforgettable quality, camellia-smooth skin, almond-shaped hazel eyes flecked with gold, a vulnerable mouth, a determined chin.

". . . see you in court, Counselor." She hung up, looked at me politely. "May I help you?"

"I'm Henrietta O'Dwyer Collins. A friend of Don Brown's."

She had a sudden quick intake of breath, those gold-flecked eyes widened, then her face closed in, smooth, impervious. "I'm terribly busy this morning. I'm due in court." She reached for a brown manila file, grabbed it.

"How do you weigh evidence, Miss O'Keefe?"

She pushed back her chair and stood, holding the folder against her as if it were a shield. Anger and misery flickered in those remarkable, pain-filled eyes. "Evidence? In one of my cases?"

I stood, too. "Yes, Miss O'Keefe."

The tension eased out of her body. "I don't understand . . . why are you asking me about my work? What does that have to do with Don?"

"Everything."

She shook her head and her honey-bright hair swayed. "I study the record. I look at the physical evidence. I interview witnesses."

"When you interview witnesses, what are you looking for?"

"The truth, of course." Her tone was impatient.

"Yes, of course. The truth. Tell me, Miss O'Keefe, how do you know whether people are telling you the truth?"

She wasn't quite patronizing. "It comes with experience. You can pick up when people are lying. Lots of little tip-offs. They sound too earnest, look at you too directly. Sometimes they'll talk too fast. Sometimes they won't look at you at all."

I smiled. "It takes a lot of intuition."

She tucked the folder under one arm, ready to walk out, terminate this interview. "You can call it that."

"You have to have confidence in your own instincts."

Her eyes blazed with sudden understanding. "Oh. So that's why you're here. Look, I told Don, it's no use. No use at all."

"Please, Miss O'Keefe. Let me finish."

She took a step toward the door, then stopped and stood quite still.

Was it respect for my age? Or was it deeper, a pain-filled heart's desperate reluctance to make an irrevocable decision?

I made my bid. "Don believes in your instinct. He wants you to look at what happened one more time, one last time. And this time, listen to your heart. This time, begin with the premise that Jack O'Keefe was innocent."

"The premise . . ." She began to tremble.

I knew then that no matter how much Kerry had suffered, she'd never questioned the facts as they had appeared — even though every fiber of her being rebelled at acceptance.

Her eyes bored into mine. "But there's no reason to think he was innocent. Is there?"

"Yes. Oh, yes. You, Kerry. Your heart says your dad couldn't have done it. Just as your heart says Don is the man for you. Come on, Kerry, give your heart a chance."

The icy wind moaning through the leafless trees sounded like a lost child's cry.

Kerry O'Keefe stood with her hands jammed deep into the pockets of her navy cashmere coat. She didn't wear a scarf. Her cheeks were touched with pink from the cold. She stared at the ruins, her face empty, her eyes as dark and desolate as the blackened remnants of the chimney.

She spoke rapidly, without emotion, as if this were just one more report at one more crime. "The fire was called in at ten past midnight on Friday, January fourteenth, nineteen eighty-three. A three-alarm blaze. It took almost two hours to put it out. The firemen didn't find the bodies until almost dawn. They had to let it cool. Three bodies. My father, Jack O'Keefe. My mother, Elizabeth. My sister, Jenny." She half turned, pointed toward a well-kept two-story Victorian frame house clearly visible through the bare trees. "My grandparents live there. They thought we were all dead, that they hadn't found my body yet." She shivered. "I'd spent the night with a friend. I came home about nine. I saw our house — smoke was still curling up like mist from a river — and I ran up the drive to my grandparents' and burst in. My grandmother screamed. She thought I was a ghost." Kerry once again faced the ruins. "I didn't know what had happened until after the day after the funeral. That's when the story came out in the newspaper saying the fire was set with gasoline and autopsies revealed traces of a narcotic in the bodies." She saw my surprise. "Yes. Percodan. A prescription for my grandmother. For back pain. They said Dad must have dropped by her house, taken the stuff that day. Only a few tablets were missing. But it wouldn't take many. It's very strong stuff. That was in the newspaper. But the rest of it never came out in the paper."

I waited.

She faced me. "But people knew. Everybody knew. The bank examiners found two hundred thousand dollars gone. Dummy loans. Made by my dad."

Kelly turned up the collar of her coat, hunkered down for protection against the bite of the wind. Her voice was as cold as the wind. "I heard my parents quarreling that night. Just before I left. Mother's voice was — I don't know — stern. Determined. She said, 'Jack, you've got to face up to it. You don't have any choice.' And Daddy" — her voice wavered — "Daddy sounded so, so beaten. He said, 'Liz, how can I? How can I?' "

Kelly crossed her arms tight against her body. "I can still hear his voice. But what I don't understand, what I'll never understand, is how could he do it? How could he kill Mother and Jenny?" Her tormented eyes swept from the ruins to my face. "And me. I would have died, too. He must have thought I was in my room, asleep. It was just a last-minute thing, the call from Janet. She asked me to spend the night. I ran down to the kitchen and asked Mother and she said okay and I hurried up to my room and packed my overnight bag and went down the back stairs. Janet picked me up in the alley."

I was familiar with these facts. Don had brought me the fire marshal's report, a copy of the autopsy reports, and the file from homicide.

Because, of course, it was not simply arson, it was murder.

The official conclusion: The bank examiner discovered the dummy loans. Jack O'Keefe, facing disgrace and probable prosecution, drugged his family, waited until they were asleep, then splashed gasoline throughout the downstairs portion of the house. He lighted a candle, wrapped a string around its base. The string led from the kitchen through the dining room to velvet drapes that were also doused with gasoline. O'Keefe hurried upstairs and went to bed. There were traces of Percodan in his body, too.

Was he already groggy when he slipped beneath the covers?

Was he asleep before the blaze erupted in sudden, demonic fury?

Although his body and the bodies of his wife and daughter were badly burned, the cause of death was asphyxiation from the smoke that roiled up from the blaze below.

Now, twelve years later, wind and rain and sun had scoured the ruins, but thick deposits of carbon on the remains of the chimney still glistened purplish black in the pale winter sun.

Despite the tumbled bricks, the occasional poked-out timber, I could discern the outline of the house, imagine the broad sweep of the porch and the jaunty bay windows, estimate the size of the living room and dining room, glimpse a bone-white remnant of the sink in the kitchen.

I looked thoughtfully toward the substantial Victorian house that belonged to Jack O'Keefe's parents.

The ruins would be visible from every window on this side of the house.

I pointed to my left. I could see the roof of a house over a brick wall. "Who lives over there?"

"Uncle Robert and Aunt Louise. My Dad's brother." There was no warmth, no fondness in Kerry's voice. "They built the wall a few months after the fire."

I wasn't sure I would blame them for that. Who would want an ever-present reminder of that violent night?

Who did want an ever-present reminder?

"Why are the ruins still here?"

Kerry's face was icily determined. "Grandmother. Then me."

"Why?"

"I don't know what Grandmother thinks. I don't believe anyone's ever known. I remember her, before the fire, as bright and cheerful and fluttery. But she's like a ceramic piece. The color is all on the surface, a surface you can't get past. All I know is she wouldn't let anyone touch any of it — not a piece, not a scrap."

"Didn't the neighbors complain? Don't they now?"

"No. Oh, they might not like it. I suppose a lot of them don't. But it's been so many years now, most people don't even notice. You see, we're the O'Keefes. *The* family in Derry Hills. For good or bad. The richest. The most powerful. Even though Grandad sold the bank a few months after — after the fire. But Uncle Robert's on the board of directors. And so am I. Uncle Robert's president of the country club. Last year he

138

headed up the community drive. And no one would want to talk to Grandmother about the ruins."

"You said the ruins stood because of your grandmother — and then because of you."

"Uncle Robert was the executor of the estate. He did what Grandmother told him to do."

But he built a wall. Brown winter tendrils of ivy clung to it.

I glanced from that wall to Kerry's face. "You own the property now. Why don't you have the ruins knocked down?"

Her pale face was stubborn. "Then it would be green and grassy — and I might forget."

Abruptly, Kerry turned, headed back toward my car.

I caught up with her.

She slammed into the passenger seat.

I slid behind the wheel.

She glared at me. "This is stupid. Stupid. And it hurts too much. Because I thought my dad loved me, loved all of us. He was my best friend, the greatest guy I ever knew. When he laughed . . ." She swallowed harshly and stared out the winter-grimed window of the car, stared out at ruins and heartbreak. When she spoke again, her voice was dull, exhausted. "I was wrong about my dad. So how can I ever believe in . . . anything."

That was why she'd told Don she wouldn't marry him. That was why these grim ruins stood.

If Jack O'Keefe was not the man she'd believed in, how could Kerry be sure about Don?

About any man?

About any person?

Ever.

Her face streaked with tears, Kerry grabbed the door handle.

"Wait, Kerry. Answer one question. Just one. You spent

the night at Janet's. How did you sleep?"

She struggled to control her ragged breathing. "Oh God, I hate to remember. I don't want to remember! We were having so much fun. We stayed up all night and talked and talked and talked. That's why I slept so late —"

"You stayed up all night?"

She heard the excitement in my voice.

"Yes. You know how it is —"

"You weren't tired? Fighting off sleep?"

Her mouth opened. Her eyes widened. She turned, stared at me. But she wasn't seeing me. "Oh, my God. If I wasn't sleepy — because I should have been, shouldn't I? If Daddy intended for all of us to die, I should have been drugged, too! The police believed Daddy took the Percodan from Grandmother's house and ground it up and put it in our drinks at dinner." Then the eagerness seeped out of her face. Her lips quivered again. "But it could have happened after dinner."

"How?"

"Cocoa." Her lips quivered. "It must have been in the cocoa."

"Cocoa?"

"It was a family thing. In the winter, we always had cocoa at night, sitting around the fire in the living room." She glanced toward the chimney, a sentinel against the pale blue winter sky.

"But you weren't there that night. And, if your dad planned for his family to die, it would be very important to him to be sure you drank the cocoa. But, if he was innocent and you didn't come downstairs for cocoa, it wouldn't matter, would it? He'd simply think you'd already gone to bed. Am I right?"

Kerry's hands came together tight and hard.

She wasn't listening.

She was thinking.

I gave her a moment, then I laid it out.

"If Jack O'Keefe didn't doctor the cocoa, someone else did."

Her eyes locked with mine.

Then I looked back at the ruins of the house, the once-substantial, old, and comfortable house. In a little town, back doors often aren't locked.

It could have been even easier, someone dropping by that winter afternoon. I envisioned a gloved hand lifting the canister lid, dropping in the finely ground powder, giving the canister a shake. Cocoa would better hide the bitter taste, too.

"You see, Kerry, if we're right about your father, then it was terribly, critically important to someone to be sure no one woke up when the fire broke out."

While I waited to see the president of the Derry Hills National Bank, I considered who might have doctored the cocoa.

Happily for Kerry, I was confident I could exclude several names immediately.

The cocoa wasn't doctored by anyone in the house.

How could I be certain?

Because Kerry lived.

The police had accepted the idea that Jack O'Keefe preferred to die and for his family to die rather than to face disgrace.

But that tortured reasoning made no sense, fulfilled no logic, unless everyone died. The police assumed Jack O'Keefe simply didn't know Kerry was gone for the night.

But on that fateful evening, Kerry's feather, mother and sister knew Kerry had drunk no cocoa.

If one of them were the murderer, he or she could easily

141

have brought a cup of cocoa upstairs to Kerry. Once it was realized that Kerry was absent, the macabre plan would have been delayed until the next night when Kerry, too, would have been home.

So, I didn't put Jack or Elizabeth or Jenny O'Keefe on my list of suspects.

If the dead could not be blamed, who could?

I intended to find out.

The office door opened and Ray Vickery, the president of the Derry Hills National Bank, walked toward me. An eager smile touched Ray's always-genial face. His handclasp was strong and warm.

"Henrie O. It's good to see you. Always good to see you." His eyes said even more.

I had occasion in the past to be of service to Ray and his wile, Eleanor, and their gratitude continues.

I could count on Ray.

He welcomed me into his office, offered me a comfortable red wing chair. He sat in its twin.

I came straight to the point.

"Ray, were you with the bank twelve years ago — when Jack O'Keefe and his family died?"

His mobile face was sorrowful. "That was awful. Yes. The bank belonged to the O'Keefes then. I'd been here about seven years when it happened." He shook his head slowly. "I still have trouble believing it."

"Why?"

"Jack O'Keefe — well, he was a fun guy, loud, always joking. A big, good-looking man. Blond, blue eyed, with a grin bigger than Texas. And later, everybody agreed he'd never really settled down, worked like he should, like his father and brother thought he should. Jack was too busy sailing or mountain climbing or building a glider or hiking with his girls or white-water rafting on the Colorado. But he was a fun guy — I couldn't believe it when he set the house on fire. His wife, the girls. And only Kerry left and that just by a stroke of luck. They say it's made Kerry a real loner. Her grandmother worries about it. She won't let anybody get close to her. If Jack had just thought . . ." Ray sighed.

"So Jack was a flake. What made him a crook?"

Ray shrugged. "Who's to know? I mean, it was such a shock. To all of us. But there wasn't any doubt about it. Two hundred thousand missing, and fake loans signed by Jack. The family hushed it up, of course. Old Man O'Keefe made up the losses. But it knocked the stuffing out of him. He sold the bank soon after. It wasn't six months later they found his skiff dumped over in the lake. His body surfaced three days later. He drowned. But I thought he did it on purpose. He was crazy about Jack."

"Who was in the loan department besides Jack?"

"Robert, Jack's brother." He frowned in thought. "And I think Gordon Evans was in loans then, too."

I took my notebook out of my purse. "Ray, some new evidence has turned up. Jack O'Keefe didn't set that fire. And that makes me wonder if he stole the money. Could someone else have signed his name to the fake loans, made him a patsy?"

Ray's mobile face reflected his response: shock, rejection, uncertainty, consideration. He rubbed his cheek thoughtfully. "It would have taken some doing. But, sure, it could have been done. Because Jack was such a loose guy and spent so much time out of the office."

"What happened to the evidence?"

He looked blank.

"The bank examiner found these dummy loans. Where would those papers be?"

It took three hours, and we didn't find the originals. But the yellowed Xerox copies in the dead files in the basement suited my purposes just fine.

Ray Vickery agreed to my plan. I knew he would. "I owe it to Jack," he said simply.

I called Don. He heard me out.

"Henrie O, it could be dangerous."

"I don't think so. But I'll be careful."

"You promise?"

"Yes."

"Henrie O, thanks."

I stopped first in Gordon Evans's office.

Evans was a lanky, somber-faced man about ten years younger than I. His handshake was limp and his mustache dispirited.

But he wasn't stupid.

When I finished speaking, he leaned forward, his gray eyes cold. "Anyone in the bank could have used Jack's office. Not I alone. And I resent the implication that I might have been involved." He reached for a sheaf of papers. "Now, I have matters —"

"Of course, there's a simple solution. Mr. Vickery has agreed to make a search of the bank's dead files tomorrow. He will then submit the papers to a document examiner along with samples of Jack O'Keefe's handwriting. If the signature is not that of Jack O'Keefe — if his name is forged on those documents — we will be sure of his innocence." I smiled. "You won't object to providing a sample of your handwriting, will you?"

"I shall do nothing of the kind. Good day, Mrs. Collins."

Alma Hendricks scooted her chair closer to mine in the

bank's employee coffee room. She poked her thick-lensed glasses higher on her beaked nose and glanced uneasily around, then spoke rapidly. "Nothing ever came out in public, but everybody in town knew. I felt so awful for the family."

"You did Jack O'Keefe's secretarial work?"

"Yes. You could have knocked me over with a feather." Her green eyes stared at me earnestly.

"Did you like him?"

Sudden tears filmed her eyes. She swung away, grabbed some Kleenex, swiped under her glasses.

So. "Some new evidence has surfaced, regarding the fire. Now there is some question whether Mr. O'Keefe actually stole that money."

She listened intently as I described the search that would be made of the dead files.

Antiques, brocaded chairs, and a variety of small tables jammed Iris O'Keefe's living room. The smell of rose pot-pourri mingled with a violet cologne. But neither could quite mask the sweet thick scent of bourbon.

We were about the same age. An ormolu-framed mirror reflected us. Funny how we often see what we wish in the quick early morning scan of a mirror. Intellectually I know I am old. But it always surprises me — shocks me — to see the lines in my face, the silver in my once raven black hair.

We were a contrast, no doubt about it. I always look impatient. I *am* impatient. My eyes are dark, my face strong boned, my body always poised to move.

Iris O'Keefe's white hair straggled, though it looked as if it had been ineffectually brushed. Her blue eyes peered at me muzzily, but that was alcohol, not age. A heavily veined hand plucked nervously at the unevenly tied white silk bow at the

145

throat of her wrinkled navy dress.

". . . will exonerate your son. We'll know definitely to-morrow when we look at the documents."

Her shoulders sagged. Slowly, wearily, without saying a word, her face drawn, she struggled to her feet and walked unsteadily across the room, habit steering her safely past the bric-a-brac-laden tables.

After a moment, I rose and followed her.

She stood by the one window with the drapes full open.

Not a tree, not a shrub marred the view of the burned-out house.

She shuddered, long, slow, deep shudders.

"Mrs. O'Keefe —"

"Leave. Leave now. Leave me."

"That's all over. Over!" Louise O'Keefe's hair curled in obedient, glistening waves. Her patterned black-and-russet silk dress was stylishly short, but Louise O'Keefe still had the figure to display her legs. She had the glisten of wealth, that unmistakable patina created by fine clothes, expensive cosmetics, superb hairdressing, exquisite jewelry (gold shell earrings and a gold pin crusted with rubies), and the confidence money buys.

Skillfully applied makeup softened the sharpness of her features. Her face was long and thin (thin, of course), her gray eyes remote, her mouth tight.

"No, Mrs. O'Keefe. It isn't over."

"It was twelve years ago." She smoothed back a wisp of hair. "Jack was a thief. And he couldn't face up to it."

I rose, but I kept my eyes on hers. "Whatever he was or wasn't, Mrs. O'Keefe, we're now certain he was not an arsonist — and thereby a murderer. Whether he was a thief will be determined tomorrow, when we study the documents."

She stood by the Adam mantel, one heavily beringed hand clutching it. "We — who is we? What right have you to make these accusations?"

I gave her a cool smile. "There are no accusations yet, Mrs. O'Keefe. But tomorrow . . ."

I waited patiently outside the door to the men's grill. If you want to find sexism alive and thriving, try your nearest country club. The grill was a fitting background for men of wealth: paneled walls, hunting prints, elegant Oriental rugs, and walnut card tables. The cardplayers were sixtyish men in argyle sweaters, fine wool slacks, and Italian loafers.

Often at this time of the day, I was hard at work in my office at *The Clarion*. The newspaper is produced by the journalism department at the college, but it serves the town of Derry Hills. I was op-ed editor this semester. It was strange to contrast the pulsing, scarcely leashed tension of *The Clarion* — of any daily newspaper office — with the muted, relaxed bonhomie here.

The contrast reminded me that life has infinite variations, and it's unwise to assume your pattern is all that exists.

Finally, my quarry laid out his hand, then rose from the table near the fireplace. Robert O'Keefe had thinning blond hair and a petulant face. He might once have been attractive, but his stocky body was flabby with a paunch that even good tailoring didn't quite hide.

When he came through the doorway, I stepped forward. "Mr. O'Keefe, may I speak with you for a moment?"

He took me to a petit-point sofa in an alcove off the main reception area.

His face didn't change as I spoke, but the long slender hands in his lap gripped each other tightly.

". . . sure you'll be delighted if we can clear your brother's name when we find those files tomorrow."

Slowly his hands relaxed. Eyes as shiny and unreadable as blue marbles slid across my face, flicked toward the grandfather clock in the corner.

"Interesting." His voice was bored. "Too bad poor Kerry's going to be disappointed." He pushed back his chair, stood. "Got to get back to the game. Good to talk to you, Mrs. . . . uh —"

"Collins."

"But the truth of it is, Jack took the money."

And he turned and walked away.

The phone call came at six the next morning.

But that was all right. I was already drinking my second cup of Kona.

I picked up the receiver.

"Henrie O, Christ, it worked!" Don was pumped up. "So what do we do now?"

Ray Vickery agreed to loan me the boardroom at the bank.

"I'd say this is bank business." His voice was grim.

"Thank you, Ray." I hung up the phone, made my calls in quick succession. It was an invitation no one quite dared to refuse. I set the meeting for 11 A.M.

I arrived ten minutes early.

Don was waiting in the parking lot.

He opened my car door, his face grim.

"Henrie O, I got word just a few minutes ago. Those signatures on the dummy loans — they're Jack O'Keefe's." Despair etched deep lines in his face. "The examiner's sure."

I'd considered that possibility already. And thought it

through. There was nothing to say about it. Now.

Instead I asked briskly, "But you brought the videocassette?"

"It's in the car. But what difference —"

"Get it, Don."

Don stood by the oversize television. It was equipped with a videocassette player. He held a cassette in his hand.

I was at the door of the boardroom.

Kerry O'Keefe arrived first. She looked gorgeous in a black-and-white rayon suit with red trim, but her face was pale and strained and the glances she sped at Don alternated between hope and uncertainty.

Don's somber face offered her no encouragement.

Gordon Evans walked in, his body stiff, his face resentful. "I am here under protest." The gray pinstripe did little for his sallow coloring. It was a rack suit, the trousers not quite long enough to break.

I raised an eyebrow. "Surely you'd like to know the truth of what happened with those loans — since you worked in that area, too."

"I do know the truth."

"Perhaps. And perhaps, Mr. Evans, you will discover that certitude sometimes does not cover a multitude of sins."

He took a chair in the far corner, crossed one leg over the other, and watched me with distaste.

Don shot me a curious, puzzled look.

Kerry jumped up from her chair. "Grandmother!"

Iris O'Keefe wavered unsteadily, but with dignity, in the doorway. "Kerry, my dear. You're here, too?"

Kerry took her grandmother's arm and carefully shepherded her to a chair beside her own.

Iris O'Keefe hunched in the chair. Her thin fingers

plucked at the pearl necklace at her throat.

Alma Hendricks hesitated in the doorway.

"Come in, Alma. I'm so glad you could join us."

"Good morning, ma'am, Mrs. O'Keefe, Miss O'Keefe." Alma slid into the chair opposite Kerry's.

Angry voices rose in the hall.

We all looked toward the door.

Robert and Louise O'Keefe, their faces flushed, stepped inside and abruptly stopped talking.

The instant of silence was full of tension.

"So what are you staring at?" Louise demanded sharply, her angry eyes snapping from face to face.

"If you'll take your seats . . . ," and I motioned to two empty chairs with a direct view of the television set.

Robert O'Keefe glowered at me. Louise tossed her head. But they sat down.

"First, I want to be sure we all know one another."

Robert crossed his arms. "Mrs. Collins, certainly we all know —"

Sometimes I don't mind being rude.

This was one of those times.

I interrupted. "Yes, of course, you know the family members, the bank staff. But, Mr. O'Keefe, I don't believe you've met Don Brown. Don, I would like for you to meet," and I introduced them, swiftly in turn, "Robert and Louise O'Keefe, Iris O'Keefe, Gordon Evans, and Alma Hendricks, Lieutenant Don Brown of the Derry Hills Police Department homicide unit."

Robert O'Keefe's eyes widened.

Louise O'Keefe drew her breath in sharply.

Iris clutched her granddaughter's arm. "Homicide? Homicide? What does that mean?"

I closed the door to the conference room and turned to

150

face my audience. "Ladies and gentlemen, in the public mind, Jack O'Keefe is guilty of theft, murder — by arson — and suicide. I propose to prove that Jack O'Keefe was innocent on all counts."

Kerry leaned forward, her chin cupped in her hands, her heart in her eyes.

"The original police investigation, following the arson, discovered that two hundred thousand dollars was missing through fake loans signed by Jack. When Percodan was discovered in the bodies, the police concluded that Jack stole his mother's prescription, doped his family, then arranged for the fire because he couldn't face disgrace. Kerry O'Keefe's escape was believed to be simply good fortune. While it certainly was that, Kerry's escape was the first proof of Jack's innocence. You see, Kerry wasn't drugged."

Iris pressed trembling hands against her cheeks. "What do you mean? What are you saying?"

"I mean that someone took the pain prescription from your house, ground it into a powder, then dropped by Jack's house and mixed the drug into the top level of the cocoa canister, knowing that the Jack O'Keefe family drank cocoa every night.

"But Kerry drank no cocoa. Jack would have known that, would have had to know it, if he planned to kill his family that night while they slept. So Jack didn't do the drugging. Nor did anyone else in the house because, once again, it would have been a twisted response to disgrace and the intent would be for all to die, and Kerry wasn't there.

"So, someone came by and left without knowing that Kerry would not drink cocoa that night."

"This is absurd." Robert stood.

"Sit down, Mr. O'Keefe. You don't want to miss the main event."

151

His glance locked with mine. Slowly, he sat down.

Louise's face flushed. "This is so insulting. I demand —"

"To know the truth. Good. Don, please begin."

Don lifted the remote. The television turned on and then the VCR began to play.

Darkness.

I began to speak. "Everything hinges on whether Jack O'Keefe dummied those loans."

Nothing but darkness.

"I spoke yesterday with two men who could have arranged the theft to look like Jack's work, Jack's brother Robert and Gordon Evans."

"I object. I object —"

"Quiet, Mr. Evans. I merely said you had the opportunity. I also spoke to Alma Hendricks, both because she could have stolen the money and because she would spread the word of my search to others in the bank, and the fact that the documents would be unearthed today."

The video picture was black, but door hinges squeaked.

"I alerted Iris O'Keefe and Robert's wife, Louise. And finally I arranged for a video camera to record if anyone came to the basement dead files here in the bank last night."

A light came on. The grainy picture flickered, then came into focus on a row of filing cabinets in the dimly lit room.

A figure dressed in black hurried to the cabinets, pulled out the drawers in quick succession, scanning the folder tabs. It didn't take long. Not quite nine minutes. Then a folder was snatched up, the searcher whirled and hurried to the door, the light went out.

The film continued to whir.

Robert O'Keefe jumped to his feet, his face convulsed. He stared down at his wife. "You fool. You stupid fool."

"I had to get them. You —"

152

"Goddamn it, Jack signed —"

He broke off.

"Yes, Mr. O'Keefe? Won't you continue? Please tell us how you persuaded your brother to sign the false loans that you had prepared." Because Robert was right. Handwriting comparisons proved the papers were indeed signed by Jack. But I knew that Jack didn't kill his family. So he must not have been the creator of those dummy loans — even if he did sign them.

"Oh, my God," Louise moaned. "I thought —"

"Shut up, for Christ's sake," her husband ordered.

"Yes, Louise, why don't you tell us about it?" I asked.

"Louise, don't say a goddamn word."

I looked from husband to wife. "Not much communication in your marriage. Right? But Louise knew who would take money — and it wasn't Jack. I don't suppose the two of you ever talked about it. What did you think, Robert? Did you really believe your brother killed himself and his family? Or was it such an enormous stroke of luck for you that you never permitted yourself to think about what really happened?"

Tears slid down Iris's withered cheeks.

"Or why don't you tell us, Iris. You've always known, haven't you? That's why you wouldn't let anyone clear away the ruins from the fire. You wanted Robert to see it day and night. But he built a wall."

"Jack was gone. I couldn't lose Robert, too. But I knew Jack didn't take any money and he'd do whatever Robert asked him to do. I knew that's the way it must have happened, Robert bringing in the loans, spinning Jack a story, asking him to sign the papers. But even knowing it, I couldn't lose Robert, too. I couldn't." She buried her face in her hands.

"Mother, Mother." Robert's voice shook. "Mother, I

didn't do it! I swear before God. I didn't do it. Not the fire. I didn't."

Iris's hands fell away. She stared at her older son.

He hurried to her. "Mother, I swear to you."

She looked into his eyes, then she made a noise deep in her throat as her head swung toward her daughter-in-law.

"That's right, Iris." I spoke clearly. "Robert took the money. But Louise drugged the cocoa and set the fire."

It bothers Don a lot that we could never prove murder against Louise O'Keefe. All we had was circumstantial evidence. We were certain, but that isn't enough in a court of law, of course.

She could claim she went after the files because she was trying to protect her husband. Not true, of course. She was trying to protect herself. That was always her goal, to protect the life and social position and security of Louise O'Keefe. And she was willing to destroy a young family to save her husband and her elegant way of life.

Everyone ultimatly gets what they deserve.

Louise O'Keefe is no exception.

And neither is Robert. He has a great capacity for not accepting reality. He should have known that Jack didn't drug the cocoa or set the fire. But he didn't want to think about it, refused to think about it. If he had thought too hard, he would have known the answer.

When he finally knew what had happened, he jettisoned Louise.

And there were no thefts to prove against Robert at this late date, the money long since made good, the statute of limitations long since past.

Louise and Robert are divorced now.

She got quite a nice settlement. She's living in the Canary

154

Islands, a hard-faced, wealthy woman.

But what has her crime gained her?

Oh yes, Louise will get what she deserves, is getting it, has gotten it.

What matters, what really matters, is love.

And love triumphed here.

Kerry and Don's wedding will be in June.

I wouldn't miss it for the world.

REMEMBRANCE

Dislike was instantaneous. And mutual.

Natalie Wherry Pearson's high-bridged nose and chiseled lips were elegant and haughty, her face as serenely arrogant as those pictured in the family portraits that lined her study. Directly behind her desk was a portrait of Colonel Amos Wherry, who died on Omaha Beach. Natalie's father.

I had now lived in Derry Hills long enough to become familiar with the local icons. Amos Wherry was a brave man, by all accounts. The glass-encased medals beneath the portrait attested to that. But it didn't mean Amos Wherry was a likable man, not if the artist's brush was true. I saw the supercilious curl to Wherry's mouth, the posture of command born not of rank but of lineage.

I was underwhelmed. I've never excelled in deference, and obeisance to wealth and position ignites in me a contrariness that borders on the pugnacious.

This visceral response isn't unique to me, of course. All reporters have a stripe of irreverence in their mental makeup. It usually keeps them from turning into toadies, a danger for those who associate, even in an adversarial way, with the rich and powerful.

Natalie Pearson knew I was disdainful. That accounted for the tightening of those thin coral lips, the firming of her chin. She glanced down at my card, lying face up on her black-lacquered antique Chinese desk with its lovely inlays of copper. On the card, beneath my name, Henrietta O'Dwyer Collins, I had written, "I wish to speak with you concerning Judith Montgomery."

She picked up the card. "I'm rather rushed this morning, Mrs. Collins. Since Miss Montgomery is no longer in my employ, I don't believe there is any point in our conversing." Her sharply planed face was all bones and unguent-smoothed skin. Her silvered hair fit her head in sleek waves designed by a stylist at an expensive salon. Glacial gray eyes surveyed me.

I smiled, even though I knew my eyes were as icy as hers. "But you've agreed to see me, Mrs. Pearson. That's quite interesting, you know."

Sudden red patches of anger flamed in her gaunt cheeks.

First score to me.

But now was the time to be wily. It wouldn't help Judith's cause for me to be summarily dismissed.

Before she could speak, I continued briskly. "I'm sure, of course, that your willingness to see me reflects your status as a community leader, your family tradition of noblesse oblige."

I kept my expression bland, a look perfected through years of interviewing.

As I had expected, after a flicker of surprise, she fished as nicely as a striped bass on a lazy summer afternoon.

Those thin red lips curved into a tight bow of satisfaction. "Yes. Yes, of course. Although I don't quite see that much can be done for poor Judith." Her voice was as cool as shaved ice.

"If you could just give me the circumstances . . ."

Old fish can be cautious. She was close to taking the lure, but not quite. "What is your interest in this unfortunate matter, Mrs. Collins?"

"Judith Montgomery is one of my students." And, I didn't add, a rather prickly one, charming one moment, confrontational the next. But, nonetheless, a student who had caught my attention and who now had asked for my help.

It still seems odd to think of myself as a teacher. I spent almost a half century as a reporter, and, after my retirement, found myself in a new career at a small liberal arts college in Missouri as a member of the journalism faculty made up, with glorious élan, of old professionals. This semester I was teaching basic reporting. I still see myself as a writer who teaches, not a teacher who writes.

The fact that *The Clarion*, the Derry Hills daily newspaper, was a product of the journalism school kept me firmly rooted in news reality. It bridged town and gown in a way unusual for a college community.

"At the college." Her tone warmed a degree.

I could see a cloak of respectability settling around me.

Useful things, occupations. But deceptive, too. Doctor. Lawyer. Indian chief. Reporter. Professor. The mind responds with a stylized image. That's why con artists dress so well, smile so often.

"I am a trustee, you know." A be-ringed hand reached up to smooth an almost invisible strand that had dared to straggle loose from her spray-stiff coiffure.

"Of course."

Actually, I'd learned it only that morning after skimming through *The Clarion* file on Natalie Pearson. Then I'd dropped by the desk of Vicky Marsh, who writes the kind of personal column found only in small-town newspapers.

I wasn't especially interested in what had appeared in Vicky's column. I wanted the information that never surfaced, the behind-the-hand whispers that rustle across a small town like discarded newspapers on a windy day.

I got a lot.

Natalie Pearson would be shocked at what I knew.

But that could come later. Right now I wanted entrée.

"I understand you hired Judith to serve as your social secretary on a part-time basis."

"Yes. It is my custom to employ a student in that role. This is the first time I've ever had a bad experience. I do appreciate the college being concerned about this matter."

I could have corrected her, made it clear I did not represent the college.

I could have, but I didn't. I had in no way suggested that I represented the school. It wasn't my job to correct her misperceptions.

"It is always a matter for concern when a student is suspected of theft. You understand that she will be suspended if charges are filed?"

Once again high red flagged her sharp cheeks.

"I am sorry to say," the words came quick and sharp, "that the police have declined to file charges. They say there is insufficient evidence." That high-bridged nose wrinkled in disdain. "However," her tone was grudging, "they've assured me they have ways of finding out when stolen goods change hands. Chief Holzer feels confident the thief will ultimately be caught."

I wished I had heard the exchange between Mrs. Pearson and Derry Hills Police Chief Everett Holzer.

Holzer and I are not simpatico. In his view, it's a (white) man's world. Everyone else (women, blacks, gays, the elderly, et al) simply get in the way and cause no end of trouble because of their uppity ways. Holzer believes the fifties marked the height of civilization.

So yes, Holzer is a chauvinist pig.

But he's smart and he's honest.

If Mrs. Pearson accurately recalled his words, if Holzer spoke of "the thief," it indicated the police were not convinced of Judith Montgomery's guilt.

159

"Perhaps we can help the chief."

Her eyes widened in surprise. "How would that be possible?"

"We can work together to find out the truth."

"But what can we do?"

"Talk to people. Someone else in the house may have noticed something."

"It's Judith," she said harshly.

"Then I know you'll be glad when that is proven."

"I want it over. Over." There was a flash of sheer unhappiness in her cool gray eyes.

Why should she be distressed? Judith Montgomery was the one in trouble.

"Tell me what happened."

She took a deep breath. Her voice was clipped. "It was the night of the Hospital Ball, October fifteenth."

One week ago.

"We have it here, of course. The board counts on it." She gestured toward French windows to her left. "We have so much room. The terraces are quite perfect. And the weather is usually pleasant in October. We have a seated dinner. Three hundred this year, I believe. And an orchestra. And dancing. And, of course, I wore the diamond and ruby necklace. I always wear it at this kind of event. Everyone expects it." She said it perfunctorily, without pleasure. As if it were a burden.

"So everyone who attended the ball could have seen the necklace, known it was here in the house."

"Oh yes. But the ball ended. As balls always do." There was the faintest undertone of sadness and regret. Her thin mouth drooped.

Did she wish for life to be filled with light and music, beautiful clothes and handsome people? Was it only then that her dreams were met?

She put the letter opener on a tray, also black and lacquered. She laced together her thin, heavily ringed fingers. Sunlight glanced off those diamonds. "I was very tired. So tired. And there was the usual commotion, the caterers striking the tables, the staff cleaning. But finally, the house was quiet. So you see, it doesn't matter that everyone saw it at the ball. The ball was over." Again, that breath of regret. "I'd asked Judith to stay the night. There are always so many little things a secretary can see to. I was in my room and I just felt too weary to come down and put the necklace away. I rang for Judith. She knew the combination, of course. She took the necklace — and that's the last time anyone has seen it." She said it matter-of-factly, as if it didn't matter a whit to her.

Perhaps it only mattered to Judith.

Judith, of course, had told me what happened next: She'd come downstairs, placed the necklace in the safe, and gone straight up to the room assigned to her. ". . . a tiny hot little hole up on the third floor."

Natalie Pearson's eyes dared me to disagree.

"When did you discover the necklace to be missing?"

"The next morning. The door to the safe was ajar." She pushed back her chair, walked to the fireplace. Her silk dress, a striking pattern of cream and black, glistened in the sunlight spilling through the terrace windows.

I joined her at the fireplace.

She tugged and a square of paneling swung open, revealing the dull gray metal of the safe.

Instead of a dial, an electronic pad was inset to the left.

Her fingers punched the numbers, 5-3-9-1-0.

The Clarion files included her birth date, May 10, 1939.

The door opened and a light came on, revealing three shelves.

She pointed at the top shelf. "There's where I keep my jewelry. I found the safe door open and the case on the floor."

"What else was taken?"

She swung the door shut. "Oh, I checked at once. But only the necklace was gone."

I looked at her curiously. "Don't you find that surprising?"

She shrugged and the silk rustled. "I suppose she was afraid to take more. Perhaps something disturbed her. Or perhaps only the necklace was wanted. It's very famous, you know. It's called Remembrance. My grandfather had it made for my grandmother when he came home safely from World War One. There have been many stories written about it. Perhaps Judith was commissioned to steal it."

I didn't argue. But, with a quick memory of Judith's defiant face, her dark blue eyes blazing, her lips tight in a defiant frown, I had difficulty casting her as anyone's accomplice. Judith was a loner as, of course, are many aspiring journalists, aloof enough to welcome a life of observation. But I had difficulty also in being sure of my judgment of Judith. I thought she was innocent because I didn't pick up either the cockiness of a clever criminal or the too-cautious fear of the guilty. What I sensed was anger, pulsing as steadily as a heartbeat.

Moreover, early in the fall Judith had found my purse in the parking lot — I still wasn't clear how it had been taken from my locked office while I was in class — and nothing was missing. Not that I would have expected anything to be, but once a thief, always a thief, and she need not have returned the purse at all, had she wished to strip it of cash and credit cards.

But there was something about Judith I couldn't gauge.

However, I simply said mildly, "Leaving the safe door open immediately exposed Judith to suspicion. If the door had been shut, when might you have discovered the necklace to be missing?"

Her eyes swung toward me, widening in surprise. Clearly, this had not occurred to her. "Why . . . I suppose . . . not until the Hall of Fame dinner. Next week."

I let her think about it.

She spoke quickly. "But no one else knows the combination, only I and my secretary."

I made no comment. Her family and staff would know her birthday and I felt sure if those dates were the basis for this combination, she'd used them elsewhere. "Do you have voice mail?"

"Yes."

"What is your pass code? One, nine, three, nine?"

Her silence answered me.

I didn't bother to ask about her credit card PIN. If it wasn't the same, I'd be very surprised.

Anyone with access to the safe could have tried various combinations: her birthday, the home address, hell, the telephone number. Savvy burglars do a little homework before breaking in.

But if I'd harbored any doubts about Judith's innocence, the open safe door answered them. All Judith had to do was swing the safe shut and she would be no more suspect than anyone who'd been in the house until the next time the safe was opened. To be sure, Judith would have been the last person to have handled the jewels, but that proved nothing.

In my interview with Judith, she'd sworn she'd closed the safe. ("Mrs. Collins, I pulled on the handle to be sure.")

"It's an interesting point." I paused, then said, as if the thought had just come to me, "I suppose a necklace that famous has always been a security concern?"

She stood as stiffly as a dog scenting a snake-infested log. I

163

pressed on. "When did you install a safe here in the library?"

"Some years ago." Her tone was wooden.

"Since the earlier theft of the necklace? From your mother's bedroom?"

Her face drained of color, leaving her cheeks as pasty as puddled candle wax.

It was so quiet I could hear her thin, quick breaths.

"The necklace *was* stolen some years ago, wasn't it? The police were called in, then suddenly the matter was dropped. Is that right?"

"No. No. There was a mistake, that's all. The necklace was simply mislaid."

"But wasn't there some question of someone on the staff being involved?"

I could hear Vicky Marsh's low breathless voice, "Henrie O, it was a four-alarm scandal. Some people thought Natalie's mother sold it for gambling debts. Another camp was sure Natalie's older brother got drunk and gave it to a current girlfriend. All anyone can be sure of is that Calvin Wherry, her grandfather, called the cops, then it was dropped like a rock. But the maid and chauffeur were gone the next week. Everybody clammed up. And six months later, Natalie married Tolman Pearson, the most boring old bachelor in town but a golfing buddy of Natalie's grandfather. They say she cried all night before the wedding. He must be twenty-five years older than she is." Vicky pushed tortoiseshell glasses higher on her nose. "No children. But her brother still lives with them. Old Mrs. Wherry's in a rest home, gaga, so I hear."

Mrs. Pearson turned away, walked stiffly back to her desk. "It was a long time ago. No one knows exactly what happened. But the necklace turned up. So it doesn't matter." She faced me. Her arms pressed tightly against her body.

If it didn't matter . . .

I smiled. "Funny, the stories that get around. But this time there has definitely been a theft?"

"As I said," her tone was venomous, "the necklace was simply mislaid some years ago. Now it has been stolen."

"But you want to find out what happened?"

"Of course."

"All right, I'll be glad to help, if I can." I spoke as if I'd been invited. "I'll talk to the others who were in the house." I kept my voice easy. "They may have seen something which will give us information."

"It's Judith. Of course it is." She rubbed one temple. "All right, talk to them. I want it settled."

The piercing whistle eased as the woman picked up the tea kettle. "Only way to make tea. Good hot water."

Steam plumed in the air as she splashed the boiling water into two pots. "No tea bags in this kitchen, thank you, ma'am." She brought the tray to the sunny breakfast table where I waited.

Ruth Fitch settled into the chair opposite me, her pudgy face pink with exertion. "Well, we've had us a week, that's for sure. I had to make the tea double strong the morning the necklace went missing. I thought Mrs. Pearson was going to faint. She was white as a ghost. Whiter! And that girl was just downright rude."

"Judith?" I poured the tea through the silver strainer.

The housekeeper nodded vigorously, her gray curls bouncing. "Yes, ma'am. When Mrs. Pearson asked if she knew where the necklace was, that girl flung up her head and snapped back that she'd put it away and if it was gone, someone else had taken it, and she didn't like the suggestion she'd had anything to do with it and she wasn't going to stay

165

someplace where her honesty was doubted and she quit. And then she whirled around and ran out of the house. Set off all the alarms, too. And that was upsetting. She didn't even take her overnight bag. We had to send it the next day. And poor Mrs. Pearson, she didn't know what to do. Mr. Pearson came wandering in and he said I'd better call the police. Then the police came . . ."

Ruth Fitch had a runaway tongue, but it didn't take long to learn what she knew:

The burglar alarm didn't go off that night.

Mr. Pearson was interested in the missing jewelry, but Mrs. Pearson didn't want to talk about it, and she shut herself up in her room and said she had a sick headache.

Mrs. Pearson's brother, Harley Wherry, was, as usual, under the weather. (I took this as a euphemism for drunk.)

The catering staff was gone before the house was locked for the night.

Five people slept in the Wherry house the night of the theft: Judith Montgomery, Natalie Pearson, Tolman Pearson, Harley Wherry, and Mrs. Fitch.

The Pearsons occupy separate suites.

No, so far as she knew, Judith didn't know the code for the alarm system.

It wasn't like the good old days with a big staff, including a full-time maid and a chauffeur. No indeed. Now a cleaning service came in every week, a girl came in twice a week to dust, Mrs. Fitch handled the housekeeping, except for large parties, and Mr. and Mrs. Pearson drove themselves.

I sipped at the Earl Grey. "Were you working here when the necklace disappeared some years ago?"

She glanced over her shoulder, then spoke softly, "I'm surprised Mrs. Pearson told you about that. Did you know she's always hated that necklace? Ever since that time? It was the strangest thing. To this day nobody knows what really happened. Later everybody guessed that Terry Parker — he was the chauffeur — took it. No one ever saw him here again after it was gone." She pulled her chair closer to mine, with another swift glance at the closed kitchen door. "But Leola, his wife, was as honest as anybody ever could be, and she left, too. She was the maid. I heard she took their little girl and moved to Springfield, but nobody knows for sure. Years later, somebody told me Leola lived in Springfield, and she'd remarried, so I don't know what happened to Terry. He was too good-looking to ever last for any woman. You know the kind, eyes that tell you you're the most gorgeous woman in the world and a wicked smile, the kind that makes women forget they've got any sense at all. Oh, he could charm everybody. And laugh! He'd get you laughing till you almost cried. He always had a kind word for everybody. Leola adored him and so did their little girl. I remember he always called her Baby. I thought to myself, a schoolgirl should have a name, but that was Terry, making everybody feel special. He called Leola Dream Girl." She ducked her head. "Why, he called me Petunia." Her cheeks dimpled. "Anyway, the necklace was kept in Mrs. Wherry's jewel box. It disappeared and then everybody was so shocked when it turned up the next week, hidden in the toe of one of Mrs. Wherry's dancing slippers." Suddenly her pink mouth formed a sudden perfect O of surprise. "Why, it was after the Hospital Ball that time, too! Why, isn't that the strangest coincidence!"

Coincidences do happen.

But I always give them a second look.

Tolman Pearson sighted along the imaginary line from his golf ball to the hole. He had beautiful form, firm wrists, his arms and shoulders moving together, just like a pendulum.

Easy to describe, difficult to do. The ball rolled obediently eight feet and curled into the cup.

"Change the holes every week. Still, you get to know the turf. But it's nice to have my own putting green."

Only the top of the three-story stone house was visible from the putting green, which was over a hill from the terraces.

"You're a good golfer." I didn't make it a question.

"Yes. Best sport in the world. Nothing else can compare."

He was seventy-nine and looked sixty-five. Indolence agreed with him.

"I'm interested in the disappearance of your wife's necklace."

He bent down, picked up the ball, walked a few paces, dropped the ball over his shoulder. "Don't mind if I putt, do you?"

I didn't suppose it mattered to him if I did. "Of course not."

Once again, he eyed the imaginary line. "Quite a magnificent necklace, you know." He studied the grass. "Funny thing is, it disappeared for a while the year Natalie and I got married. She told me Harley pinched it, but her grandfather made him put it back. I tried to talk to Calvin about it, but he wouldn't ante. Suppose it was true about Harley. But, there it is, it was a long time ago." Once again, that sure, confident stroke, and the ball rolled to the cup, dropped in. "Don't suppose it matters. Natalie doesn't like to talk about it." He walked to the hole, picked up the ball. "Actually, I don't even think she would have called the police this time if I hadn't insisted. I came downstairs for breakfast and found everyone in a panic. But you can't lose a fortune and not do something. The insurance fellows wouldn't like it."

"So you've made a claim for the necklace."

168

Pale blue eyes swung toward me. For an instant, they lost their good-natured gleam. "Of course."

Harley Wherry was amiably drunk, but it was such an habitual state there was only the slightest thickening to his voice. ". . . so that's why old Tolman's never wanted to make any investments with me. Trust my dear little sister to queer my pitch. But," he moved languidly in the massive red leather chair in a dim corner of a downstairs clubroom, "that's all right. Poor old Nat. She's never had much fun. I've always had fun. My number one rule in life is to do whatever the hell I want to. Makes sense, right? So I'll let Tolman keep on thinking I'm the light-fingered Harry. Thing about it is, I think Sis stole the jewels the first time around. And, somehow, the Old Man — that's my grandfather, and he was the closest thing to a Prussian general you ever met — caught her at it. Why else did she marry Tolman? She sure as hell didn't want to." A chuckle ended in a hiccup. He reached out a thin, languid hand, so like his sister's but ringless, and picked up a full tumbler. He lifted it and drank. "But this time, it has to be the secretary. Too bad. Cute little thing." His mouth curved in a salacious smile. His face was almost a replica of his sister's except his cheeks sagged with dissipation, and his eyes were rheumy. "Can't see why Sis would do it. Of course, I never knew why she did it the first time."

Don Brown looks like an average thirtyish guy, almost nondescript, not too tall, slender, with a narrow, often weary face. But a perceptive viewer will note the quick intelligence in his eyes, the deliberate lack of expression, the wiry athletic build of a long-distance runner.

He's a cop, a good one.

And he's my friend, one of the best. A good enough friend

169

that he now calls me Henrie O, the nickname given to me by my late husband Richard. Richard said, "Sweetheart, you pack more surprises into a single day than O. Henry ever put in a short story."

Don Brown and I met when I'd first moved to Derry Hills and a young blond woman was strangled in the apartment next to the one where I was staying temporarily.

We've come a long way since that day. I'd thought him too young to be a detective. He'd thought me too old to be of any assistance. We were both wrong.

On Sunday afternoon, he lounged comfortably in a rattan chair on my screened porch, a mug of coffee cradled in his slender hands. "I copied the file." He nodded at the Manila folder on the rattan coffee table. "Sue Rodriguez has the case. She thinks it's clearly an inside job, but it's a puzzler because the primary suspect, Judith Montgomery, doesn't strike Sue as stupid. So, why didn't Montgomery shut the safe, delay the discovery? Moreover, there are no fingerprints on the safe door and the buttons on the electronic panel were smudged. The last person to punch the numbers wore gloves. Why would Montgomery wear gloves? She was supposed to put the necklace away. Her prints should be there. Moreover, she slammed out of the house the next morning — apparently they made her mad — and she was wearing, according to the housekeeper and Mrs. Pearson, a thin chambray blouse and jeans tight enough to fit an eel and carrying a tiny purse. The necklace is big. No way she could have taken it out in a pocket or in that purse. Judith Montgomery didn't know the house alarm system and it hadn't been turned off when she left. When she yanked open the front door, the alarm sounded and Mrs. Fitch had to turn it off. So Montgomery didn't snitch the necklace and pass it to a confederate. Any opened window or door would have sounded the alarm."

"We can't be certain she hadn't somehow learned the alarm code." I sipped at my coffee and pushed the plate with sugar cookies closer to Don.

He took one. A crumb straggled down his chin as he continued. "True. But if Montgomery took the necklace, she's made no move to unload it. Sue's had her under around-the-clock surveillance." He finished the cookie. "So now, Henrie O, tell me how you got involved."

"Judith's one of my students."

"Investigating a jewel theft isn't in your job description. I guess your reputation as a sleuth is getting around."

I shrugged it away, but I suppose it was flattering to think students saw me as something other than a teacher or a retired reporter. "I'm afraid I haven't come up with much this time."

I told him what I'd learned. Not enough to clear Judith. Not even enough to implicate anyone else, and the list of others had to be confined to Natalie Pearson, Tolman Pearson, Harley Wherry, or Mrs. Fitch, and a less likely crew of jewel thieves I'd never seen.

I shook my head. "Nothing makes sense, Don. Why? Why would any one of them do it? Money? The family has money. As for Judith and Mrs. Fitch, how could they make the right kind of connection to fence a necklace like that?"

I refilled our mugs. "Don, there's something odd about the whole setup. I keep thinking there's some connection to the disappearance of the necklace some years ago. I found a story in *The Clarion*, October seventeenth, nineteen eighty-three. There was only one story, then the investigation was dropped. There was no hint it was thought to be an inside job."

Don drank his coffee, his eyes squinted in thought. But, finally, he shook his head. "Got me, Henrie O. It has a funny feel to it. But you'll get there. You always do."

I didn't share his confidence.

Monday morning after my nine-o'clock class, I returned to my office to find two messages.

I called Don first.

"Henrie O, talk about twists and turns! In Sue's mail this morning, there was a typed note with this message: *The necklace is hidden in Natalie Pearson's closet. Ask her why.* Sue's already had the note to the lab. It's written on Tolman Pearson's stationery and it has his fingerprints on it. Sue's huddling with the chief now."

"The insurance company will find this quite interesting."

"Won't they?" Don agreed. "And, of course, it's a misdemeanor to report a false crime. I'd say Natalie Pearson's got some problems."

I've been around investigations of all kinds for a good many more years than Don. "Actually, Don, I doubt it. I'll bet you a ticket to the Cards' opening day next spring that it will be déjà vu all over again: The lost shall be miraculously found and no more will be said."

There was an instant of silence. "It would simplify life for the chief, wouldn't it? I'll let you know, Henrie O."

The second call was to the registrar's office in Greene County. I wrote down the information I'd asked for — the issuance of a marriage license sometime after 1983 to Leola Parker.

I wanted to talk to Leola Parker, find out more about handsome Terry, who was seen no more after the first disappearance of the necklace. And if Leola had moved to Springfield, been rumored to have married again, there was a good chance that second marriage took place in Springfield.

It had.

Sometimes basic reporting, going after facts to flesh out a story, can turn up surprising leads. I stared down at the names I'd written:

Leola Baker Parker to John Milton Montgomery.

Oh, oh, and oh.

I tapped my pen against the paper.

I ran through some facts in my mind:

1. The open safe door.
2. Smudged fingerprints.
3. Leola Parker was an honest woman.
4. Natalie Wherry wept the night before she wed.

I now had an idea why.

But I still needed certain facts.

Mrs. Fitch had her own telephone line at the Wherry house. When she answered, I had one question.

What time did Natalie Pearson eat breakfast the morning the jewels were discovered missing?

As she concluded, I said, "Thank you, Mrs. Fitch. I'll —"

"Mrs. Collins, have you heard? Mrs. Pearson found the necklace in her closet. Why, it's just the strangest thing! In the toe of a pump, just like last time! Mrs. Collins, have you ever heard of such a thing?"

"I imagine it will turn out to be some kind of a joke, Mrs. Fitch."

"Well, Mrs. Pearson doesn't think it's funny!"

"I'm sure she doesn't. Nor," I said a trifle grimly, "do I. Thank you, Mrs. Fitch."

I hung up the phone.

I had one more person to talk to — if she would see me.

Our shoes grated against the pebbled walk. The Italian terraces rose behind us. There was no one near.

Natalie Pearson walked with her head down, her hands

clasped tightly behind her back. "Mrs. Collins, I have to know *why*. Not because it matters legally. The matter is officially closed, both by the police and the insurance company. Actually," Natalie Pearson's voice was bitter, "everyone seems to think I took the necklace and hid it, even though that makes no sense at all." Her eyes glittered with anger. "But I have to know why. Why would this young woman whom I don't know involve me in this — this grotesque charade? Why, Mrs. Collins?"

"I believe I know."

She stopped, faced me, her gaze demanding.

But this time I didn't see pride or arrogance. This time I saw pain and despair.

"I will explain what happened, Mrs. Pearson, if you will tell me the truth about the first disappearance."

A pulse throbbed in her throat.

I spoke quietly. "Terry Parker took the necklace from your mother's room. Is that right?"

A breeze rustled the cedars behind us. In the sunlight, her quite perfect, lifeless hair was touched with gold.

I could see that she'd had a fragile beauty when she was younger, before her eyes lost hope.

Natalie Pearson met my gaze squarely. "No, Mrs. Collins. I took the necklace. I gave it to Terry."

We gazed at each other.

Her mouth quirked in a wry, sad smile. "You don't look surprised."

"No. I understand he was handsome. And charming."

"Oh yes. He made love to me. We were going to run away together. I gave him the necklace and the next night I was to meet him at the train station." She stared down at the shadows splashed along the sidewalk. "He didn't come."

Three little words, and the sorrow and loss they conveyed

174

could never be summed up or judged or understood.

"And the necklace?"

"The next week Leola Parker came to see my grandfather. I don't know how she knew about the necklace. She must have found it in Terry's things and demanded to know what it was all about. She gave the necklace to my grandfather and told him it was all my fault, that I'd persuaded Terry to take it and that Terry had now deserted her. My grandfather said I had a choice." Her voice was toneless, all the passion and pain leached away by the passage of time. "Be publicly revealed as a woman involved with the family chauffeur — or marry Tolman."

"You married Tolman, and all of this was behind you — until now."

"Yes. Now, Mrs. Collins, tell me why this has happened."

"Terry Parker — what did he look like?"

"He was very handsome. Black hair. Dark blue eyes. High cheekbones. A magical smile and a funny way his mouth crooked when he thought everything was wonderful . . ." Her voice trailed away.

She could have been describing Judith Montgomery.

"Oh, my God. It's Baby," she whispered.

I found Judith in *The Clarion* newsroom, at one of the desks used for general reporting.

She looked up from her computer as I stopped beside her.

"If you have a moment, Judith?"

"Oh yes, Mrs. Collins. What's happened?"

"Quite a bit." I led the way to my office and closed the door. I settled behind my desk.

She sat demurely in a chair, facing me.

But she was electric with excitement, her eyes bright, a becoming flush in her cheeks.

"Have you heard that the necklace has been found?"

Pleasure glistened now in her eyes. Pleasure and an almighty cockiness. "Oh, really? Then they owe me an apology, don't they? I'll demand it. And if they don't — if *she* doesn't apologize — I'll write a story for *The Clarion*."

"No."

Suddenly, her face was still, smooth, stiff. "No? Why not? I've been accused of theft. And they had no right. It's just like —" She stopped short.

"Yes, Judith? Like what?"

She stared at me, knowing something was wrong.

"Why don't you tell me about it — Baby."

Her face twisted with fury. "*She* took the necklace. Years ago. *She* took it. But she blamed my father — and so he ran away. That's what happens when people are rich and powerful, they can put the blame on someone else. Mother told me all about it, how *she* went after my dad, turned his head, persuaded him to run away with her. It's all *her* fault."

"Fault." I sighed. "That's what you've done, isn't it? You've blamed Natalie for your dad's running away. But think a little further, Judith; he didn't have to run away. Your mother returned the necklace. Your father left because he wanted to. Maybe he changed his mind about Natalie, maybe your mother faced him down. It doesn't matter. Yes, Natalie took the necklace, but she took it for him, to have him."

"No." It was a child's cry. "No. If it weren't for her, I would have had my dad, he wouldn't have gone away."

"Oh yes. Someday he would have. Because that's who and what he was. Your mother blamed Natalie because she didn't want to blame him. Everyone always made excuses for Terry Parker. Wherever he is now, you can bet he's left behind people who loved him. And he's left behind a legacy of bitterness. You spent years thinking about it, and thinking how you

176

could pay back the woman you blame for losing your father. That's why you came to school here. That's why you applied for the job as Natalie Pearson's secretary. Tell me, how many jobs did you turn down, for one reason or another, until you got what you wanted? You became her secretary and you waited for the right opportunity. The night you put the necklace away, you added sleeping pills to Mrs. Pearson's drink."

Her eyes widened, her mouth opened.

"How did I know? Because she overslept the next morning, by more than an hour. When she came down to breakfast, she mentioned feeling headachy to Mrs. Fitch. That could have been dangerous, Judith. You don't know what medicines she takes. But you were focused on your plan.

"That night, as she slept heavily, you crept into her room and hid the necklace in her closet, in the toe of a shoe, just as you'd heard that the necklace was found so long ago. From Mrs. Fitch, I imagine. I imagine you polished it so it would have no fingerprints. You made yourself a suspect, but you were careful to make it look wrong, the safe door open, no fingerprints on the door, the fingerprints smudged on the electronic panel. And the next morning, leaving in tight clothes with a small purse, not taking your overnight bag, setting off the alarm. You thought of everything."

She eyed me carefully. "You can't prove anything."

"I don't need to. I know. And you know."

She shoved back her chair, her face defiant. "What are you going to do?" She was poised to run.

"It is a crime to lie to a police officer during the course of an investigation."

"So."

"It could be grounds for suspension from school."

She waited, her body tense. "What are you going to do?"

"That depends upon you, Judith. You see, I'd like for you

to let go of the past, focus that thought and energy and passion on the future. Your future. You're smart, quick, clever. For example, you wanted someone to take up your cause. That's where I came in. You took my class and very quickly you figured out that I have a passion for the underdog and I thumb my nose at the powerful. You figured out a way to use me. First, you set it up so that I would be sure of your honesty. What did you do? This is an old building, did you try a bunch of keys until you found one that opened my office, then wait for a good time to snatch my purse?"

Her eyes flickered.

"I thought so. And then you called on me to help an underdog in need. And I couldn't wait to put on my Superman cape and get into the fray."

Something in my tone surprised her.

I managed a wry grin. "Yes. I'm at fault here, too. How rebellious do I come across in class? I need to give some thought to that. You see, Judith, as hard as it ever is to know someone else, it is harder to know ourselves. So let's make a deal: You put the necklace — Remembrance — behind you for good, for always, and look to yourself for the direction of your life, not your father or your mother or Natalie Pearson. And I promise that I won't — next time — assume that the underdog is always right."

As I told Don later, one is never too young to change — or too old to learn.

DEAD IN THE NET

I rode in the ambulance with Bettina. Her hand trembled in mine. She was immobilized on the gurney to prevent further injury. I'd complimented her that morning on her tennis dress, a white cotton pique with matching bluebells on the collar and the pocket of the skirt. She'd looked especially vibrant at breakfast, her bright, quizzical, inquiring blue eyes probing my face, her silvery hair swept up in coronet braids. She'd peppered me with questions as befitted a former reporter. A fine reporter, one of the best I'd ever known, curious, intense, fair, clever. Now her face looked sunken. Bereft.

I understood. At our age, injury can't be shrugged away. It can take months — or never — for damaged muscles or — God forbid — broken bones to heal. The bleak emptiness in Bettina's face was her spirit saying farewell to a last remnant of youth, the exhilaration of playing tennis, the surge of pleasure at a good shot, the rueful exclamation at a mishit. Of course, it was only a remnant. We couldn't, no matter our skill, dash about the court as we had many years ago. But to be able to walk onto a court to play was perhaps more precious now than before. Yesterday in our doubles match, I'd announced that I was no longer a Galloping Gazelle, that I now played with Stately Grace. Midway through the game, I forgot my resolution and dashed toward the net. Bettina laughed and said, "Face it, Henrie O, you have a Galloping Gazelle trapped in a Stately Grace body." Yes, the Galloping Gazelle would be there until my last breath. But that's one of the great secrets of age. Our hearts are always young. My dark

179

hair is streaked with silver, my lean face sharp edged, but I still move quickly because life is a race and I haven't hit the finish line yet.

At Bettina's wry judgment, everyone on the court had laughed. The memory of that laughter was a poignant companion on this doleful journey.

"Deliberate." Bettina spoke precisely in her high, musical voice, loudly enough for me to hear over the undulating siren.

I looked into light blue eyes glazed with pain, but bright with intelligence.

She gave a tiny shake of her head. "Not me. It could have been any one of us."

I knew that, knew it with a twist of sickness in my stomach. We'd gathered on the deck that overlooks the courts, filled tall plastic cups with ice water, spoken inconsequentially of the weather — but what is there to remark about weather in August in Northern California, other than choosing fleecy warmups if playing outside? — gathered up our racquets and carryalls, walked across the wooden planking to the stairs. It wasn't quite eight o'clock in the morning. This side of the clubhouse was still in deep shadow.

Bettina led the way. I could have gone first. That was less likely, of course, because I was a guest. But it could easily have been Marge Winslow, plump, bouncy, arrayed in support stockings, so the sun glistened off her legs. Or it could have been Arlene Simpson, tiny, thin, in a bright pink tennis dress. She was the least likely because, as Bettina had remarked as we waited in the lounge, Arlene was always a day late and a dollar short. She had in fact sped up to join us at the last moment.

Bettina was the first to reach the wooden stairway. She reached the third step and her foot slid from beneath her and, flailing, she fell heavily on her right side, smacking into the step, the thump as loud and shocking as her sudden scream.

We were frozen for an instant. Long enough for Bettina, crumpled now halfway down the stairs, to twist her head and cry, "Slick. Slick!"

Slick, indeed. The third step, a portion of it nearest the right handrail, was covered with a greasy film. I flung down my warmup jacket to cover the area, then moved close to Bettina. Already the skin on her right thigh was swelling, an angry purplish and red.

Now I held tight to her hand as the ambulance wheeled into the hospital emergency drive.

My warmup jacket was gone. The mid afternoon sunlight, though the soft California variety, shone on a step indistinguishable from all the rest. I knelt, stroked the wood, knew I was being watched by players scattered at wooden tables topped by bright umbrellas. For a moment, the only sounds were the thwock of tennis balls on the courts in use and the faint clink of ice in tall glasses. Players through for the day were served tea or beer in glasses, not paper cups.

"I cleaned the step. It's okay now. Oh, I'm so sorry about Mrs. Hodge. How is she?" Earnest brown eyes looked at me from beneath a frizzy brown bang. "I'm Karen Jessop. One of the pros." The thick swatch of white cream spread over her nose gave her the air of a perky chipmunk.

As is usual to me, she looked at an age to be getting a driver's license, not a grown woman who'd no doubt played college tennis, tried the minor pro tournaments, and ended up a teaching pro.

"The prognosis is good. Nothing broken. But she's in a great deal of pain. A massive hematoma. Bruised ribs. A strained shoulder." Yes, it was better by far than a broken hip, but there was always the danger of blood clots. And it would take time to heal, time Bettina should not have had to spend in convalescence.

And why?

I faced the lithe young woman. She had the bright sheen of an athlete and, though everyone now knows its dangers, her skin was ruddy from too much sun. She tossed her head and her bangs quivered. When she was five, no doubt her family found it an adorable gesture. Now it was automatic and faintly affected. When she was sixty, it would be sad.

"You cleaned it up?" I was still in my tennis shirt and shorts. I held Bettina's oversize key ring in my hand.

"Oh, yes." Her answer was swift. "Someone else might have fallen. I got right to it."

"If you cleaned it," I spoke deliberately, "you know how large an area was slick. Describe it to me. Please."

One hand nervously fingered the pleats of her tennis skirt. She looked puzzled. And worried. "There was something really greasy, some kind of film, on the step." She looked at the wooden planks, then held her hands about a foot apart.

"From front to back?" I kept my tone conversational. "Covering that entire area?"

Karen Jessop understood the implication, the deduction. "Yes." A simple answer, but it made our exchange anything but simple.

"Ma'am," she gestured toward the clubhouse, "you'd better talk to Walt."

Double doors from the deck opened into a large lounge with big size television screens at either end, scattered tables and chairs, bulletin boards listing flights of players, challenge matches, and tournament dates. The main desk was in the center of the room. A small restaurant overlooked the sparkling indoor pool. Staff offices lined the opposite wall, near the main entrance. A secretary's desk sat in the open in front of the staff offices.

I headed for the last door, the stretch of wall twice as long as the other offices, with DIRECTOR marked in red script on the pebbled glass.

"Ma'am. Please. Excuse me." The secretary was on her feet and beside me as I reached for the doorknob. "May I help you?"

"Thanks, no." I grabbed the knob, twisted it.

"Ma'am, Walt doesn't want to see anybody right now." She looked uncertain, surely unaccustomed to deflecting importunate tennis guests. Her voice was high and anxious. Her angular face was softened by huge violet eyes.

"I must speak with him. About Bettina Hodge's injury." I opened the door. I didn't mind appearing rude. I spent a half century as a reporter, scrambling for facts, more than that, for truth, which can be harder to come by. I've confronted politicians with pasted smiles, cops with seen-it-all eyes, businessmen with cash register hearts, con artists with empty souls, gentle people with outstretched hands. Sometimes you catch a quarry unaware and for an instant, before emotion is masked, truth is revealed. I wanted to see Walt Whittaker, the managing pro, without his company manner.

For a split second, I did. Walt Whittaker radiated leashed power, even with his big body slumped forward on the desk, his shoulders bunched, his hands spread flat. He was staring at a picture frame. In his freckled face, I glimpsed despair, anger, misery. More emotion than a greased step should evoke.

I stepped inside, firmly closed the door behind me.

Startled, Whittaker's head jerked up. Curly red hair swirled in tight ringlets over a broad face with light green eyes and a snub nose and a wide mouth. In a life size photo on the wall behind him, he held a huge winner's silver goblet, that wide mouth spread in an ebullient grin. A laughing woman with a heart-shaped face stood beside him, stared adoringly up at him.

Whittaker scowled, scrambled to his feet.

Now it was time to excuse my precipitous entrance. "I'm Henrie Collins. I was going to play with Bettina Hodge this morning. I came straight from the hospital."

"Oh, God." He heaved a huge sigh and the anger gave way to concern. "How is she?"

"In pain. But she should be okay. She's worried about the situation here. She asked me to see if I can find out who's causing all the trouble. Before someone is seriously injured." Bettina was sure the slick step was the latest — and ugliest — in acts of vandalism that had plagued the club recently, vandalism no one seemed to be addressing.

"Somebody could have spilled sun screen on the step." He looked at me with hopeful eyes.

There are none so blind as those who do not wish to see. "I talked to Karen Jessop. She said the slick film covered that entire portion of the step, from front to back." I didn't have to tell him an accidental spill would have been irregular, uneven.

The tennis pro's face tightened.

I ticked the incidents off, one by one. "Who spiked the drinking water on Court 3 with quinine? Nobody hurt but it's a nasty taste. Who poked nails into some of the balls in the ball machine? I understand one of the balls hit a junior, cut her arm. Who spilled oil into the pond near Court 6, killed the fish there?"

"Christ. If I only knew." A dull red suffused his face. "But nobody knows anything. Nobody's seen anything. I put up a reward. You know, for the staff. But it's like there's a ghost. I don't know what the hell to do." He flung himself into his chair, looked at me morosely.

I studied him. He'd gone a long way on looks, the boyish open face, the blazing hair bright as red neon, the full mouth with a tiny oblique scar above the upper lip that added a vulnerable quality to his undeniable masculinity. Looks and, of course, ability. I gestured toward the trophies atop the bookcases. "What do you do when it's 0-5 in games and you're at deuce in the sixth set?"

His thick red brows drew down in a tight frown.

"Do you turn and run from an overhead smash? Do you give up when it's love forty?" I waited for his answer.

Now his face was crimson. "I won state three years straight when I was a junior." It was a growl. He was on his feet. "I won Nationals twice. I played the circuit for seven years and got to the second round at Wimbledon. I played with the flu. I played with a sprained ankle. I played with an inflamed appendix. Hell, I played drunk, mad, sick. Nobody's ever called me a quitter."

"Then don't quit now. Every question has an answer. Somebody did these things." I held his gaze. "We can figure out who."

His face changed as I watched. The despair and anger gave way to careful, considering thought. He shoved a big hand through the thick tangle of red hair. "So who're you? What can you do?"

He didn't want a resume. I knew what he wanted. "I spent most of my life as a reporter. I know how to ask questions. I don't give up."

Our gazes locked. He saw a sixty-something woman, dark hair frosted with white, dark eyes that have seen good and bad and lived with both, a lean and angular woman always poised to move. I saw a rangy, boyishly attractive man, his freckled face marred by a scowl. I also saw the beginnings of

185

hope in despairing eyes.

"Okay. Yeah." He came out from behind his desk. "Come on."

I followed as he plunged out into the lobby. It was hard to keep up. We came out onto the porticoed main entry. The La Mesa Tennis Club, as befitted its name, was perched on a promontory that poked out into the Pacific. Rugged cliffs tumbled on the north and south sides. The clubhouse faced west. The second floor of the club contained four indoor courts with a seagull's view of the crashing waves. Nine outdoor courts, in rows of three separated by dark cedars, were squeezed onto the headland. Past the courts, the narrow tongue ended on a sharp point with a spectacular view of the surging ocean. The town of La Mesa was about thirty miles north of San Francisco on Highway One and this was one of its best tennis clubs.

The wind whipped Walt Whittaker's white shirt and shorts, ruffled his red curls, snapped the fronds of nearby palms. The sharp scent of the sea was almost overridden by the lush sweetness of the dark red roses blooming beside the entrance.

He pointed past the almost full parking lot. "There's one road that leads in here. We have a gated entry."

I'd already figured that out. "Has to be a member, an employee, a delivery person."

"The vandal came through the front door or a delivery entrance at the side." We checked out the fences that ran from either end of the redwood clubhouse to the cliffs. There was a gate in the north fence, but it was locked. There was a buzzer. A small sign beneath it said: Deliveries 3 to 5 P.M. only. Ring.

He swung around, headed back to the entrance. He stared at the ground as he walked. "Goddam."

I waited until we were in the tiled lobby. "Tell me."

186

"The timing." His voice was reluctant. "None of it could have been done by a delivery person. Would be hard for them to do anyway. I mean, they take stuff to the service door, they aren't wandering around the club grounds. But the ball machine's in use until nine at night. And the water barrels are freshened every night."

"Was the tainted water —"

"Last Wednesday morning. Court Three. You'd have thought we'd dished out cholera. Christ, one of the local councilwomen drank it and she was sure she'd been deliberately poisoned. She ran a bunch of the stuff to a local lab. That's how we knew it was quinine. The ball machine was two days later."

"First thing in the morning?"

"Yeah." He looked bleakly around the lobby. His gaze stopped at the central desk. A slender young man with wire frame glasses and a mop of long black hair lifted a hand. "Yo, Walt."

"There's always someone on duty?"

"Yeah." Another unhappy affirmative. "From seven-forty-five when we open to midnight. Seven days a week."

"Okay. Let me see if I've got it right. Last Wednesday the water in the dispenser on Court 3 was tampered with. Friday, some of the balls in a ball machine were spiked. How about the fish pond?"

"Rafael found the fish belly up Saturday morning. But —" He shook his head. "Let me check the court sheets."

It turned out not to be simple.

Court 3 was in constant use, which would presuppose players drinking from the dispenser, from eight A.M. to nine P.M. on Tuesday. The water was tampered with between nine P.M. Tuesday and ten A.M. Wednesday.

The ball machine was used at eight A.M. Friday and it was

187

fine. The spiked balls came out during a three o'clock clinic. The nail-sprigged balls must have been added between ten A.M. and three P.M. Friday.

A gardener clipped hibiscus near the pond Friday afternoon and it looked clear.

That brought us to this Tuesday morning and the greased step. The last players came in from the outdoor courts at eleven o'clock Monday evening.

"No rhythm to it," I murmured.

He shook his head irritably. "We can't plot where everyone in the club was for all those times."

I didn't disagree, though we certainly could make that effort. But that wasn't the point of my questions. I'd learned what I needed to know about times. The vandal had to be someone who could move about the club at almost any time without causing notice. That limited the possibilities to the staff or to the juniors in summer clinics or to players who played almost every day.

Walt's secretary approached. "Walt, Sharon wants you on the phone."

"Hey, Walt," a wiry white-haired player waggled his encased racquet, "I need some help with my overhead. You free tomorrow at nine?"

"Sure, Carl. Tell Karen to put it on my schedule." Walt looked past the player at Terry, holding up the cordless phone, then told me, "I need to talk to my wife —"

It interested me that in the midst of dealing with big time trouble at his job, Walt Whittaker would stop to take a call from his wife.

I nodded briskly. "Of course. Walt, I'd like to see the pond. Why don't you meet me there when you're free?"

"Fine, fine." He reached for the phone, turned away. But not before I saw his features soften. "Yeah. What's up?" He

188

walked toward his office.

I asked directions, found my way to the pond and realized anew why northern California is a world-class destination. Bougainvillea spread over a low stone wall that encircled the sparkling pond. Just past the pond, the headland jutted to a point. I passed a clump of bent cypress and climbed a tilted slab of rock. I could see forever, the dark blue Pacific ocean stretching endlessly away. Below huge waves crashed into sharp edged rocks that tumbled at the base of the sheer cliff. The ever present breeze was sharp enough to make me shiver but it was definitely invigorating, the smell of the sea mingling with the darker scent of the cypress. A few feet more and a sign warned starkly: DO NOT PASS, CRUMBLING SOIL.

I didn't waste time. I had my questions ready when Walt came. It wasn't seeing the pool that mattered to me, of course. I wanted Walt to myself and this was the loneliest piece of land on the club grounds.

He carried a brown wicker picnic hamper. It looked small in his big hands. He looked at me uncertainly. "I've started coming out here for lunch whenever I can. It gives me a break. I've got plenty for both of us." He climbed up on the tilted slab, shaded his eyes, looked out at the surging water. The breeze tugged at his clothes. "I'm king of the world here."

But I heard uncertainty beneath the bravado.

He flipped open the hamper lid, pulled out a checked tablecloth. "Terry thinks I deserve the best." He anchored the cloth with loose rocks. There were blue plastic plates and real silverware. "Roll-ups okay? Chicken poached in wine with tarragon then grilled."

It was mid afternoon. It seemed a century since Bettina and I had arrived at the club early this morning. I was ravenously hungry. But if he wanted a meal in peace, I wasn't the right companion. "You may not want to eat with me when you hear my questions."

He flipped the tabs on a couple of cans of cola. "Lady, it can't get any worse."

I was terse. "Sure it can. For starters, who hates you?"

His head jerked up.

I looked into shocked eyes. "It's pretty simple, Walt. The vandal has to be a member or an employee. That lets out a former employee with a grudge or a business that could profit if the club closes down or gets sold. A few more incidents like you've had and you'll start losing members faster than Wall Street treasure hunts after the Dow plunges. So who's the goat if things get even nastier?"

He stared out at the water, the food on his plate untasted. His broad face creased into lines of misery. Abruptly he surged to his face. "Goddam it. Goddam it!" He swung his arm and the can of cola pitched high in an arc, glinting in the sun, then disappeared over the side of the cliff. His mouth quivered. "God, I love this place. Why would anybody do this to me?"

"That's what I want you to tell me. What have you done to somebody that's turned them into a slimy creature willing to destroy and hurt anyone, everyone just to get at you?"

We didn't eat, after all. He talked, slowly, jerkily, hands tightly clasped, and I listened.

Bettina looked very slight in the hospital bed. Her face was grayish white, but her bright blue eyes looked at me clearly. When I finished, she spoke with a touch of her old vigor. "Excellent, Henrie O. I can't see that you missed anything. It has to be an inside job. But what a vicious way to try and destroy Walt." A tiny smile tugged at her lips. "Appealing, isn't he?

190

All that curly red hair and boyish charm. Still, I was a little surprised when the board picked him to be director over Heather Hernandez. But I guess there's a glass ceiling everywhere. And Peter Vance had been there longer. But Peter's been a little short on charm since he lost out to Walt on Sharon. Oh, what a mess misguided love makes of our lives." A grin. "Sounds like Shakespeare, doesn't it? Age becomes me. Lordy, I can't help myself."

I laughed. "You're feeling better." Then I wished I hadn't said it when I saw the flash of darkness in her eyes. Oh, yes, better, but it was going to be a long time before Bettina played tennis again.

Her thin face sharpened. "Henrie O, promise me you'll be careful. Very careful."

I looked at her in surprise.

Her blue eyes were anxious. "I have a bad feeling, Henrie O. And not just because I got hurt. There's a blind rage in all of this. And I don't think it's finished."

I took her hand, squeezed it. But I had no comforting words. I was afraid she was right. Blind rage . . .

The next morning was one of those August days that belies the image of sunny California. Fog hung dank and cold and thick, wreathing the cypress, hiding the void where the road snaked alongside the cliff's edge.

I called the club, asked Walt's secretary when he would arrive. She said nine o'clock. I timed my arrival at his home for a quarter after nine. I wanted to talk to his wife and I wanted to talk to her without warning. No one can have a better idea of a man's friends and enemies than his wife. Walt had given me, reluctantly, painfully, two names, Heather Hernandez and Peter Vance, teaching pros at the club. Sharon Whittaker might well have other suggestions to offer.

191

There was a bell pull beside the heavy oak front door. I tugged the strap, heard a faint peal within.

The door opened and a slim young woman with long brown bangs and straight hair tucked loosely behind her ears regarded me warily. "Yes?" She wore an oversize white shirt with the tail out, blue chambray slacks and espadrilles.

"I'm Henrie Collins, a friend of Bettina Hodge —"

Her face changed, warmed. "How is she? Is she all right?"

I smiled. "I'm supposed to pick her up at the hospital this afternoon to bring her home. She's going to have to take it easy for a while, but she's going to be okay."

"Thank God." Her relief was evident.

"You know what's been going on at the club." I made it a statement.

One slim hand fingered the top button of her shirt. Her angular face was suddenly stiff.

"May I come in?" I spoke pleasantly, not urgently.

She stared at me through the screen. "Why do you want to talk to me? I'm not out there much anymore."

"I'm helping Walt investigate." It wasn't a lie. "I'm sure you want to help, too."

"You're helping Walt?" She brightened. "Of course. Come in." She led the way through a cluttered living room, magazines haphazardly stacked, books in piles, to a small tiled sunroom though it wasn't sunny now. We settled in white wicker chairs. She looked at me eagerly. "Walt's asked you to help him?"

That might not be absolutely accurate. But it was close enough. "You know how upset he's been about the things that have happened. But the slick step makes it clear the vandal doesn't care who gets hurt. It's got to stop. Do you have any ideas about the vandalism?"

Her eyes fell away from mine. Her face thinned, took on

192

the brooding quality of still water at midnight.

I've asked questions for a long time. I've gauged every kind of response. I couldn't take it to the bank, but I was suddenly certain that she knew something. If only I could persuade her to tell me.

"It's awful." She caught a strand of her long hair, wound it around her finger. "I've been so worried. And Walt wasn't doing anything. But now —" she looked at me hopefully "— maybe you can help him."

I smiled. "I'll try. It looks like it has to be an employee —"

She drew her breath in sharply.

"— or someone who plays almost every day."

She clasped her hands, slim, young hands with beautifully kept nails, tightly together. "I can't imagine anyone doing things like that." Her voice quivered.

"How about Heather Hernandez?"

"No." The denial was swift, definite. She pushed up from the chair, paced to the window, the window that looked out into gray nothingness. "Sure, Heather hated being passed over. But she'd never do anything that would hurt anyone. And she loves the club. It's her life. She's terribly upset over the problems."

I stood, followed her to the window. "Peter Vance wanted to marry you."

She faced me. One slim hand caught my arm, clutched it painfully tight. "Listen to me, Peter's the most decent, kindest man I've ever known."

I looked into strained brown eyes. "He's very unhappy now, isn't he?"

She pressed her fingers against her face.

"Is that why you quit teaching at the club?" I saw the flicker in her eyes, knew I was right. "Because Peter was so distraught over your marrying Walt?"

"Not Peter." Was it a plea? Her hands clenched into fists. "I can't believe it's Peter. I thought —" she broke off, shook her head. "But I must have been wrong."

"What did you think?"

"Oh, I don't know, I just don't know." She turned and ran. Her footsteps clattered down a hall way. A door slammed.

It was time for me to leave. I wasn't certain what I'd learned. But I knew what Sharon Whittaker feared. I was in a hurry now to meet Peter Vance.

Driving on a cliff road in fog pumps adrenaline. I watched the center line, clung to it, eased my way along the coast, in a cocoon of gray. I didn't relax until I reached the entrance to the club. I was driving Bettina's stickered car so the guard waved me past the checkpoint. Only a few cars were in the lot.

Peter Vance was teaching a class of juniors on indoor Court 1. A loft with webbed chairs and water dispensers overlooked the indoor courts. All the courts were full, the first with the clinic, the second with two college age men in an intense singles game, the third and fourth with women's doubles. I leaned on the wide wooden railing and looked down.

"Watch the ball. Always watch the ball." Peter Vance was compactly built, sturdy chest and thick legs. Thinning blond hair topped a pudgy face, a face designed for easy laughter, dimples, a broad mouth. He smiled, but it sat on his face like a health inspector in a greasy spoon. His instructor's patter was automatic, mindless. "Turn and swing, Sandy, turn. Okay, watch your court position. Don't get caught there, Ellen. Come on in. Punch the ball. That's the way. Good volley. Okay, let's do some serves."

When the session ended and the kids pelted toward the exit, his face was unguarded, a tight frown, lips turned down.

"Mr. Vance." I hurried down the steps. My tennis shoes made no sound on the green surface. The singles match continued, the women laughed and chattered as they gathered up their racquet covers and warmups.

Vance's eyes scanned me. If he made a judgment, I didn't read it.

I looked straight at him, into morose blue eyes. "I'm Henrie Collins and —"

"Yeah. I know." It was a small community. Sure he knew. "What's the deal? You figured it out yet?" It wasn't quite smart ass.

I held his gaze. "I'm close. Maybe you can help me."

"Yeah. Well, probably not. Walt's the man to talk to." He half turned, grabbed a towel, scrubbed his damp hair.

I don't like being dismissed. And I had a clear memory of Bettina's pain. "I guess Walt is the man. He got Sharon, didn't he?"

The towel masked his face. He stood motionless. Finally, slowly, his arms dropped. How had I ever thought his face good humored? His narrowed eyes blazed, his cheeks flamed, his jaw jutted.

"So what the hell is it to you?" He flung the towel away.

"Makes me wonder." I folded my arms. "Walt Whittaker will be fired if the club starts losing members, won't he?"

"Could happen." Was there a note of pleasure? "He's handled it all wrong." Peter snagged a cup from the between courts dispenser, pushed the button for water. He downed the cup in one swallow, took a satisfied breath. "He should have grilled everybody, maybe got a night watchman."

I didn't like the satisfaction in his voice. "You're not sorry to see him in trouble, are you?"

He stepped toward me, stood so close I could see the rigid tendons in his neck. "Lady, I'd like to see him in hell. He's a

195

lousy, no good son of a bitch. Did you know I got him the job here? I'll bet he didn't tell you that. And he knew I wanted to date Sharon. Did he give a damn? He went after her right from the first. And after they got married, he didn't want her here at the club, didn't want me to see her or talk to her."

"If it makes you so miserable," and I knew I was looking at misery, at a heart writhing in pain, "why don't you quit?"

Peter's shoulders slumped. "Yeah. Maybe I should. But I want to be here when and if she ever figures out she made the mistake of her life. I want to be here for her." He grabbed up his racquets, head down, he began to walk toward the exit.

Heather Hernandez put down the telephone, looked at me with searching brown eyes. She was a big woman, built like Pam Shriver. Or a Wagnerian soprano with muscles. She made her small office — room enough for a desk, her chair and an extra plastic chair — look even smaller. "I hear Bettina's going to be fine." Her voice was surprisingly light and high.

"She was lucky. Somebody else may not be so lucky, if the tricks don't stop." She hadn't invited me to sit down. I smiled, slid onto the chair.

She didn't smile in return. "I told Walt this was the silliest stunt yet."

"Stunt?"

"Encouraging you — a stranger — to try and figure out what's going on here." She didn't say it, but her eyes made it clear: I was a nosy old woman and whatever I did would be a waste of time.

"So maybe you've figured out who's behind the vandalism." My gaze was metallic.

Her face had all the elasticity of a Roman statue. She leaned back in her chair. "Have you talked to Peter Vance?"

"Yes." I looked bland.

Her massive shoulders lifted in a shrug. "He hates Walt. With good reason. But nonetheless . . ."

"You hate him, too." I held her gaze and felt cold at the malevolence in her dark eyes.

After a moment, her wide mouth stretched in an unpleasant smile. "Not enough to ruin the club. I'm the one who's made it what it is. Eventually, the board will see that. I'll be the next director. Now, I've got to see to the ordering. There are a million and one details to this job. And I do it right." She pulled a folder close, bent over it.

A rattle at the door.

Walt's secretary stuck her head inside. "Heather, quick. There's trouble on Court 9. Hurry . . ."

Gauzy swirls of thinning fog decorated the cypress trees. The oyster gray sky was lightening in patches, but dense fog still hid the end of the point and the ocean. The crashing surf sounded dully through the mist. I couldn't keep up with Heather's long stride, not even when I broke into a lope. But I reached the court, the last one, in time to see Walt Whittaker, his face suffused with rage, shout into a cell phone.

". . . every name. Nobody gets out of here without giving their name. Nobody."

I looked past him at the court. Bright red paint hung in wet globules from the center net, spread in an irregular patch on the forehand service square.

Walt clicked off the phone, faced Heather. "Get back to the clubhouse. Get the name of every person — staff, member, guest — and where they were between —" he glanced at his watch — "eleven-thirty and now."

It was ten minutes past noon.

Walt's choleric flush deepened. He glared at Heather. "Including yourself."

Heather was as tall as Walt. She drew herself up, her powerful body poised as if to attack. "Be careful, Walt. Be very careful." Then she swung away.

Walt's hands clenched into fists.

I tried to lower the level of tension. "How did you get the time frame?"

It took a moment for him to respond. He breathed deeply. "Rafael was out here clipping. He went to the maintenance shed about eleven-thirty. He came back here a few minutes ago and found this —" He flung his hand toward the oozing paint. "God dammit, we've got to do something. Have you talked to them? Which one of them's doing it?"

Yesterday he'd fought like a tiger resisting the idea of a personal enemy, reluctantly giving me the names of Peter Vance and Heather Hernandez. Now that he'd crossed that bridge, admitted to himself the vandalism was directed at him, he was ready to bring his suspicions out into the open.

"I've talked to them." To morose and brooding Peter, to self-absorbed and satisfied Heather. "Let me see if anybody can pinpoint where Peter and Heather were during the time period."

"Do it fast." He was long past politeness. He glanced at his watch. "Sharon's coming in for lunch. I'd almost call and tell her not to come. But she told me she has some ideas. We'll be out at the point. Why don't you join us?"

I wouldn't miss it. "Has Sharon decided to tell what she knows?"

Maybe it was one shock too many. He turned toward me like a man who'd just been punched in the gut. His big face flattened. His eyes narrowed.

I didn't back away. "I talked to her this morning."

"You talked to Sharon?" He stepped toward me. "Why the hell did you do that?"

"To see if she had any ideas about this stuff." I tilted my head toward the paint-stained court. "Obviously she does. Did she call you, set up having lunch?"

Slowly, he nodded. And scowled. "Okay, that does it." His voice was truculent. "It's that sorry bastard. She's finally come to her senses about him. All right." He slammed a fist into his hand.

I reached out, touched a tense, muscled arm. "Don't say anything to Peter. Let's find out what she knows first."

Rafael showed me the storeroom. It was a low slung gray metal building screened by purplish red crepe myrtle. He unlocked the door, held it open for me. He could have been anywhere from forty to seventy, his face lined, his black hair streaked with silver. But he moved fast and talked faster. "No, senora, we don't have any red paint. White. Blue. No red."

There was no can of paint discarded at the court. It could be anywhere, stuck into shrubs, thrown over the cliff. Even if a search unearthed the container, I doubted we could learn much from it. Only a fool would handle it without gloves and in this day of huge discount do-it-yourself stores, tracing it to a purchaser would be impossible.

As for Peter Vance and Heather Hernandez, both had been in and out of the main building during the morning and could have tossed the paint. Both angrily denied doing so.

The fog still swirled as I walked toward the point. The muffled surf sounded ominous and was a dour counterpoint to my thoughts. What did I know? What did I have? Damn little. We could draw a tight circle around the likely suspects. But we needed to stop this stream of viciousness. Red paint.

Did that signal danger?

Walt stood by the tilted slab, his face creased in a tight frown. Sharon shrugged, turned away from him. She reached down to the brown wicker picnic hamper, lifted the lid.

A chocolate cloud erupted from the hamper with a high shrill buzz, a hideous enveloping wavering mass of enraged wasps. The wasps swarmed over Sharon, covering her hair and face and arms and body. She screamed and flailed and stumbled away, fighting, crying, and then she slumped to the ground.

Officer Benita Chavez's long thin face was stern. "A hornet's nest. In the hamper."

Walt Whittaker lifted a tear-stained face. "It was meant for me. And it got Sharon. If only she hadn't come in for lunch. If only . . ." He buried his face in his hands.

Peter Vance's stocky body quivered, one bone wracking shudder after another. He stared dully at the still mound beneath a tarpaulin brought from the maintenance shed.

Heather Hernandez stood with her powerful arms folded, her brown eyes fastened in sick fascination on the wicker basket and the broken hornet's nest.

Officer Chavez lifted her head. We all heard the siren. "Lt. Fenton will want to talk to all of you." She'd heard everything we had to tell, the vandalism that caused serious injury, then death. "Please remain here —"

I spoke quietly. "Officer Chavez."

The young policewoman looked at me inquiringly. Walt Whitaker glared at me with red-rimmed eyes. Peter Vance's gaze was dull and disinterested. Heather Hernandez's dark eyes darted from face to face.

Walt burst out, "It's too late. Sharon's dead! What difference does it make now." He lifted a shaking hand, pointed at

Peter. "It's you!" His hand jerked toward Heather. "Or you! One of you killed her and when I know —" He broke off, his chest heaving.

"We'll know." My voice was crisp. The greatest, most satisfying shot in tennis is the overhead smash. The ball arcs above you. Timed right, your racquet connects at the top of your swing, and the ball cannons over the net, out of reach, unreturnable. There is a surge of power, an exhilaration afforded by no other stroke. But you only get one chance and if you miss, the opportunity is gone forever. It's the kind of shot you have to take without thought or planning because there is no time to deliberate. The ball is there and you go for it. "We'll know. I want Officer Chavez to obtain a search warrant to check out the desks and lockers used by Peter Vance and Heather Hernandez."

Peter Vance continued to stare dully at the tarpaulin. Heather Hernandez's face twisted with fear.

"You'll find gloves or a rag smeared with red paint, something that will link one or the other to the vandalism and so to Sharon Whittaker's death." I looked into one particular face and I saw the tiny flash of satisfaction. "But when you find the incriminating evidence, Officer Chavez, the carefully planted evidence, I request that you submit it for DNA testing."

Walt Whittaker's broad, boyishly handsome face froze.

I pointed at him, just as I would lift my left hand to finger an arcing ball. "That's right, Walt. You used gloves, of course, when you created this trail of vandalism. But did you know that it only takes a single touch to leave a tiny dusting of DNA? That's true. The wonders of science, Walt. A single touch will prove you killed your wife."

He backed away from us, his face disfigured with fury. "She was going to leave me. For him." The hatred was scathing, virulent.

201

Officer Chavez's hand dropped to her gun.

Walt Whittaker stood for an instant, like a dangerous bull, seeking escape. Then he turned and ran.

"Halt. Halt!"

But it wasn't a gunshot that stopped him. Peter flung himself after Walt, ran with fury, and slammed the big pro into the ground.

I helped Bettina out of her wheelchair, into the passenger seat. "You're moving pretty well."

"Henrie O!" Her blue eyes widened. "Tell me all about it."

We reached her home, a cheerful wooden house framed by bougainvillea, as I finished speaking. I turned off the motor. "Walt was just a little too clever."

She opened her car door. "But Henrie O, how did you know?"

I got out, came around to help her. "When Sharon died from the stings, I realized it was a culmination, a carefully planned chain of events that resulted in her death. And if it was deliberate, if it was murder, who had a motive? Who was jealous and possessive and always had to win? And who would know whether she was allergic to wasp or bee stings? Who is the first suspect when a wife is murdered? Her husband. Yes, Walt was a little too clever. Although it could appear that the swarm of hornets was another in a series of pranks and one that turned deadly, I'm sure the police will discover that Sharon was allergic to stings. And the timing of the paint on the court made a difference."

Bettina edged out of the car, used her new cane to stand. She clung to my elbow as we moved slowly up her walk. "Why is that?"

"The court was defaced within a narrow time frame. I

thought that was curious because none of the other incidents could be pinned down that closely. There had to be a reason." I held open the front door for her. "What did it accomplish? The timing made it absolutely clear that Peter and Heather could have thrown the paint. And whoever threw the paint was, of course, the person who planted the hornet's nest in the hamper. Now why set it up so particularly? I decided the plan had to be to plant something incriminating on one of them. As it turned out, there were paint-smeared gloves in Peter's locker."

Bettina looked at her own row of senior trophies atop a bookcase. "Walt always had to win. I know that. Poor Sharon." Her thin face tightened. "I'm so glad you caught him. Henrie O, it would have been so easy for him to get away with murder. Whatever made you think of DNA? And how did you know about the new research?"

"I read a wire story in your local newspaper about the new discovery just before we went out to play doubles that morning." Old news hounds always keep up. "Australian scientists have determined that simply touching everyday objects leaves traces of DNA." Yes, it had been nice timing. "A smashing story, I thought."

LIFE-INTEREST

Diana glanced toward Ralph as she pushed the tiller. His eyes met hers, with undisguised love and desire. Happiness flooded her, because, suddenly, she knew this was right and all the sad and lonely nights were . . . Without warning, pain pierced the back of her head, exploded in her skull. She lifted a hand uncertainly, then tumbled backward into the achingly cold water. The pain devoured her, yet it was overborne by the scarlet burst of fear as she gasped for air and pulled water into her lungs. Then nothing . . .

The words, ugly, hurtful words, buzzed into her mind.

"Is she dead?"

That was Elinor's high, cool voice.

Buddy answered her. "No, worse luck," he drawled. "The good doctor got her out. She's unconscious. He thinks it's a stroke."

Diana wanted to cry out, ask what had happened, but she couldn't speak or move.

"Too bad she wasn't out in the boat alone." That was Elinor again.

"Shh, somebody might hear you . . ."

Diana wanted to tell them that she could hear, but the muscles in her throat lay as limp and useless as dead fish at the tide's edge. A siren shrilled, and Buddy and Elinor moved away on the wooden dock. The sound of running feet, then firm hands lifting her up.

"Hurry, for God's sake!" Ralph swore steadily in a hoarse,

shaken voice as hands fumbled to lift her.

Hurry.

Three weeks later, Diana stared angrily across her room. Hurry. God, how she wished they hadn't hurried. If the surgery had been delayed, perhaps she would have died. Who wanted to live like a crippled bird? Half her body lay immovable. She had always prided herself upon her swiftness, her grace, and now she lay like a mummy, alone in a room that had once harbored such happiness.

Diana's gaze moved restlessly around the room. They'd been so pleased to bring her home from the hospital, and it should have made her happier. But how could she ever be happy again? She'd thought, in that instant before her body betrayed her, that she might find happiness with Ralph, her dead husband's friend. Her friend. She had had an instant's peace from the sorrow she'd borne since Harry died. Dear Harry. If she could have smiled, she would have. To think of Harry always brought a smile to her heart. It was impossible to believe he was gone, that she would never again see his blunt, determined face and hear his boyish laughter. He had always been boyish with her, even though he had been so much older. She'd never thought of his age when they married, even though he had grown children her own age from his first marriage. None of that had mattered because Harry Jessop lived a vigorous, youthful life, and he gloried in having a young vibrant wife at his side at both the home and office. He admired her brilliance as a corporate lawyer and her passion as a lover. Even in his final illness, he'd laughed, fighting to live. If he were here now, he would urge her to fight because Ralph and the other doctors had told her she could relearn how to walk and talk, that it would come if she tried, but the battle didn't seem worth the effort, not any more.

The hall door clicked open.

Diana's eyes narrowed as the nurse walked in.

Nurse Mapes didn't smile. Her eyes darted around the lovely room, and her mouth tightened. It was disgusting how much money some people had — not that it was doing Mrs. Jessop much good right now.

Nurse Mapes picked up Diana's flaccid right hand. Pulse steady. Color good. Then she reached down and lifted the coyer to straighten Diana's right leg. Mustn't let it go rigid. Time to bundle up Mrs. Jessop and wheel her onto the balcony.

"Ready for a little air, aren't we?"

The nurse chattered as she helped Diana sit up and slip into the wheelchair.

Diana's green eyes glittered angrily. The woman was a clod. She treated Diana like a stuffed doll, never looking in her eyes. No one, Diana thought bleakly, really looked at her now. Not even Ralph — and he had looked at her so longingly before. There had been a sense that in the fullness of time, Diana and Ralph could make a new beginning — until that day on the sailboat.

But Diana felt a surge of happiness when she was rolled onto the balcony. She loved the crashing of the surf, the sea-scented air, the ruggedness of the cliff below the balcony.

Too soon, Nurse Mapes returned to wheel her back into the bedroom. The nurse shut the French doors to the balcony. Diana hated having the doors shut, and she couldn't say so. It was infuriating not to be able to control so simple a thing as the opening or closing of doors. Maybe her speech therapist could help her learn to say door or open. But the therapist came daily, did her job efficiently, and Diana felt no nearer ever to speaking again.

In the afternoon, her physical therapist, Ruthie Harris,

rushed in, running a little late as usual, but smiling and cheerful.

"Hi, Mrs. Jessop, I'm sorry I'm late. How's everything today?" She looked at Diana, really looked at her. "You don't look happy. Is anything wrong?" Then she shook her head. "Dumb question. You're sick of all this, aren't you? Well, don't worry. It's a long road, but we're going to make it."

Ruthie massaged and exercised each limb. Her face glistened with sweat by the end of the session.

Diana took a deep breath, and despair swept her. She could just manage to move her left arm and leg. She could hear and understand everything, but she couldn't write a single word with her left hand. Every time she tried, the pen made meaningless marks. As for her right side — there was nothing. Ruthie worked and worked with her right arm and leg, but there was nothing.

Diana closed her eyes. Her throat ached with unshed tears.

"Hey Mrs. Jessop." Ruthie's voice was soft. "Don't you think I know my job? Give me a little credit."

Unwillingly, Diana looked up.

"I'll tell you," Ruthie said firmly, "you're ahead of a lot of my patients. Your muscles are strong. Tell me, were you a jogger?" She paused. "Give me a blink for yes."

Diana blinked once.

"Oh hey, that's swell. Now we can talk. Are you a jogger? One blink for yes, two for no."

Diana blinked twice.

"No?" Ruthie looked surprised, then she nodded. "I remember. I used to see pictures of you in the paper. You ride."

Diana blinked once. Then her eyes filled with tears.

"I know," Ruthie said gently. "But you'll ride again. I know you will."

The next afternoon, Ruthie surged into the room then paused and looked sharply at Diana. "Hey, you're in a rare temper, aren't you?"

Diana blinked once, furiously.

Ruthie looked around the dim room. "Oh, I'll bet you don't like it so dark. Shall I open the curtains?"

Diana blinked once, then stared hard at Ruthie.

Ruthie cocked her head. "Okay. You want the curtains open." A blink. "But that's not all." A triumphant blink.

Ruthie looked slowly around the room then back at the French doors. "Do you want the doors open to the balcony?"

Diana blinked once, firmly.

Ruthie hesitated. "They've always been closed. Is that really what you want?"

Diana blinked again with great precision.

Ruthie smiled. "I've got it. You like the doors open, but the nurse doesn't know, and you can't tell her. Did you used to keep them open?"

Diana blinked yes.

Ruthie was still massaging when Nurse Mapes walked in, crossed to the French doors, and started to shut them.

"Wait. Mrs. Jessop wants the doors open."

"Really. I suppose she told you that?"

"Yes, she did."

"Don't be silly. She can't talk."

"She understands every word she hears. She blinks once for yes and twice for no. I just asked her about the doors. Look, I'll do it again." Ruthie turned toward Diana. "Mrs. Jessop, do you want the French doors open?"

Diana blinked once and delighted in Nurse Mapes' discomfiture.

The nurse looked irritated. "Too much air isn't good. I'll

check with Dr. Halsey."

That evening, Ralph shrugged impatiently when Nurse Mapes asked if it would be all right to leave the French doors to the balcony open.

"God yes, what earthly difference could it make?"

The open doors delighted Diana, and Ralph sensed her happiness. For the first time since her stroke, he gave a genuine smile. "Listen, I'm proud of you, Diana. You're a fighter. You're going to get well."

Diana's days took on a sharper focus. One wonderful day, she managed to slightly move her right foot. She squeezed a little rubber ball to strengthen her left hand, and she and Ruthie played Scrabble — and Diana always won. She was getting better, but she still couldn't speak.

Hal Jessop's visits were the highlight of her week. He burst in, hurried, intense, and he reminded her so much of his father. He was the only one of Harry's children who didn't resent his remarriage. Buddy and Elinor hated Diana. Diana had always known that, but Buddy and Elinor's hateful words as she lay on the dock proved it for all time.

She pushed that thought away and concentrated on Hal's report about the company. When he left, he took with him the air of excitement and eagerness which had permeated her days when she was running the company. But Hal paused at the door and said firmly, "You get well, Diana. We need you at the office."

All right. She was going to do it. She was going to get back to work. She'd done very well today in her session with Ruthie.

Dear Hal. Harry would be so proud of him. As for Buddy and Elinor . . . Diana shivered and pulled up an afghan. Buddy and Elinor wanted her to die.

The warmth of the afghan soothed her, and Diana drifted into sleep.

"Oh, she's asleep." Elinor's voice.

Diana began to wake.

"The nurse said it was okay to wake her up," Buddy said impatiently. "Hey, Diana."

Diana looked up.

Buddy brightened. "Hey, Diana, Hal says you're doing great."

Diana's green eyes narrowed. Fat lot Buddy and Elinor cared. Buddy's narrow face was creased with an ingratiating smile, but his blue eyes were cold and watchful. He was a small, wiry man and didn't look at all like his father. Elinor was more like Harry, tall, slim, and redheaded. Her elegant russet sweater emphasized the richness of her copper hair. She might have been a beautiful woman except for the petulant droop of her mouth.

Buddy bent nearer. "Elinor and I need a little help, Diana. Some money."

Diana's face remained impassive.

Buddy said urgently, "A lot of money. Look, I went to see Mr. Oliphant, but he said you had to agree."

So Buddy had been to the lawyer. Buddy should have known it was useless. Diana had a life-interest in Harry's estate and, so long as she lived, she controlled all income and principal. At her death, the estate would be split between Hal, Buddy, and Elinor.

No wonder Buddy and Elinor were disappointed when Ralph pulled her out of the bay.

"Hal says he can talk to you," Buddy continued. "I mean, I know you can't talk, but he seems to understand you. We'll tell him what we need and have him ask you. Okay?"

Elinor tugged on Buddy's sleeve. "I don't think she hears you."

Buddy turned toward his sister. "God, Elinor, I've got to get some money."

Diana heard the desperation in his voice. So Buddy was in trouble. Well, let him get out of it the best way he could. She couldn't tell them to leave, but she didn't have to listen. Diana closed her eyes.

"If only she'd died . . ." Buddy's voice trailed away.

Silence. An ugly, ominous, menacing silence.

Diana slitted her eyes. Buddy stared down, his head jutted forward, his eyes hooded, then, he whirled around and pulled his sister across the room.

Diana's heart fluttered and her lungs ached for air as she strained to hear the whispers.

Buddy's face was inches from his sister's. "Nobody'd be surprised if she had another stroke."

Elinor shrugged her shoulders.

"Don't you understand? If she dies, nobody's going to be surprised."

Elinor lifted an eyebrow. Buddy grinned.

Through her narrowed eyes, Diana watched the idea possess them.

Then Elinor shook her head. "Doctors are smart, Buddy."

Buddy grabbed his sister's arm. Diana hated the look on his face, the wolfish, hungry look.

Horror exploded in Diana's mind. No. This couldn't be happening. These were Harry's children, Buddy and Elinor. She knew them. No.

Elinor hissed, "They'd do an autopsy."

"Not if they think it's a stroke. Come on, Elinor. It'll be easy. All you have to do . . ."

211

Elinor began to back away. "Not me, Buddy. No way. No way."

He gripped her arm and kept her from the door. "All you have to do is get one of Ken's syringes."

Elinor pulled free, and her heels clicked sharply against the floor as she hurried, almost ran, to the door, Buddy close behind her, determinedly behind her. Before the door closed, Diana saw Elinor's face and in it, read her own death warrant.

Diana's heart thudded irregularly. She struggled to pull herself upright. Then she reached out with her left hand and pushed at her bell. Her breathing was shallow and irregular. God, what was she going to do? She knew that Elinor would help Buddy, especially if all it took was one of her husband's diabetic syringes. What did Buddy plan? To give Diana insulin? Oh no, no, it would be cleverer than that. Buddy didn't want her in a coma, he wanted her dead, and a syringe full of air shot into the bloodstream would create an embolism. There would be no trace, nothing but a hypodermic mark, and who would look for that?

Nurse Mapes yanked open the door. Diana had interrupted her afternoon coffee. The rich always thought they could have anything anytime the . . . For God's sake! She hurried across the room and picked up Diana's wrist. Her pulse was 140. What in the world . . .

"Mur . . ." Diana heard her own voice, thick and heavy and slow. "Mur . . ."

"Hush now," Nurse Mapes said sharply. "What's happened here? Why are you upset?"

Diana tried to slow her breathing. She stared up into the woman's heavy, red face. "Mur . . ."

"This is a fine how do you do. Doctor will be very unhappy if he finds you like this."

Diana stared up, her eyes wide and strained.

"What do you want?" the nurse asked. "Do you want to see Dr. Halsey?"

Diana blinked once, very carefully.

Ralph came just after six. He was frowning. "Hey, what's wrong with my favorite patient? Ruthie says you're doing great."

She tried to speak, but again it was guttural, hoarse noise, not a word, and meaningless. She stared at Ralph, willing him to understand, her eyes wide and staring. Again, she made that noise, "Mur . . ."

He winced. He hated seeing her like this. She knew it, understood it. It made him cry inside to see her struggle.

"Take it easy. Quiet now, Diana."

He asked questions. About the food, the room, her muscles. Diana blinked and frowned and struggled. Perspiration darkened her fine blonde hair. Her green eyes pled.

Ralph tried. He tried hard, but, finally, he gave up. Perhaps it was because he was so tired. He'd been four hours in surgery, and the patient died on the table. Perhaps it was because he hated seeing Diana like this, hated seeing her trying so frantically, so desperately to communicate.

"Look, this is madness. We aren't getting anywhere."

She arched her head forward. She was panting, and her one moveable hand opened and closed spasmodically on the bed.

He reached for his bag. "I'm going to give you something to help you . . ."

The cry she gave was so deep, so wrenching that he stopped and faced her again.

"You don't want a shot?"

She blinked twice, and stared at him, her eyes imploring.

"You must relax. Will you lie back now and rest, be quiet?"

Slowly, Diana put her head back against the pillow. She sighed and forced herself to breathe slowly, evenly.

Ralph hesitated for a long moment, then closed his bag. "All right, Diana, that's better." He leaned down then and kissed her cheek. "I'll come by in the morning. Maybe I'll be able to figure out what's wrong."

Morning. Diana lay there and stared at the closed door. If she rang for the nurse, it would be pointless. It would only bring Ralph back, and this time there would be a hypodermic, and she wouldn't even know when Buddy came. Buddy would come in the night, of course, steal quietly down the hall and into her room. Even if she rang for the nurse, he would have time. It took only an instant to give an injection.

Perhaps it would be easier so. Let Buddy give her a shot, and that would be the end of it.

The answer exploded inside. No. Never. She wanted to live. Despite the struggle, despite the pain, she wanted to live. She wanted to see the golden spill of color at dawn. She wanted to hear the thunder of the surf. She wanted to remember Harry and all their days of happiness. She wanted to think and feel and laugh and cry. She wanted to see Ralph and the love in his eyes.

She wanted to live.

Her heart thudded again, irregularly hard, then, the fingers of her left hand cut into the palm. She mustn't give way to panic. She must think it through, find a way to save herself. It was all up to her.

There wasn't any way. She was doomed. Tonight, Buddy would move from shadow to shadow and come into her room, carrying death. There wasn't any way in the world that she could . . .

Oh God, why did she think of it now? Why hadn't the idea come to her when Ralph was here, when she was trying so hard to communicate? Because there was a way.

Diana looked across the room at the clock. It was almost seven now. Was there time? Could she do it? And would she be able to persuade Nurse Mapes, force Nurse Mapes to call Ralph back?

It was few minutes before nine when Diana finished. She'd fallen trying to get out of bed and into the wheelchair. From there, she'd crawled to the game table and pulled herself up. Once her hand jerked spasmodically and the little golden pieces tumbled away. Tears of despair burned her eyes, but she started over. And then it was done. It took half an hour to get back into bed. She pulled herself awkwardly with her left arm and pushed with her left leg. She'd stopped by the desk that had belonged to Harry on her return trip, but, finally, she was done. She rang the bell.

Nurse Mapes glared down at her. "What happened to your face?" She bent nearer. "You've got a bruise there." The nurse looked around the room.

Diana held her breath. Nurse Mapes mustn't be the one to see the game table. Diana knew she wouldn't believe, wouldn't act. No, it had to be Ralph.

The nurse took Diana's pulse, and a little flicker of worry cut through her irritation at being called. "Now, I'm going to have to call doctor if you . . ." She paused and looked down at Diana's frantically fluttering eyes.

"Do you want me to call doctor?"

Diana carefully and slowly, so very carefully and slowly, blinked once.

The huge house lay dark and quiet on the bluff above the Pacific.

Buddy Jessop nosed the outboard into the cove. He ran the motor just above an idle the last 100 yards. The boat slipped silently up to the wooden pier. As he tied the boat,

Buddy patted his jacket pocket and felt the hypodermic.

His sneakers made no sound on the wooden pier or the cut-out steps in the face of the cliff. He was almost to the top when his foot stubbed on something uneven. He took a pencil-sized flashlight from his pocket and turned it on. A rock slide partially blocked several of the steps, but he picked his way past. Good thing he didn't mind heights. Right now, he didn't mind anything. He'd fix those steps when he got the place. He could negotiate with Hal and Elinor over who got what. There would be plenty to go around. He turned off the light as he reached the top. Below him the surf boomed against the sharp-edged rocks at the base of the cliff. There was plenty of moonlight to show the way. He looked up. Yes, Diana's windows were open. It was going to be so easy.

He climbed the wooden trellis and at the top gripped the balcony railing and swung lightly over. The night breeze stirred her curtains. He took one quiet step after another then pushed past the curtains into the room. A thin bar of moonlight illuminated the bed and a still figure lying there.

He began to breathe more quickly. His heart raced. He crossed quickly to the bed, in a hurry now. He took the syringe from his pocket, and pulled up the plunger, filling the syringe with air.

The bedside lamp flared on, and a strong hand gripped his wrist. Pain radiated up Buddy's arm. He looked dumbly into Ralph's angry eyes then, beyond the bed, at Diana sitting in her wheelchair. She slumped a little, but her left arm rested on the wheelchair arm, and she held the pistol unwaveringly.

Ralph pushed up from the bed and shoved Buddy away. "You little bastard."

Buddy stumbled backwards and came up hard against a chair. He regained his balance, realized his arm was free, and he still had the syringe. He tried to hide it behind him.

Ralph looked at him in disgust. "That won't help. I know," and his head jerked toward the game table next to Buddy.

Buddy looked down. The Scrabble tiles were uneven, but they told the story.

MURDER BUDDY HYPO

Ralph took a step toward Buddy, "Diana did that, Buddy. She had to crawl across the room. She crawled to the game table, then she got Harry's gun out of his desk." Ralph bit off the words. "I wanted to call the police, but Diana . . ."

"The police," Buddy blurted. He stared at Diana. His eyes fell to the gun. Then he said knowingly, confidently. "You won't shoot me, Diana." He turned and lunged for the French doors and the balcony. "You won't shoot."

He swung himself lightly over the railing and swarmed down the trellis. Hell, they couldn't prove anything now. He paused at the top of the cliff to fling the syringe out into the night. They'd never find it. They'd never prove a thing. He heard a call behind him.

Buddy plunged down the rock cut steps, moving fast.

Too fast.

He didn't remember the blocked steps until his toe caught on debris, and then it was too late. Forever too late.

Buddy's frenzied, final shout tore across the night silence.

Diana heard it and shuddered. Harry's son. How could it have happened? How could Buddy and Elinor have hated her so much?

"Diana." Ralph called her name strongly, then he was beside her, touching her.

Diana swallowed and looked up. She saw concern and understanding, and, more than that, she saw love and admiration. In this room this night, she'd encountered evil, but now a man stood beside her whose presence affirmed everything

217

that was good. Ralph was here. He was here because she'd fought to live.

"Ra . . . lph."

She said his name, and it was a triumph.

UPSTAGING MURDER

Laurel Darling Roethke was a latecomer to mysteries, but, as with all her enthusiasms, she gave her new interest her all. She subscribed to both *Ellery Queen Mystery Magazine* and *Alfred Hitchcock Mystery Magazine*, belonged to the Mystery Guild, and was on the mailing list of a half dozen mystery bookstores, from Grounds for Murder in San Diego, California, to The Hideaway in Bar Harbor, Maine. Her heart, of course, belonged to Death on Demand, the mystery bookstore so ably directed by her dear daughter-in law, Annie Laurance Darling. She adored Annie, though it was a bit of a puzzle that Max had chosen such a serious young woman to be his wife. Oh, well, one could never quite understand the squish of another's moccasins.

Still, it was Max's love for Annie that had led Laurel to the mystery. A true thrill was discovering the delights and plea-sures of mystery weekends, from the Catskills to the Sierras, from the Louisiana bayous to the Alaskan tundra.

Annie encouraged her, of course. Dear Annie. So thoughtful to send a brochure on that Tibetan weekend, Murder at the Monastery. But she was already committed to Death Stalks the Smokies at this gorgeous inn in southeastern North Carolina, and it would only make sense to visit Annie and Max on her way home. She was so near.

So far, this weekend had been such a wonderful experi-ence, a welcoming dinner devoted to one of Laurel's favorite authors, Leslie Ford, with choice tidbits about three of Ford's most famous characters, Grace Latham and Colonel Primrose and *dear* Sergeant Buck.

Laurel hummed vigorously as she inspected her image in the mirror. What was it that lovely police chief, the guest of honor, had murmured as they danced last night? That she had a Grecian profile and hair that shimmered like moonlight on water? How sweet! Men were so often obtuse, but they added such spice to life. She brushed a soupçon of pale pink gloss to her lips, nodded in satisfaction, and turned toward the door. Not that she expected to encounter anyone else abroad at this hour, but a woman owed it to herself always to look her best.

She slipped quietly down the hall. After all, you couldn't be too careful at mystery weekends. Everyone was so determined to win. Very American, of course, the spirit of competition. Some people (her mind skittered to Henny Brawley, one of the most avid mystery readers to frequent Annie's store) would do almost anything to win. So Laurel felt it was quite fair to scout out the territory in advance.

The Big Ben-like tone of the grandfather clock on the landing tolled the hour. Boom. Boom. So *quiet* at two A.M. Then she paused, one hand lightly resting on the heavy mahogany newel post at the foot of the stairs. Switching off her pencil flash, she cocked her head to listen.

A footstep.

No doubt about it.

How odd.

Perhaps another mystery competitor. She felt a quiver of disappointment. She'd so often triumphed because most people, face it, were slugabeds. She, of course, scarcely needed any sleep to function quite successfully. Darting into the cavernous library, which also served as the inn's lobby and as an auditorium, she found shelter behind heavy red velvet drapes as another stealthy footstep sounded.

Her heart raced in anticipation. Perhaps this weekend

would be decidedly special. There were many reports of ghosts in these backwoods. Could it be that she would soon witness a spectral apparition? Laurel considered herself something of an authority on unearthly visitants. She was quite familiar with the works of the Society for Psychical Research, having read the ambitious, two-volume, 1,400-page work, *Phantasms of the Living*, published in 1886, and certainly she was cognizant of the apparitional research of that modern giant in the field, Dr. Karlis Osis.

Eagerly, she peered from behind the drapes. When a gray-robed figure glided into view, she was at once disappointed, yet intrigued. This was no ghost. After all, apparitions have no need of flashlights. But this was decidedly curious! Something was afoot here, no doubt about it. The dimly seen gray figure in the long, sweeping, hooded robe aimed a pencil flash, a twin to the one Laurel carried, down the center of the huge room. Laurel followed the bobbing progress of the light to the small stage where the mystery play would be presented tomorrow night. Such a clever idea, as touted in the brochure. As is customary at mystery weekends, a murder would be discovered shortly after breakfast, teams formed, and an investigation begun. The young actors hired to play suspects' roles would provide grist for the weekend detectives' mills. But, in addition, this weekend would feature a suspense play to be presented after dinner and before the announcement of the winning detective team at, of course, the stroke of midnight.

The hooded figure ran lightly up the steps and the pencil flash illuminated a narrow portion of the stage. The set included a yellow pine nightstand beside a rickety wooden bed with a pieced quilt cover. The figure placed the flash on the bed, the sliver of light aimed at the nightstand.

A gloved hand pulled open the drawer and lifted out a pistol.

221

Laurel strained to see the robed figure, dimly visible in the backwash of the flash, the sharply illuminated gloved hand, the gun. A crisp click, the gun opened. Another click, it shut. The gun was replaced in the drawer, the drawer closed and the pencil flash lifted.

The hooded figure passed very near, but there was no visible face, just folds of cloth. There was an instant when Laurel could have reached out, yanked at the robe, and glimpsed the face of the intruder. She almost moved. To unmask the villain now — and the click of the pistol signaled unmistakable intent to Laurel — would perhaps protect the victim in this instance. But what of the future? Laurel remained still and listened to the fading footsteps, and then the figure was gone.

The police chief, such a handsome man and, understandably, a bit confused as to the purpose of her visit, welcomed her eagerly to his room. She soon put things clear, however. Then it took a bit of persuasion, but finally the chief agreed to her plan.

"Damned clever," he pronounced. "And, now, my dear, perhaps, after all your exertions, you might enjoy a glass of wine?"

Laurel hesitated for a moment but, after all, nothing more could be accomplished in her quest for justice until the morrow. She nodded in acquiescence, bestowing a serene smile upon her coconspirator. She couldn't help but appreciate the enthusiastic gleam in the chief's dark eyes.

Over a breakfast of piping hot camomile tea and oat bran sprinkled with alfalfa sprouts, Laurel studied the program of *Trial*, described as "a drama of life and death, of murder and judgment, of passion and power. An abused wife, Maria, is on trial for her life in the shooting death of her husband. A vindictive prosecutor demands a death for a death. Her fate will lie in the hands of the judge." Laurel thoughtfully chewed another sprig of alfalfa and committed to memory the five young faces of the cast.

Kelly Winston, the abused wife, had sharply planed, dramatic features and soulful eyes. She was a drama graduate of a Midwestern college. Beside her studio picture was a single quote: "I want it all."

"Hmm," Laurel murmured as she admired the really very handsome features of Bill Morgan, the abusive husband slain by Maria. Such an attractive young man, though, of course, handsome is as handsome does. His quote: "George M. Cohan has nothing on me!"

Handsome was not the word for Carl Jenkins, who portrayed the prosecutor. His dark face glowered up from the program, thin-lipped and beak-nosed. "I'll see you on Broadway."

Walter Sheridan beamed from his studio picture, apparently the epitome of charm, good humor, and lightheartedness. He played the judge. "Life's a bowl of cherries."

Jonathan Ravin's face was young and vulnerable. His chin didn't look as if it had quite taken shape. He played the hired man who excites the husband's jealousy. "All I need is a chance."

Laurel did suffer a few pangs of envy as the weekend detectives began their investigation into the murder of a rich playboy at a Riviera château. (The roles played during the day investigation differed, of course, from the roles in that evening's play.) Laurel found the thrill of the chase hard to ignore. But a greater duty called. She consoled herself with thoughts of that great company of fictional sleuths who, like the company of all faithful people, surely were at her shoulder at this very moment (figuratively speaking): Mary Roberts Rinehart's Miss Pinkerton, Patricia Wentworth's Miss Silver (though why one should be dowdy with age mystified Laurel), Heron Carvic's Miss Seeton, Gwen Moffat's Miss Pink, Josephine Tey's Miss Pym, and, of course, Leslie Ford's Grace Latham. (Good for Grace. She, at least, made time in her life for men.)

But Laurel's plan of necessity required that she not be at the forefront of the mystery weekend investigations. In fact, she lagged, and only approached one of the young people playing the mystery roles when the investigators bayed through the inn in search of further elucidation.

She approached by herself, bearing goodies. Did anyone ever outgrow cookies and milk, even if, at later ages, these translated to gin and tonic?

Kelly Winston, who played a countess in the investigations, occupied one alcove in the library. As Laurel approached, the actress made a conscious effort to erase a tight frown and look aggrieved, in keeping with her role of the countess whose diamond tiara had been stolen.

Laurel proffered an inviting Bloody Mary with a sprig of mint. "Hard work, isn't it?" she said cheerfully. "I do so admire you young people. And the life of an actress! So much to be envied, but often such difficult demands, especially when emotions run high. It's so hard with men, isn't it, Kelly?"

Kelly looked at Laurel in surprise, but the drink was welcome. "Aren't you doing the mystery weekend?"

A light trill of laughter. "In a way, my dear. But I'm a writer too. Fiction, let me hasten to add. And I dearly enjoy getting to know my fellow human beings on a personal level. And I can tell that you are *so* unhappy."

The dam burst. Laurel made gentle, cooing noises, such

an effective response, and presented an ingenuous face and limpid blue eyes. Kelly admitted that it was too, too awful, the way Walter was glooming around. After all, they'd only dated for a couple of months. Of course, he had helped her get the mystery troupe job, but that didn't mean he owned her, did it? More empathetic coos. And Bill was just the cutest guy she'd ever met!

Laurel found her next quarry, Bill Morgan, with an elbow on the bar. He accepted his drink with alacrity. He was a strapping young man, six foot four at least, with curly brown hair, light blue eyes, and a manly chin. Laurel's glance lingered. She did so admire manly chins. "I do think Kelly is such a dear girl! I hope Walter isn't making things too difficult for you both."

Bill, who was clearly accustomed to female attention from ages six to sixty, expressed no surprise at Laurel's personal interest. He drank half his Bloody Mary in a gulp. "Oh, Kelly's just being dramatic. Actually, it's Carl who gets on my nerves. I didn't even know she'd been involved with him until he got drunk the other night and told me I was a dumb sh—" He glanced at Laurel, cleared his throat. ". . . jerk to get involved with her. He said she went through men like a gambler through chips." He downed the rest of the drink, then looked past Laurel at the main hall and began to wave. "Hi, Jenny. Hey, how about later?"

A tiny, dark-haired girl with an elfin grace paused long enough to blow him a kiss. "Terrific. See you at the pool."

Laurel waited until Bill realized she was still there, not a usual situation for her. Of course, he was crassly young. When he smiled at her dreamily, obviously still thinking of Jenny, she said bluntly, "Do you think Walter is jealous?"

Bill looked at her blankly. "Jealous?"

"Of you and Kelly," she said patiently.

"So who cares?" he asked lightly.

"And Carl?" Laurel prodded.

"Oh, he's just a drunk." Then he frowned. "But kind of a nasty one."

Carl looked like he could be a nasty drunk, with his dark, thin face, prominent cheekbones, and small, tight mouth. As Laurel approached, he smoothed back patent-slick hair (he played a French police inspector in the mystery skit). He stared at the Bloody Mary suspiciously.

"So what's in it?" he snapped. "Ipecac? Valium?"

It was Laurel's turn to be surprised. "Why should I?"

"This isn't my first mystery weekend. People are crazy. They'll do anything."

Laurel lifted the glass to her lips, took a sip. "One hundred percent pure tomato juice, vodka, and whatever," she promised, and smiled winningly.

Carl gave a grudging smile in return. "You aren't one of the nuts?"

"Do I look like a nut?" she asked softly.

He took the Bloody Mary.

"Actually," Laurel confided, "I'm a writer and I'm doing an article on how women mistreat men. Don't you think that's a novel idea? So often, it's the other way around, don't you think?"

Although he looked a little confused, he nodded vehemently. "Damn right. Women mistreat men all the time. Wish they'd get some of their own back."

"Your last girlfriend?" she prompted.

His face hardened. "Should have known better. She two-timed me and made a play for Walter. My best friend. But he's finding out. She isn't any damned good. She'll dump Bill, too, one of these days."

"Isn't it hard, having to act with her?"

226

Carl looked at her sharply. "Hey, what the hell? How'd you know it was Kelly? Hey, lady, what's going on here?"

"That's what I'm finding out," she caroled. Laurel gave him a sprightly wave and wafted toward the hall. She ignored his calls. A determined sleuth is never deflected.

The abandoned Walter, a French chef in the daytime skit, was short, plump, and genial. His spaniel eyes drooped at the mention of Kelly. "Gee, I wish I'd never gotten involved with her. She just seems to irritate everybody. It hasn't been the same since she came aboard."

"Were you deeply in love with her?" Laurel asked gently.

A whoop of laughter. "Lady, love is a merry-go-round. You hop on and you hop off. No hard feelings."

She found the fifth member of the troupe, Jonathan Ravin, beneath an umbrella at poolside. He played Oscar, a Polish expatriate. Long blond hair curled on his neck. He had unhappy brown eyes and bony shoulders.

He shook away the Bloody Mary. "I never adulterate my tomato juice."

"Oh, I certainly understand that," Laurel said sympathetically. "So dreadful what is done to food today. I cook only organically grown vegetables."

After a lengthy discussion of the merits of oat over wheat bran, Laurel segued nearer her objective. "Do your friends eat as you do?"

"My friends?"

"The other actors, Kelly and Bill and Carl and Walter."

"They aren't my friends," he burst out bitterly. "I thought Bill was. But when Kelly came along, he didn't even have time to play checkers anymore. Why did Walter have to bring her in? We had a wonderful time before she came."

Mystery teams sat together at dinner, passing notes, engaging in intense conversations with occasional loud out-bursts of disagreement. But when the solutions were turned in at eight P.M., there was a general air of relaxation.

Laurel had not even sat with her team. Admittedly a dereliction of duty on her part, but more serious matters dominated. Instead, she settled early at the table closest to the stage, her police chief friend beside her. Their chairs were only a few feet from the downstage-left stairs. As the houselights dimmed, she sat forward, chin in hand, to observe.

As the play unfolded, she was impressed with the skill of the young acting troupe. Kelly was superb as the abused wife on trial for the murder of her husband, the handsome, strapping Bill. Slender, blond Jonathan was an effective hired man, who served as the object of the husband's jealousy. The play began in the courtroom where the widow was on trial for her life for the murder of her husband. She claimed self-defense. Plump Walter, as the judge, looked unaccustomedly stern in his black robe. The prosecutor, played by the dark-visaged Carl, was determined to see her executed for the crime. As Carl badgered her upon the witness stand, she broke down in tears, screaming, "You can't know what it was like that night!" The stage went dark. An instant passed and the spots focused downstage on the partial set containing the old bed and the nightstand. Kelly raised up in the bed. She was dressed in the cotton gown she had worn the night of the shooting.

Laurel slipped to her feet and moved toward the downstage-left steps. The police chief, with footsteps as light as a cat's, followed close behind.

Onstage, the door to the bedroom burst open. The husband, played so well by that handsome young man, Bill Morgan, lunged toward the bed. His face aflame with jealousy and anger, he accused her of infidelity. Denying it, Kelly rolled off the bed, trying to escape, but her husband bounded forward. Grabbing Kelly, Bill flung her toward the bed and began to pull his belt from its loops. With a desperate cry, she turned toward the nightstand and yanked at the drawer. Pulling out the gun, she whirled toward Bill — and Laurel was there.

Firmly, Laurel wrested the gun from Kelly's hand. She stepped back.

"Lights." (It had only taken a moment that afternoon to convince Buddy, a charming young hotel man, that a new wrinkle had been added to the evening's entertainment. So many people, it was sad to say, were so credulous. Really, it was no wonder criminals found such easy pickings.)

The stage was bathed in sharp white light.

"What the hell's going on?" Bill demanded.

Laurel held the gun with an extremely competent air. (After all, she had been second highest overall for women at the National Skeet Shooting Association World Championships in San Antonio in 1978.)

"So boring," Laurel trilled, "when everything always goes on schedule. Let's be innovative, listen to the inner promptings of our psyches. What would happen at this moment if this gun were turned upon another? Let us see." She smiled kindly at Bill Morgan, the handsome young man so accustomed to female adoration. "Not you, my dear. You've had your close call for now. But what about Carl? Does he hate you for taking Kelly away?" She swung the pistol toward the dark-visaged actor.

He squinted at her beneath the bright lights. "Lady, you *are* a nut." He folded his arms across his chest and shook his head in disgust.

The barrel poked toward him for a moment.

"No," Laurel said crisply, "not Carl."

The barrel swiveled up to aim at the black-clad judge. "Walter."

"Jesus, lady, get the hell offstage!"

But he made no move to duck or move away. Laurel smiled benignly. "It is important to be open to life. You passed a romantic moment with Kelly, did you not? But you see all liaisons as impermanent. So I think I shan't shoot at you."

She sighed and turned the gun toward the slender young man. Jonathan brushed back a wisp of blond hair. "This isn't funny, even if you think it is," he said pettishly. "What if we don't get paid for tonight?"

"Ah, the Inn will not be unhappy. Mystery lovers prefer excitement in the raw. They wish to experience life upon the edge. And we are now so close to true drama."

She swung around and leveled the pistol, aiming directly at Kelly's heart.

"I believe you will be the victim tonight, my dear. One two . . ."

Kelly lifted her hands, stumbled backward, turned and began to run. "Stop her, somebody. Stop her before she kills me!"

As Kelly fled down the steps into the hall, Laurel called after her. "My dear, how interesting that you should be afraid. Because all the players know this gun is loaded with blanks."

The police chief, nodding approval at Laurel, hurried after the escaping actress.

Bill's eyes widened like a man who sees an unimaginable horror. "The gun. Blanks. You mean . . ."

Laurel nodded. "I'm afraid so, my dear. She put in real bullets. She would have killed you, of course — and claimed

230

it was an accident, that some malicious person must have made the substitution. It would have been so difficult to prove otherwise. But, fortunately, I was abroad in the still of the night. And the dear police chief and I, such a cooperative man, removed the bullets, just in case, you know, that I didn't move swiftly enough tonight. Though everyone who knows me knows that I am always swift. We have the bullets she put in place of the blanks. They are Exhibits A, B, and C, I believe. The police are *so* efficient."

"Real bullets?" Bill repeated thinly. "My God, why?"

"Oh, my dear young man. You are so young. It would be well to understand that a woman who goes from man to man must do so at her own volition. A woman such as Kelly could never bear to be cast aside." She beamed at the handsome young man. "There is much to be said for constancy, you know." (She forbore to mention her own marital record of five husbands and — but that would be another story entirely.) "In any event, you should be quite safe now. Such a *public* demonstration of evil intent."

HER GOOD NAME

Annie Laurance Darling willed the telephone to ring.
But the undistinguished garden-variety black desk telephone remained mute.

Dammit, Max could at least call!

The more she thought about it, the more she wished that she had gone. Of course, it was undeniably true that Ingrid wasn't available to mind the bookstore, but it wouldn't have been a disaster to close for a few days in November. She didn't let herself dwell on the fact that Saturday had been her best fall day ever. She'd sold cartons of the latest by Lia Matera, Nancy Pickard, and Sara Paretsky.

But there was Max, off to Patagonia and adventure. And here *she* was, stuck in her closed bookstore on a rainy Sunday afternoon with nothing to do but unpack books and wonder if Max had managed to spring Laurel. Even Laurel should have known better than to take up a collection for Amnesty International in the main hall of the justice ministry in Buenos Aires! A tiny worm of worry wriggled in Annie's mind. She knew, of course, that her husband was absolutely capable, totally in command, unflappable, imperturbable. Annie snapped the book shut and bounced to her feet. But oh, sweet Jesus, who knew what kind of mess Laurel had —

The phone rang.

Annie leaped across the coffee area and grabbed up the extension behind the coffee bar. She didn't bother saying "Death on Demand." The finest mystery bookstore on the loveliest resort island off the coast of South Carolina wasn't open.

"Hello." She tried not to sound concerned. But maybe if she caught a jet tonight —

"Maxwell Darling." The tone was peremptory, cut-through-to-the-bone direct.

Annie's shoulders tensed. She immediately recognized the dry, crackly voice that rustled like old paper. What did Chastain, South Carolina's most aristocratic, imperious, absolutely impossible old hag, want with Annie's husband?

"Miss Dora, how are you?" Annie could remember her manners even if some others could not. Annie could imagine the flicker of irritation in Miss Dora's reptilian black eyes.

"No time to waste. Get him to the phone."

"I wish I could," Annie snapped.

"Where *is* he?"

"Patagonia."

A thoughtful pause on the other end, then a sniff. "Laurel, no doubt." The old lady's voice rasped like a rattlesnake slithering across sand as she disgustedly pronounced the name of Max's mother.

"Of course," Annie groused. "And I darn well should have gone. He might need me. You know how dangerous it is in Argentina!"

A lengthening pause, freighted with emanations of chagrin, malevolence, and rapid thought.

"Well, I've no choice. You'll have to do. Meet me at one-oh-three Bay Street at four o'clock."

Annie's eyes narrowed with fury. Miss Dora was obviously the same old hag she'd always been. And just who the hell did she think she was, ordering Annie to —

"A matter of honor." The phone banged into the receiver.

Annie stalked down the storm-dark street, the November rain spattering against her yellow slicker. Clumps of sodden

233

leaves squished underfoot. The semitropical Carolina Low Country was not completely immune to winter, and days such as this presaged January and February. Annie felt another quiver of outrage. Why had she succumbed to the old bat? Why was she even now pushing open the gate and starting down the oystershell path to 103 Bay Street?

The aged, sandpapery voice sounded again in her mind: *A matter of honor.*

The sign to the right of the front door hung unevenly, one screw yielding to time and weather. An amateur had painted the outstretched, cupped hands, the thumbs overlarge, the palms lumpy. The legend was faded but decipherable: HELPING HANDS.

Annie was almost to the steps of the white frame cottage when she saw Miss Dora standing regally beneath the low spreading limbs of an ancient live oak. Annie was accustomed to the gnomelike old lady's eccentric dress — last-century bombazine dresses and hats Scarlett would have adored — but even Annie was impressed by the full gray cloak, the wide-brimmed crimson hat protecting shaggy silver hair, and the ivory walking stick planted firmly in front of high-topped, black leather shoes.

A welcoming smile tugged at Annie's lips, then slid to oblivion as Miss Dora scowled and thumped the stick. "You're late. The carillons play at four o'clock."

"Carillons?"

A vexed hiss. "Come, come. We'll go inside. Wanted you to hear the carillons. It's too neat, you know. The shot at precisely four o'clock. Know it must have been then. Otherwise somebody would have heard." Thumping stiffly to the door, Miss Dora scrabbled in her oversize crocheted receptacle. "No one's taking Constance's character into account. Not even her own brother! Blackening her name. A damnable lie." She jammed a black iron key into the lock.

As the door swung in, Miss Dora led the way, a tiny, limping figure. She clicked on the hall light, then regarded Annie with an obvious lack of enthusiasm. "Would do it myself," she muttered obscurely. "But sciatica. With the rain in November."

The parchment face, wrinkled with age, also held lines of pain. Annie almost felt sorry for her. Almost.

The stick swished through the air. "A dependency, of course. Small. Cramped. Cold floors in the winter. Constance had no use for her own creature comforts. Never gave them a thought. Sixty years she took care of the poor and the helpless here in Chastain. Everybody welcome here." The rasp muted to a whisper. "And may her murderer burn in hell."

The hair prickled on the back of Annie's neck. She looked around the dimly lit, linoleum-floored hallway. Worn straight chairs lined both sides of the hall. Near the door, turned sideways to allow passageway, sat a yellow pine desk.

The stick pointed at the desk. "Manned by volunteers, ten A.M. to four P.M., every day but Sunday. Emma Louise Rammert yesterday. You'll talk to her."

The calm assumption irritated Annie. "Look, Miss Dora, you're taking a lot for granted. I only came over here because you hung up before I could say no. Now, I've got things on my mind —"

"Murder?"

Annie fervently hoped not. Surely Max and Laurel were safe! Max had promised to be careful. He was going to hire a mercenary, fly in to the secret airstrip, hijack Laurel from her captors (a potful of money always worked wonders, whatever the political persuasion), and fly right back out. Oh, hell, she should have gone! What if he needed her?

235

"Oh, who knows?" Annie moaned.

"Don't be a weak sister," the old lady scolded. "Asinine to fret. He'll cope, despite his upbringing." A thoughtful pause. "Perhaps because of it. Any event, you've work to do here." The cane pointed at a closed door. "There's where it happened." The rasp was back, implacable, ice hard, vindictive.

The old lady, moving painfully, stumped to the door, threw it open, turned on the light.

"Her blood's still there. I'm on the board. Gave instructions nothing to be disturbed."

Annie edged reluctantly into the room. She couldn't avoid seeing the desktop and the darkish-brown splotches on the scattered sheets of paper. The low-beamed ceiling and rough-hewn unpainted board walls indicated an old, lean-to room. No rugs graced the warped floorboards. An unadorned wooden chair sat behind the scarred and nicked desk. In one corner, a small metal typewriter table held a Remington — circa 1930.

Gloved fingers gripped Annie's elbow like talons. The walking stick pointed across the room.

"Her chair. That's the way the police found it."

Propelled by the viselike grip, Annie crossed the few feet to the desk and stared at the chair. The very unremarkable oak chair. Old, yes. But so was everything in the room. Old, with a slat missing.

The ivory stick clicked against the chair seat. "No pillow. Constance always sat on a pillow. Bad hip. Never complained, of course. Now, you tell me, young miss, where's that pillow? Right at four o'clock and no pillow!"

Annie was so busy wondering if Miss Dora had finally gone around the bend — which would be no surprise to her, that was for sure — that it took her a moment to realize she was "young miss."

Annie slanted a sideways glance.

Miss Dora hunched over her stick now, her gloved hands tight on the knob. She stared at the empty chair, her lined face sorrowful. "Sixty years I knew Constance. Always doing good works. Didn't simper around with a pious whine or a holier-than-thou manner. Came here every day, and every day the poor in Chastain came to her for help. No electricity. They came here. Husband beat you, son stole your money, they came here. A sick child and no food. They came here."

A tear edged down the ancient sallow cheek. "I used to tell her, 'Constance, the world's full of sorrow. Always has been. Always will be. You're like the little Dutch boy at the dike.' "

The old lady reached out a gloved hand and gently touched the straight chair. Then the reptilian eyes glittered at Annie. "Know what Constance said?"

"No." The dark little room and the blood-spattered desk held no echo of its former tenant. This was just a cold and dreary place, touched by violence.

"Constance said, 'Why, Dora, love, it's so simple. "I was hungry and you gave me meat, I was thirsty and you gave me drink, I was a stranger and you took me in. Naked, and you clothed me; I was sick, and you visited me; I was in prison and you came unto me." ' "

Beyond the dry whisper was an echo of a light and musical voice.

Miss Dora's stick cracked sharply against the wooden floor. She stared at Annie with dark and burning eyes. "A woman," she rasped, hard as stone against stone, "who saw her duty and did it. A woman who would never" — the cane struck — "never" — the cane struck — "never" — the cane struck — "quit the course."

Annie reached for the telephone, then yanked her hand

back. Dammit, she dreaded making this call. Miss Dora had almost persuaded her yesterday afternoon. Indeed, Constance Bolton's life did argue against her death. Annie studied the picture Miss Dora had provided of a slender, white-haired woman in a navy silk dress. Constance Bolton looked serious, capable, and resourceful, a woman accustomed to facing problems and solving them. Her wide-set brown eyes were knowledgeable but not cynical; her mouth was firm but not unpleasant. Stalwart, steady, thoughtful — yes, she had obviously been all of these and more. Yet — Annie glanced down at the poorly reproduced copy of the autopsy report on Constance Maude Bolton, white, female, age seventy-two — the answer seemed inescapable, however unpalatable to Constance Bolton's friends. Annie hated to destroy Miss Dora's faith. But facts were facts.

She dialed in a rush.

"Here."

"Miss Dora, this is Annie. I'm at the store. Listen, I got a copy of the autopsy report on Miss Bolton." Annie took a deep breath. "She was sick, Miss Dora. Dying. Bone cancer. She hadn't told many people, but she knew. Her doctor said so. And there were powder burns on her hand."

Gusts of polar wind could not have been colder than Miss Dora's initial silence. Then she growled, "Doesn't matter, young miss. Get to work. Think." The receiver thudded with the same force as the cane had struck the floor in that dingy office. *"Never — never — never quit the course."*

Annie slammed down her own receiver and glared at the phone, then jumped as it rang again.

"Death on Demand."

"The pillow," Miss Dora intoned. "The pillow, young miss. The pillow!" And the receiver banged again.

Annie jumped to her feet and paced across the coffee area.

Agatha, the bookstore's elegant and imperious black cat, watched with sleepy amber eyes.

"Dammit, Agatha, the old bat's going to drive me crazy!"

Agatha yawned.

"Unreasonable, ill-tempered, stubborn" — Annie stopped at the coffee bar and reached for her mug — "but not stupid, Agatha."

As she drank the delicious French roast brew, Annie stroked Agatha's silky fur and thought about Miss Dora. Irascible, yes. Imperious, yes. Stupid, no. "And about as sentimental as an alligator. So if she knows in the depth of her creaky bones that Constance Bolton wasn't a quitter, where does that leave us?"

If it wasn't suicide, it had to be murder.

How could it be?

Powder burns on her right hand. Constance Bolton was right-handed. A contact wound — star-shaped — to the right temple. Bone cancer. And the gun — Annie returned to her table and riffled through the police report — the gun had been identified by Miss Bolton's housekeeper, Sammie Calhoun. A .32 caliber revolver, it had belonged to Constance Bolton's late brother, Everett. It had, as long as Sammie worked there, lain in the bottom drawer of the walnut secretary in the library. She had seen the gun as recently as late last week.

The fact that this gun had been brought from Miss Constance's home was another pointer to suicide.

But — *if* she had been murdered — the use of that gun sharply circumscribed the list of possible killers.

It had to be someone with access to the bottom drawer of that walnut secretary.

Suicide? Or murder?

On the one hand, terminal illness, powder marks, a contact wound, a gun brought from home.

On the other hand, Miss Dora's unyielding faith in her friend's character and a missing pillow.

Annie sipped at her coffee. A pillow. There didn't seem to be any reason — She thumped the mug on the counter and clapped her hands. *Of course, of course. It could only have been done with a pillow. And that explains why the murder had to occur at four o'clock when the carillons sounded. It wouldn't have been necessary to mask a single shot. But it was essential to mask two shots. Oh, my God, the old devil was smart as hell!*

Annie pictured the dingy room and Constance sitting behind the desk. A visitor — someone Constance knew well, surely — standing beside the desk. The movement would have been snake-quick, a hand yanking the pistol from a pocket, pressing it against her temple and firing. That would have been the moment demanding swiftness, agility. Then it would have been a simple matter, edging the pillow from beneath her, pressing her hand against the gun and firing into the pillow. That would assure the requisite powder residue on her hand. The stage then was set for suicide, and it remained only to slip away, taking the pillow, and, once home, to wash with soap and water to remove the powder marks upon the killer's hand.

Oh, yes, Annie could see it all, even hear the tiny click as the door closed, leaving death behind.

But was there anything to this picture? Was this interpretation an illusion born of Miss Dora's grief or the work of a clever killer?

Annie could hear the crackly voice and behind it the musical tones of a good woman.

"I was hungry . . ."

By God, nobody was going to get away with the murder of Constance Bolton! Not if Annie could help it!

Annie focused on Miss Constance's last few days. If it was murder, why now? Why on Saturday, November 18?

The housekeeper agreed that Miss Constance was sick. "But she paid it no nevermind. Miss Constance, she always kept on keepin' on. Even after Mr. Peter was killed in that car wreck up north, that broke her heart, but she never gave in. Howsomever, she was dragged down last week. Thursday night, she hardly pecked at her supper."

Annie made a mental note about Thursday.

She compiled a list of Miss Constance's visitors at Helping Hands the past week.

The visitors were all — to the volunteers — familiar names, familiar troubles, familiar sorrows.

Except on Thursday.

Portia Finley said energetically, "We did have someone new late that afternoon. A young man. Very thin. He looked ill. A Yankee. Wouldn't tell me what his trouble was, said he had to talk to Miss Constance personally. He wrote out a note and asked me to take it in to her. She read it and said she'd see him immediately. They were still in her office talking when I went home."

It took all of Annie's tact, but she finally persuaded Portia Finley to admit she'd read that short note on lined notepad paper. "I wanted to be sure it wasn't a threatening note. Or obscene."

"Oh, by all means," Annie said encouragingly.

"It didn't amount to much. Just said he was a friend of Peter's and Peter had told him to come and see her."

Friday's volunteer, Cindy Axton, reluctantly had nothing out of the ordinary to report.

But Saturday's volunteer, Emma Louise Rammert, had a sharp nose, inquisitive steel-gray eyes, and a suspicious mind.

241

"Don't believe it was suicide. They could show me a video of it and I still wouldn't believe it. Oh, yes, I know she was sick. But she never spoke of it. Certainly *that* wouldn't be motive enough. Not for Constance. But something upset her that morning and *I* think it was the paper. *The Bulletin*. She was fine when she came in. Oh, serious enough. Looked somber. But not nervy. She went into her office. I came in just a moment later with the mail and she was staring down at the front page of *The Clarion* like it had bitten her. Besides, it seems a mighty odd coincidence that on the afternoon she was to die, she'd send me off early on what turned out to be a wild goose chase. Supposed to be a woman with a sick child at the Happy Vale trailer court and there wasn't anybody of that name. So I think Constance sent me off so she could talk to somebody without me hearing. Otherwise, I'd of been there at four o'clock, just closing up."

Was the volunteer's absence engineered to make way for suicide — or for an appointment? Constance Bolton, had she planned to die, easily could have waited until the volunteer left for the day. But if she wanted to talk to someone without being overheard, what better place than her office at closing time?

Annie picked up a copy of the Saturday morning *The Bulletin* and took it to the Sip and Sup Coffee Shop on Main Street.

The lead story was about Arafat and another PLO peace offer. The Town Council had met to consider banning beer from the beach. Property owners attacked the newest beach nourishment tax proposals. Island merchants reported excellent holiday sales.

A story in the bottom right column was headed:

AUTOPSY REVEALS CAR OCCUPANT
MURDER VICTIM

Beaufort County authorities announced today that a young man found in a burning car Thursday night, originally thought to have died in a one-car accident on a county road, was a victim of foul play.

Despite extensive burns, the autopsy revealed, the young man had died as a result of strangulation. The victim was approximately five feet seven inches tall, weighed 130 pounds, was Caucasian, and suffered from AIDS.

The car was found by a passing motorist late Thursday evening on Culowee Road two miles south of the intersection with Jasper Road.

The car was rented at the Savannah airport on Thursday by a Richard Davis of New York City.

Authorities are seeking information about Davis's activities in Chastain. Anyone with any information about him is urged to contact Sheriff Chadwick Porter.

Annie called Miss Dora. "Tell me about Peter."

"Constance's grandnephew. His father, Morgan, was the son of Everett, her older brother. Everett died about twenty years ago, not long after Morgan was killed in Vietnam. Peter inherited the plantations, but he never worked them. James did that. The other brother. But they went to Peter. The oldest son of the oldest son inherits in the Bolton family. Peter inherited from his mother, too. She was one of the Cinnamon Hill Morleys. Grieved herself into the grave when Morgan was killed in Vietnam. So Constance raised the boy and James ran the plantations. When he was grown, Peter went to New York. A photographer. Didn't come back much. Then he was killed last winter. A car wreck."

One car wreck had masked murder.

Had another?

Annie wished for Max as she made one phone call after another, but she knew how to do it. When it became clear that Peter Bolton didn't die in a car wreck — despite that information in his obituary, which had been supplied by his great-uncle James — she redoubled her efforts. She found Peter's address, his telephone number, and the small magazine where his last photograph had been published and talked to the managing editor.

But Peter wasn't murdered.

Peter died in a New York hospital of AIDS.

And Richard Davis had been dying of AIDS before he was strangled and left in a burning car in Beaufort County, South Carolina.

Richard's note to Constance Bolton claimed he was a friend of Peter's. More than a friend?

Maggie Sutton had the apartment above Richard's in an old Brooklyn brownstone.

Her voice on the telephone was clipped and unfriendly. "You want to know anything about Richard Davis, you ask —"

Before she could hang up, destroy Annie's link to Richard and through him to Peter, Annie interrupted quickly. "Richard's dead. Murdered. Please talk to me. I want to find his murderer."

It took a lot of explaining, then Maggie Sutton said simply, "My God. Poor Richie."

"Did you know Richard was coming to South Carolina?"

"Yes. He was sick —"

"I know."

"— and they fired him. They aren't supposed to, but they do it anyway. Before most people with AIDS can appeal, file a lawsuit, they're dead. Richie was almost out of money. His insurance was gone. They only want to insure healthy people, you know. Nobody with real health problems can get insurance. Richie and Peter lived downstairs from me. Nice guys." She paused, repeated forcefully. "*Nice* guys." A sigh. "God, it's all so grim. Richie took care of Peter. He died last winter. Last week, Richie told me he was going on a trip and he asked me to feed their cat, Big Boy, while he was gone. Richie said Peter had written a will before he died, leaving everything to Richie, but he didn't do anything about it then. I mean, he didn't want Peter's money. But now he was desperate. And he thought, maybe if he went down there, showed the will to the family . . ." Her voice trailed off.

The family.

The last surviving member of the family stood with his head bowed, his freshly shaved face impassive, his hands clasped loosely behind his back, as mourners dispersed at the conclusion of the graveside service on Tuesday afternoon. A dark-suited employee of the funeral home held a black umbrella to shield James Caldwell Bolton from the rain.

The day and James Bolton were a study in grays, the metallic gray of Constance Bolton's casket, resting over the dark pit of her grave, the steel gray of Bolton's pinstripe suit, the soft gray of weathered stones, the misty gray of the weeping sky, the silver gray of Miss Dora's rain cape, the flinty gray of the stubby palmettos' bark, the ash-gray of the rector's grizzled hair.

Annie huddled beneath the outspread limbs of a live oak, a thick wool scarf knotted at her throat, her raincoat collar upturned. Rain splashed softly against gravestones as mourners came forth to shake Bolton's hand and murmur condolences.

Annie stared at the man who had inherited the Bolton and Morley family plantations.

James Bolton didn't look like a murderer.

He looked — as indeed he was — like a substantial and respectable and wealthy member of the community. There was a resemblance to his dead sister, brown eyes, white hair, a firm chin. But where Constance's face was memorable for its calm pity and gentle concern, there was an intolerant and arrogant quality to his stolid burgher's face.

As the last of Miss Constance's friends trod away across the spongy ground of the graveyard, Annie left the oystershell path. Skirting behind a stand of pines, she moved into the oldest part of the cemetery, stopping in the shadow of a crumbling mausoleum some twenty-five yards distant from the new grave site.

Bolton waved away the undertaker with the umbrella.

Had any of the mourners looked back, they would have glimpsed his figure, head again bowed, lingering for a last moment with his sister.

But Annie could see his face. It was for a singular, heart-stopping instant transformed. His lips curved up in satisfaction.

Annie knew, as clearly as if he'd shouted, that James Bolton was exulting. A murderer twice over, safe, secure, successful. A rich and powerful man.

"James."

His face re-formed into sad repose as he turned toward Miss Dora.

The old lady took her time, each step obviously a painful task.

Annie slipped free of her raincoat, unfurled a navy umbrella — Sammie Calhoun had quite willingly given her mistress's umbrella to Miss Dora — and undid the scarf covering the curly white wig.

Miss Dora, her wizened face contorted in a worried frown,

peered up at James Bolton.

"James, I've had the oddest" — the raspy voice wavered — "communication. The ouija board. Last night. Never been a believer in that sort —"

"James . . ." Annie held a high, light, musical tone then let her voice waver and drop like the sigh of a winter wind. In her own ears, it didn't sound enough like the recorded interview the local radio station had found of Constance Bolton speaking out in a League of Women Voters forum on abortion. She tried again, a little louder. "James . . ."

It must have been better than she'd thought.

James Bolton's head whipped around, seeking out the sound. His face was suddenly gray, too, the color of old putty.

Annie glided from behind the cover of the mausoleum, one hand outstretched. "James . . ." Then she backed away, just as a dimly seen figure might drift forth, then disappear. Once out of Bolton's sight, she darted in a crouch from stone to stone until she gained the street. Quickly pulling on the scarf and raincoat, she hurried to Miss Dora's.

"Heh. Heh. Heh." Miss Dora's satisfied cackle would chill the devil. She poured a cup of steaming tea.

Annie sneezed. The heat against her fingers helped a little, but she didn't feel that her bones would ever warm from the graveyard cold.

Miss Dora glowered. "No time to flag. Young people today too puny."

"I'm fine," Annie retorted crisply and knew she was catching a cold. But she couldn't afford to sneeze tonight. She and Miss Dora weren't finished with James Bolton.

"Scared him to death," Miss Dora gloated. "He looked like bleached bones." Her raisin-dark eyes glittered. "Mouth open, whites of his eyes big as a platter. And when I pretended I hadn't seen or heard a thing, thought he was going to faint. That's when I told him about the ouija message: *Pillow. Find pillow.*" She cackled again.

Annie took a big gulp of tea and voiced her concern. "Miss Dora, how can we be sure he didn't destroy the pillow?"

Miss Dora's disdainful look infuriated Annie.

"Classical education taught people how to think!" the old lady muttered. "Crystal clear, young miss. He dare not leave it behind. He had to take it with him. Then what? He couldn't keep it in his house. Old Beulah Willen's his housekeeper. Not a single spot safe from *her* eyes. So, *not* hidden in his house. No incinerators permitted in the city. Besides it's too bulky to burn well. Joe Bill Tompkins drives James. So, *not* in his car. I talked here and there. He's not been out to any of the plantations since Constance died. So where is it? Somewhere not too far, young miss." Another malicious cackle. "James thinks he's so smart. We'll see, won't we?"

The rain had eased to a drizzle. Annie was warm enough. A black wool cap, thermal underwear, a rainproof jacket over a wool sweater, rainproof pants, sturdy black Reeboks. The nylon hose over her face made it hard to breathe, but it sure kept her toasty. From her vantage point she could see both the front and rear doors to James Bolton's house. She had taken up her station at nine thirty. Miss Dora was to make her phone call at nine thirty-five and play the recording Annie had made and remade until Annie's whispered, "James . . . I'm . . . coming . . . for . . . the . . . pillow," sounded sufficiently like Constance Bolton to satisfy Miss Dora.

The back door opened at nine forty. James Bolton, too, was dressed for night in dark clothing. He paused on the top step and looked fearfully around, then hurried to the garage.

Annie smiled grimly.

He reappeared in only a moment, carrying a spade.

Annie followed him across the Bolton property and through a dank and dripping wood. She stepped softly along the path, keeping his shaded flashlight in view, stopping when he stopped, moving when he moved.

Who-oo-ooo-ooo.

Annie's heart somersaulted and she gasped for breath.

Bolton cowered by a live oak.

Annie wasn't sure which one of them the owl had frightened the most.

Iron hinges squealed, and Bolton stepped through the opened gate to the old graveyard, leaving the gate ajar. He moved more cautiously now, and the beam from his flashlight poked jerkily into shadowy pockets.

Did he fear that his dead sister awaited him?

Annie tiptoed, scarcely daring to breathe. One hand slipped into her jacket pocket and closed around the sausage-thick canister of mace, a relic of the days when she lived in New York. The other hand touched the Leica that hung from a strap around her neck.

Bolton stopped twice to listen.

Annie crouched behind gravestones and waited.

When he reached the oldest section of the cemetery, he moved more boldly, confident now that he was unobserved. He walked directly to a winged angel atop a marble pedestal, stepped five paces to his right, and used the shovel to sweep away a mound of leaves.

Annie was willing to bet the earth beneath those leaves had been recently loosened.

He shoveled quickly, but placing the heaps of moist sandy dirt in a neat pile to one side.

Annie crept closer and closer, the Leica in hand.

She was not more than ten feet away and ready when he

reached down and lifted up a soggy newspaper-wrapped oblong.

The flash illuminated the graveyard with its brief brilliant light, capturing forever and always the stricken face of James Bolton.

He made a noise deep in his throat. Wielding the shovel, he lunged blindly toward the source of light. Annie danced sideways to evade him. Now the canister of mace came out and as he flailed the shovel and it crashed against a gravestone, Annie pressed the trigger and mace spewed in a noisome mist.

Annie held her breath, darted close enough to grab up the sodden oblong where he had dropped it, paused just long enough — she couldn't resist it — to moan, "Jaaammees . . ." Then she ran faster than she'd ever managed in a 10 K, leaping graves like a fox over water hazards.

The headline in next morning's *The Bulletin* told it all:

JAMES BOLTON CHARGED

IN MURDER OF SISTER

Miss Dora rattled the newspaper with satisfaction, then poured Annie another cup of coffee. The old lady's raisin-dark eyes glittered. "We showed him, didn't we? Saved Constance's good name."

For once — and it was such an odd feeling — Annie felt total rapport with the ill-tempered, opinionated, impossible creature awaiting her answer.

Annie grinned. "Miss Dora, we sure as hell did."

Annie bought her own copy of the newspaper before she took the ferry back to the island. She wanted to have it to show to Max. Especially since his telegram had arrived last night:

Retrieval accomplished. No fireworks. Boring, actually. Only action caused by fleas Laurel picked up in jail. Plus tourista tummy (me). Home soon. But not soon enough.
Love, Max.

ACCIDENTS HAPPEN

Jimmy Kramer specialized in charm. And he was careful to tailor his attitude to the customer. Businessmen liked fast, unobtrusive service and, if they were from out of town, maybe some tips on the good clubs with friendly ladies. Older women liked deference — "Yes, ma'am." "No, ma'am." But he was best with middle-aged women, especially lonely middle-aged women. They liked his Nordic blond hair, diffident smile, and muscular surfer's body. Just a suggestion of sexual attraction, that was the best.

Jimmy raked in high-dollar tips.

That's all he was thinking about in the beginning with Opal Morrison.

He knew who she was. It was a small coastal town. Excellent surf. That was the attraction, that and the fact it was several hundred miles north of Long Beach and the pregnant girl he'd walked out on.

But he quickly picked up on the locals. Opal was a successful realtor, had her own agency. Around fifty, she was just a little chunky in her fashionable suits, and her red hair had dark roots. She worked eighty-hour weeks, but she spent more and more evenings at the Casbah. Sappy name, but the owner was a pretty good guy, not hard to work for.

Pretty soon Opal came in for dinner every night, and she always picked Jimmy's corner. Pretty soon she was leaving 20 percent tips.

One evening his hand touched hers, and he gave a little squeeze. When she left, giving him a gigged-fish look, he knew he could make a move.

But Jimmy liked to be sure. He spent an afternoon in the library looking at old issues of the local paper. Interesting what you could pick up by skimming. OPAL MORRISON, REALTOR OF THE YEAR. OPAL MORRISON, FIFTH YEAR TO SELL OVER FIVE MILLION DOLLARS. Opal Morrison, owner of a $450,000 Spanish mission house.

Opal — rich, single. And lonely.

It didn't take him long. He started working out at her health club. Pretty soon they were ending up in the hot tub there after he got off work. Then she invited him to her house. And her hot tub. And so, yeah, she was fifteen years older than he, but she was pretty sexy. Not great, but okay.

They got married on a Valentine's weekend.

They'd been back from their honeymoon at Princeville for a week when she told him briskly that he would work at the agency. After all, he certainly didn't have to be a waiter anymore.

The other realtors were nice to his face, but he could feel their disdain. What the hell, it didn't bother him.

He missed surfing every day. Opal expected him at the office. But he could still surf on the weekends. Most of the time. Except when Opal planned for him to do something else.

This had been a pretty lousy weekend.

Opal was driving. She always drove.

Jimmy slouched in the passenger seat. The sleek red Mercedes hummed along in the slow lane. What a waste of horsepower.

Jimmy could feel his face tightening until a pain began to pulse in his temple.

". . . and I certainly do think you could try a little harder,

Jimmy. It isn't asking much for you to be nice to my niece."

He forced a mild answer. "I tried to be helpful." And God knows, he had. His back ached like hell from spading up that flower bed at Gina's house. And he'd damn near fallen off the roof when he rescreened that ventilator opening that the squirrel had broken into.

"Jimmy, would you sort this stuff for the recycling bin. . . . Jimmy, would you mind trimming that mimosa. . . . Jimmy, maybe next week you could reseal the deck . . ."

Opal's hair streamed in the wind.

Sounded sexy, right?

Actually, she looked like an old witch. In the unforgiving afternoon sunlight, he could see the faint pink lines below her ears from her face-lift.

"Jimmy, get my sunglasses out of the pocket."

No *please*. No *thank you* as he handed her the designer sunglasses.

"Did you find the Willet file?"

Did she think he'd managed to retrieve the missing file by ESP? Hell, he hadn't been out of her sight the entire weekend. Opal knew he hadn't found it.

"Not yet." He grabbed the newspaper.

"Maybe you could run down to the office when we get home. Take another look."

"Yeah." Jimmy kept the paper raised. He skimmed the stories. The San Andreas fault was moving, according to earthquake experts. Deaths from car wrecks had risen sharply following the increase in the speed limit. The body of a hiker had been found in the ocean near Carmel.

"Jimmy." There was the same foreboding tone his mother had used when he tracked mud across the kitchen floor.

"Yes." He managed not to hiss. Opal didn't like it when he said yeah. She said it didn't set a good tone at the office.

254

"Oh, good grief! It looks like a semi's jackknifed. I wonder if I can get off at the next freeway . . ." Opal muttered to herself.

Jimmy read a two-paragraph story:

The body of a woman hiker washed ashore at Carmel today. Esmeralda Winslow of San Francisco fell from a cliffside trail Friday.

Sheriff Dan Colby said the accident was reported by Winslow's husband, Mack.

"Jimmy. Jimmy!"

He lowered the newspaper, looked at Opal.

The afternoon sun was harsh on her raddled skin. She looked every one of her fifty years.

"Jimmy, you could at least answer me when I speak!"

"Sorry, Opal. I just noticed a story about a rise in house prices for beach properties."

. . . body . . . washed ashore . . .

Opal sniffed. "Honestly, Jimmy, that was in the realtor roundup last month. Didn't you read that material I put in your in-box?"

His in-box was stuffed with notebooks, pamphlets, and rental magazines. Nobody could have waded through all of it.

"I read it."

"Then you should have known prices were going up."

He almost blew up. What difference would it make if he did know? Opal never let him close a deal. She kept him on a very short leash. Yes, he got to drive prospects around, but when it came time to sign on the dotted line, the money went to Opal. Not to Jimmy.

Opal had all the money. Of course, she was generous. He had a nifty Porsche. But she expected him to be as crazy about her business as she was. She'd insisted that he study for the realtors exam. When he passed the damn thing, she would expect him to work as hard as she did.

It wasn't exactly what he'd had in mind. And now, more often than not, there was a sharp edge to her voice when she spoke to him. Opal never quite jumped on him. But she was always pushing, prodding, encouraging, demanding.

He wasn't willing to do battle, but he was quite adept at delaying, skirting, and ignoring.

That night, as he walked the elderly, whiny Pekinese around the back garden, he kept seeing that small story.

. . . body . . . washed ashore . . .

He waited while Peky sprayed a pottery frog.

He could get a divorce.

Actually, he didn't even have to do that. He would just walk out, never come back. Go down to L.A. Wait tables. There are always those kinds of jobs.

There would be no more cashmere sweaters. No Porsche. No silk sheets.

He would have to start over with nothing. He knew Opal well enough to be sure he'd better not take his car or take much cash out of the bank. So it wasn't his car. Or his cash.

. . . body . . . washed ashore . . .

But if something happened to Opal . . .

Jimmy didn't write anything down. He didn't keep that paper. But he started thinking.

It would have to be a good accident, look like a real accident.

The next morning over breakfast, he said casually, "Opal, I think you're working too hard. You know how the doctor said you need to walk more. How about if we go out and do some hiking on weekends?"

It got to be a regular thing. Every Sunday they went up or

256

down the coast and tramped around on the cliffs for an hour or so. Of course, on Saturdays he was still Mr. Handyman at her niece's. But he even suggested improvements. Everybody thought he was just grand. Gina took him aside one afternoon to say she'd never seen her aunt happier.

Jimmy buckled down at the office too. He worked out a new computer program for their listings. It took him several months to put it together and a lot of tedious copying.

Nora, who'd been there for six years, raised an eyebrow. "Trying for Realtor of the Month, Jimmy?"

For a moment, he shook with genuine mirth. "Nope, Nora. Just having fun."

"Oh, my," she murmured. "Being married to Opal must be the next best thing to a lobotomy."

And that was when he started bringing odd gifts and little bouquets to Opal. Just a little something every few weeks. They got to know him well at the florist. And at the nearby jeweler. Nothing terribly expensive. Just little remembrances, a ceramic hedgehog for Groundhog Day, a silver deed with her initials.

Opal blossomed, and she carped only occasionally.

Sometimes Jimmy almost forgot his objective. But he was tired of trying so hard. And he missed surfing. And he was bored with hurrying through breakfast to get to the office and update the computer program. Opal loved the damn computer program.

"Jimmy, it gives us a boost ahead of every other realtor in the county." Her eyes gleamed.

"Yeah — Yes." He automatically corrected himself now.

And on Sundays they hiked, up and down the coast. But Jimmy drove. He insisted on taking his car and driving for these outings. "More of a holiday for you, Opal."

She smiled at that and leaned back against the headrest.

257

This Sunday he was heading for a particular path, narrow and twisting, high above heavy surf crashing against black boulders. Just outside Carmel, actually.

Opal was attractive in a cream blouse and green linen walking shorts that made her look slimmer than she was.

When he pulled off the road, Opal held up her hand. "My God, Jimmy, be careful. It's a long way down."

"Hey, we've got good brakes," and his voice was exuberant.

. . . body . . . washed ashore . . .

It was more than a year ago that he'd seen the little article.

He handed Opal her backpack, slipped into his own. As he followed Opal — she went first, of course — the sun glistened on her hair. But Jimmy was concentrating on the path. A few more steps and they were out of sight of the road.

He looked past Opal, his eyes sweeping the bay. It was a small curve in the coastline. No sailboats. And no surfers here. The water was too rough, huge waves that slammed against towering rocks.

He tensed his knees, lifted his hands. He drew in a ragged gulp of breath, deep in his lungs, then slammed his palms against Opal's backpack.

Opal hurtled off the trail, plunging down toward the rocks. Her scream began deep and guttural, then exploded like a banshee's wail.

Jimmy shuddered, long quivers shaking his body. That scream . . . Finally it was quiet. Nothing could be heard but the rumble of the surf and the rustle of the cypress.

Jimmy turned and began to run back up the path.

Opal was gone. Dead and gone.

. . . body . . . washed ashore . . .

He reached the road and looked both ways.

No cars.

258

He looked up and saw a windswept redwood house on top of the ridge. It seemed to hang between the earth and the sky.

Jimmy ran toward it. "An accident!" he shouted. "An accident! Please, help me, my wife's had an accident!"

He was winded by the time he reached the house. His chest heaved. He pounded on the wooden door.

When the door opened, he couldn't speak.

"What's happened? My God, what's wrong?"

Jimmy had seen a person like this only in classy fashion ads. Or in the movies. Sleek golden hair framed a fascinating face, thin, elegant, fine-boned, intelligent, aristocratic.

The slender woman's green eyes widened in concern. She wore a golden silk blouse open at the throat and black slacks.

"My wife." His voice shook, cracked. "The cliff. It gave way."

Jimmy read the certainty of Opal's death in the sudden sharp intake of the woman's breath.

"Oh, God. Come in. I'll call. Come in." She reached out a thin, graceful hand that clasped his, drew him inside.

Jimmy had never felt smoother skin.

She ran to the phone, dialed 911. "This is Joanna Clements. There's been an accident . . ."

Jimmy didn't listen to her words. He was repeating her name in his mind. Joanna Clements, Joanna Clements, Joanna Clements . . .

She came down to the road with him, waited with him until the sheriff's car and a county rescue motorboat arrived.

Jimmy wished they'd turn off the whirling light atop the sheriff's car.

Flash. Flash. Flash.

A helicopter maneuvered just above the roaring surf.

Jimmy's head hurt.

Joanna Clements stood with her hands deep in her

259

pockets. "I wish I could help. I know this is so hard on you, Jimmy."

They were already Jimmy and Joanna.

An occasional shout rose from the beach.

Jimmy shivered.

Joanna said immediately, "You're cold. I'll be right back," and she hurried up the steep drive.

His eyes followed her. He'd never met anyone who attracted him the way she did. He loved the way she moved, her body lithe and athletic, and he was exhilarated by the brightness in her eyes. And her voice rang in his mind, husky, with a timbre that was fascinating and unique.

"Mr. Kramer."

Jimmy jerked around.

Sheriff Dan Colby was a big man with blunt features and cold light-brown eyes. He wore his round-crowned hat jammed down over his big ears, but he didn't look clownish. He looked ominous. The strap from his hat had worn a sore spot on one cheek.

Jimmy felt suddenly breathless. Afraid.

"You known Mrs. Clements long?"

"No." Jimmy wished his voice had come out stronger. He tried again, and the word was almost a bark. "No." He cleared his throat. "I'd never seen her until today. But she's been so nice, so —" He broke off. Even he could hear the too-warm sound in his voice.

The sheriff's eyes had a funny, sardonic look. He nodded slowly. "Hold out your arms."

Jimmy stared at the big man blankly.

"Your arms."

Jimmy lifted his arms. He looked, too. The sun glistened on the blond hairs along his forearms. He had good arms, strong, muscular.

260

The sheriff nodded and turned away.

Jimmy still stood there, puzzled, his arms outthrust. Why the hell did the sheriff want to look at his arms?

It was like a kick in the chest. Jesus, the man was looking for scratches. Jesus!

It was an accident, Jimmy wanted to yell after him, an accident!

Shouts rose from the beach.

Jimmy wrapped his arms tight across his chest.

The sheriff's walkie-talkie buzzed. He lifted it, held it close.

They all heard the metallic voice. "The chopper's spotted the body, Dan."

The sheriff flicked it off, looked at Jimmy.

"Opal." Jimmy buried his face in his hands. Should he break down? No. Not with that fish-eyed bastard watching him like a hawk. Maybe he should act mad. He jerked his head up. "Listen, maybe she's okay. Why can't you get her, help her?"

"Mister, nobody could survive a fall from that cliff. Not onto those rocks."

Joanna ran lightly to them, thrust a parka toward him. "Here, put this on."

The touch of her hand — Jimmy looked at her in wonder, then his eyes jerked back to the sheriff. He grabbed the parka, shrugged into it.

The sheriff stared hard at Jimmy. "Okay, Mr. Kramer, tell me how it happened."

"I've told you."

"I'd like to hear it again."

It helped to have Joanna's sympathetic face there. "We hike — hiked — every Sunday. And this was like any Sunday. We'd started out. Opal was in front of me. And all of a sudden she was falling. I think maybe the path crumbled. Right under her feet." He tried hard to look straight at the sheriff, but finally his eyes slid away.

They let him go at last. Joanna walked him to his car, told him to call her if there was anything she could do, anything at all.

Everybody was great to him the next few weeks. Opal's niece couldn't have been nicer. Of course, she inherited half the estate, so that probably made her cheerful. But she made a point of writing Jimmy a really nice note about what a great marriage he and Opal had had. Jimmy didn't mind sharing. It was a hell of a big estate. He was a very rich man now.

The women realtors brought casseroles.

Jimmy thanked them. And said bravely, "Accidents happen."

Two weeks later, he answered the front door to find Sheriff Colby standing there.

Jimmy simply stared at him.

"Can I come in?"

Jimmy licked his lips. Could he slam the door, tell the sheriff to go the hell away? But maybe he couldn't. And why would he, if everything was on the up and up?

"Sure." Jimmy led the way into the living room.

They sat in two overstuffed chairs near a long, low glass coffee table.

The sheriff took off his round-crowned hat, held it in his lap.

"So you wanted to talk to me?" Jimmy asked.

"Yeah. I been checking around. I understand Mrs. Kramer was a lot older than you."

Jimmy felt his face flush. "What's that got to do with anything?"

"I don't know, Mr. Kramer. I'm just trying to find out all

about you. And Mrs. Kramer."

"Why?" Jimmy wished his voice was stronger, firmer.

The sheriff looked around the huge room with its indirect spot lighting and luxurious rugs and crystal on side tables. "Was this Mrs. Kramer's house? When you married her?"

Jimmy swallowed. "Look, Sheriff, my wife fell off a cliff. What difference does it make whether this was her house? Or how old she was?"

"1 don't know, Mr. Kramer. But I like to fill out my files real carefully. And I'm not finished looking into Mrs. Kramer's fall."

Jimmy stood up. "I don't have to talk to you. If you want to talk to me again, you call my lawyer."

The sheriff took his time getting up. He loomed over Jimmy and his eyes were sharp and cold. "I'll do that, Mr. Kramer. I'll do that."

Jimmy took sleeping pills that night. But he kept waking up, struggling to breathe. Damn the sheriff. Damn him!

Jimmy heard later that the sheriff visited a lot of people and that they'd all told the sheriff what a devoted husband he'd been and that the difference in age between Jimmy and Opal hadn't meant a thing.

Sheriff Colby checked. And checked. And checked. But three weeks after Opal Kramer fell to her death, Sheriff Colby closed the file.

Jimmy waited another two weeks, then drove down Highway 1.

Joanna Clements opened the front door. And smiled. To Jimmy it was like watching a sunrise on a lush summer day, streaks of gold and mauve and apricot blending in iridescent glory. Her pale yellow cashmere sweater molded gently against high breasts. Tan jodhpurs emphasized her slim legs. Delicate gold earrings shimmered in the sunlight.

She looked surprised and hesitant — and pleased.

Jimmy burst into awkward, hurried, desperate speech. "I'm so sorry to bother you. But I had to come back. My pastor said the only way to come to grips with what happened was to come back here and go to the cliff. Can you understand that?"

She nodded slowly, her eyes huge with sorrow. She reached out, took his hand tightly in hers. "Yes. I do understand. My husband —"

Jimmy felt frozen. Husband.

"— was killed in a scuba accident last year. I've made myself swim there. Again and again. Oh, Jimmy, I'll go down to the cliff with you."

Jimmy came to see Joanna every weekend. He was swept by feelings he'd never known, never imagined.

They fell in love, gently, then with eagerness and passion.

Jimmy couldn't believe his luck.

Joanna — dear, sweet, beautiful, magnificent Joanna. And she cared for him. Yes, she was fifteen years older than he, but it was so different from Opal. Joanna never seemed old, she simply seemed more vital and exciting and knowledgeable than anyone he'd ever known. And he knew she would never grow old to him.

She would always be his beloved Joanna.

They waited six months to marry.

There was only one shadow on his happiness. As they walked out of the chapel, he saw the sheriff's car parked nearby. The sheriff sat unmoving in the driver's seat. Mirrored sunglasses were turned toward Jimmy and his new wife. Jimmy shivered.

They honeymooned in Kauai. Climbing, hiking, and kayaking with a vibrant companion, Jimmy realized that he'd never enjoyed himself so much in all his life.

Most of all, they loved to climb.

Upon their return, he moved into Joanna's house. One of the first things he did was to pay off the mortgage. He hadn't realized that she'd been in financial straits. And it was wonderful to be able to help her, to say, "Oh, don't worry about that, I'll take care of it." It turned out that she and her husband had been in debt — their bank had gone under — and the insurance policy on his life had been just enough to pay off most of the bills, but she still had an almost insurmountable monthly payment on the house.

Joanna had been so grateful, so thrilled. "Oh, Jimmy, I love my house and I've been so afraid I would lose it. I would die if I didn't have my house."

And he realized that she did love the house. Sometimes he almost felt a tiny quiver of jealousy. But she was so happy when she found a new vase for a sunny corner or re-terraced the hillside. The house took a lot of money. But he had a lot of money.

Every day Jimmy was struck again by his good fortune.

By now he'd almost forgotten the ache in his hands when they'd struck Opal's backpack.

And life with Joanna was filled with joy. He loved her happiness, knowing the house she adored was now hers forever.

Jimmy realized he enjoyed selling houses more than he had thought. He bought some business property in Carmel and opened his own office. And everything he did seemed to turn to gold. He made more and more money.

He'd been going to the office for several months — KRAMER REALTY was printed in gold letters on the frosted door — when he heard the main door open. He looked up eagerly.

Sheriff Colby stepped inside. He walked across the thickly carpeted floor, stood and looked down at Jimmy. Then he looked around the office. "Pretty nice."

"What do you want, Sheriff?" Jimmy hated the way his voice shook.

"Just to say hello, Mr. Kramer. Welcome you to Carmel. I suppose you know your wife is highly thought of around here."

"Joanna. I know. She's wonderful."

The sheriff nodded. "And she's a real healthy woman."

"Of course she is."

"She'd better stay that way, Mr. Kramer." And he swung on his heel and walked out.

Jimmy stared at the closing door.

He didn't tell Joanna, of course. He couldn't. And it seemed to him that he saw the sheriff just a little too often, sometimes at night, sometimes in the middle of the day.

But it didn't matter, he told himself. Sheriff Colby couldn't do anything to him.

Finally Jimmy began to relax. Time passed and he was happy, happy all the time. And so was Joanna.

The night before their first anniversary, she fixed a special dinner.

"Jimmy, I have a wonderful idea for tomorrow."

"Whatever you want. Whatever in the whole world you want, Joanna."

"I want us to go together on the path and take flowers for Opal."

Jimmy didn't want to seem reluctant. After all, they'd gone swimming several times where Joanna's husband, Roger, had drowned.

"We have to remember those we've loved," Joanna said solemnly.

"Of course we do," Jimmy agreed resolutely. "After all, accidents happen. But that was yesterday. Today belongs to us."

"But we won't forget Opal. And Roger."

The next day, their first anniversary, was perfect — the soft blue sky cloudless, the air soft and warm. Even the wind-swept cypress looked benign in the soft air.

Jimmy went first along the narrow path, carrying a spray of orchids. Joanna followed, with a small bouquet of violets.

The surf boomed. Glancing down at the glistening boulders and the roiling water, Jimmy felt a surge of sheer pleasure. He was living a dream come true. Nothing could ever be better —

The violent push struck him in the small of the back.

His arms flung wide, but there was nothing to grasp. As his body turned and began to plummet, he glimpsed Joanna's face, the elegant features smooth and satisfied, a tiny smile curving her lips. Always graceful, she swung her hand and the violets curved out into space.

He heard his own scream and felt himself falling faster and faster.

The scream ended abruptly.

Joanna turned and walked swiftly up the path toward her house. Her beloved house. All hers.